the **3O**-
day
engagement

the 30-day engagement

WAVERLY DECKER

CALHOUN HOWARD
New York, New York

Cover image of two women © 2023 by Ivanna Nashkolna
Ring image in title © irinadanyliuk via Canva
Cover © 2023 Calhoun Howard LLC

For information about this book, rights inquiries, and for permission to use portions of this book other than for review purposes, contact
Calhoun Howard LLC
2248 Broadway #1330
New York, NY 10024
permissions@calhounhoward.com

The publisher is not responsible for websites that are not owned by the publisher.

Library of Congress Control Number: 2022942921
ISBNs: 979-8-9866210-0-5 (paperback), 979-8-9866210-1-2 (ebook), 979-8-9866210-2-9 (downloadable audio)

calhounhoward.com

First Edition: February 2023

10 9 8 7 6 5 4 3 2 1

for everyone who got there a little late

april

one

EVERY SUMMER, WW AND PARTNERS held a lunch with all the interns. These interns, alternately awkward or overconfident, with a few partners and VPs, shuffled into the wood-paneled conference room for a sandwich and a seltzer water, and sat together at the long, polished table in the company's largest meeting room, which technically overlooked Bryant Park but actually faced the upper floors of a dozen other charmless midtown Manhattan office buildings. A few platitudes were shared, a few handshakes exchanged, and then everyone went back to work, the interns to be mentored by the most junior analysts in the most isolated cubicles, far from the real action.

But one phrase from that lunch had stayed with Emory Jordan since she was hired as an intern twelve years ago. She'd carried it with her as one of the few women to work at WW and Partners—

through her years as an analyst, while climbing her way through the associate ranks, and into her years as a VP. The advice had come from the current WW himself, William Wils. William was the third WW in a line of men with the same initials who had all, in their occasionally unorthodox ways, invested in business when venture capital wasn't a career, it was what you did with your family money. William's sage advice: *Treat every presentation like it's a matter of life and death.*

When Emory's turn came for a presentation twelve years later, last on the agenda at the Tuesday morning meeting that William presided over so he could personally screen potential investments before floating the companies to his partners, she did, indeed, steel herself for battle. She was expected to model good presentation skills for the junior staff—and not only sell William on the company that he might later pitch to the partners, but also demonstrate that she had investigated the potential investment inside and out.

Instead of leaning back in her chair, loosening her tie, and folding her hands behind her head, as so many of her male peers did, she took one deep, quiet breath, tilted up her chin, and stood from her rolling conference room chair gracefully. (Rule one of many she'd made after learning the hard way: Never let go of the armrest until you have fully risen or are securely seated, lest you fall on your ass.) She forced her clenched jaw into calm relaxation as she passed by the analysts lining the back wall, where she'd stood herself in the best dress pants and button-down she could afford when she was a new employee, hoping that some of her research would lead to a deal. (Rule two: No nervous smiles or frowns.) She flattened her palm against the side seam of her skirt until she accepted the passing of the projector remote. (Rule three: No visible shaking.) Then she took her place next to the screen, at the far end of the room from where William sat in front of the imposing double doors, so she could easily gesture to her presentation slides.

Battle time. Her left heel was screaming, wounded already— her shopper at Bellworthy's had picked out some perfectly professional nude pumps to go with her new sand-colored skirt suit. She'd worn them around her Brooklyn apartment and they'd seemed fine, so she hadn't ferried them in a separate bag and donned the last bit of her armor at the office.

(Rule four: No wardrobe or grooming distractions.) A small error of strategy. Emory could recover.

She had to. A successful presentation about Neighborhood Answering would crack open the door for two smart, worthy women to get their burgeoning company in front of WW and Partners, and maybe secure an influx of money that would catapult them from startup to wildly successful. It was their dream, and so it was Emory's job to be their trusted ally.

Unfortunately, early April was the worst time to present at the Tuesday hell meeting, no matter how compelling the project at hand, because this season brought slanting sun through the windows and right into her eyes. She took a step in one direction, and then the other, trying to find a place where she could be seen and heard but not have to squint. (Rule five: No obvious discomfort. See also rules two, three, and four.) She *needed* her position at the helm, needed to ensure that William caught every word she floated down over the bagel trays and cups of coffee and folders full of paperwork. Emory turned her head slightly to the side—good enough—and launched into her well-practiced offensive.

By the end of it, she was on a high. The company had a solid team behind it and plenty of growth potential. A note of pride on their behalf crept into her voice. "Ms. Chu and Ms. Nadeem have built their virtual doorman company to scale quickly and efficiently, and they've taken to heart the challenges that plagued earlier companies in the space. They offer a low-cost, high-margin service that's out of reach for the average New Yorker. There will be someone within a few blocks able to check the security cameras or come out in person, around the clock. Someone to answer the buzzer or to watch you safely enter your apartment, even if it's a small building, and even if it's the middle of the night. With the package lockers in apartment lobbies, and the option for apartments to receive regular patrols, and the rest that I've detailed for you, their company can be a one-stop shop for landlords of all sizes who want to increase their security and customer service."

Emory had considered including a few sentences about a time when she'd been followed home to her first apartment, and even practiced those lines down to breaths and silences. In the icy air-conditioning of the conference room, with everyone staring at her, she diverted around the minefield. That story would make her a tasty treat for her peers, and of the five other VPs, four of them would eat her alive if given a good bottle of barbecue sauce. (Rule six: Do not admit any weakness.) There was another gut punch in her presentation's arsenal: protection for wives and daughters and sisters. And using that angle felt like telling girls to not dress like sluts or to not get tipsy and was complete bullshit.

She was stone. (Rule seven, but it was really more of a self-admonition than a rule: Rocks don't sweat.)

The projector remote in her hand was slippery, though. Rocks felt pressure. They had fault lines. Emory didn't want to crack when she had the full attention of the room. But she knew what they wanted to hear. They wanted to hear that they were invincible, and heroically, they could save everyone else. *Wives and daughters*. A false flag operation to draw them in.

But that wasn't her style, no matter how much Emory wanted the room's approval. Instead of speaking aloud the miserable lever about women as victims of crime that she knew—and hated—by heart, she clicked through the next slides of familiar NYC landmarks, mixed in with neighborhoods less familiar to her audience that mostly lived in Manhattan and rarely ventured beyond it. "Because employees will be working in the neighborhoods where they live, Neighborhood Answering will convey a sense of community even while expanding on a national scale. They're set up to start operations in cities in New Jersey and Connecticut next year, and are developing a more focused, concierge-style offering for those in rural areas, in standalone homes, and so on. Other potential lines of business include virtual office services like mail handling and phone lines for small businesses, supporting entrepreneurs who don't need a corporate office space."

Emory pointed out figures in the financial projections and wrapped up her pitch right as the room shifted from paying attention to idly chatting while they flipped through their copies of her deck and the Neighborhood Answering business plan. William was leaned over listening to Tim, another WW and Partners VP. Tim, like all the VPs, was in contention for promotion to junior partner, and they each wanted that coveted, rare opening for themselves. Of course he wouldn't let any opportunity to connect with William pass him by.

Nothing like someone talking over you before you even finish. "Any questions?"

Bryce, who had been a VP since Emory had started at WW and Partners, spoke first. "Not a question, more of a comment. Some of this undercuts coworking spaces and bigger offices. We don't want our real estate partnerships to think we aren't prioritizing them."

Emory did not sigh or roll her eyes. Bryce managed their relationships with several of New York's biggest commercial real estate services. What he didn't have was a sense of scale. "We're not really talking about big firms skipping out on having offices in midtown. The office services are for, say, sole proprietors who never had a corporate headquarters and won't ever need one."

Another VP—Adam Carrington, a nephew of one of the partners who'd made VP nearly five years before anyone else had, and Emory's absolute least favorite colleague—spoke up. "So why don't people move if they're getting packages stolen?" He nudged Bryce. "I mean, if you live in a crappy building with no security in a bad neighborhood, what do you expect?"

The first two years she'd worked at WW and Partners as an intern and then an analyst, Emory lived deep in Queens, where you had to take a bus to get to the subway. Hers wasn't a bad neighborhood; it just wasn't a *great* neighborhood. She'd had her packages delivered to the office during the day and spent her nights chasing down cockroaches. And sure, the minute she'd received a respectable raise she'd moved out. "This is an accessible luxury product for locations where dedicated security staff isn't an option." She flipped back through the slides to the demographic and financial overviews and tried to come up with a response beyond *I'm sorry some people aren't rich enough for you.*

Carrington always activated her *shut up, jerk* instinct. Post-presentation question time was meant to be a chance to catch any oversights, and Carrington's most frequent contribution to the strength testing of investments was proclaiming that if he didn't want something, it was worthless. He ran a hand over his bristly blond crewcut and blathered on. "And won't Chu and Nadeem take the company and run off to Japan or India or wherever? Like, we'll invest and they'll—"

Adam Carrington, worst of the VPs. There was an uncomfortable murmur from the analyst lineup, but not one loud enough to

7

distract Carrington from his smug suppositions. Emory didn't like where this was going. Or what he was implying.

She wondered if he'd say this sort of thing out loud if they weren't both white. Or if the room was more diverse.

The answer was: almost certainly. "Their families are from China and Pakistan, and they were both born here. They're staying."

Fortunately, the bagel tray was circulating, and he stopped putting his foot in his mouth long enough to fill it with carbs. Across the table, Jeff Lieberman, the one VP that Emory actually *did* like, raised his eyebrows in commiseration. She wanted to throw her hands to the ceiling, but that would break the Emory presentation code.

Tim appeared beside her. He'd moved from his right-hand man position at the end of the conference table down to the screen awfully quickly, or she'd been more distracted by Carrington's mouth flatulence than she realized. If Tim had already finished pitching himself to William, something bigger was on his mind.

"Good presentation," Tim said, taking the remote out of her hand. "We need to check on the score now."

Emory looked to the other end of the room for confirmation. William nodded from his presiding position. They'd recently invested in a sports data company, so there was constant gambling talk at the coffee maker.

"Isn't it just an exhibition game today?" she asked, wondering what about a score for a sport she couldn't even remember, on another continent, on a weekday, could matter at that exact moment.

Tim swapped the input over to television. Instead of the game, entertainment news took over the screen. A young, lithe reporter flirted with the camera.

"It's probably blacked out here." Carrington stated the obvious.

"So all we're going to get is this garbage." Not even Bryce, the VP who Emory suspected was funneling most of his salary into sports betting, got up and left, though. If they couldn't have sports, they'd take beauty.

Then another beauty appeared on the screen, in tabloid shots of her in a bathing suit, in a clip of her walking down the red carpet, in a scene with her strutting away from an explosion in a form-fitting bodysuit with a cape trailing behind her. She was tall—a smidge over Emory's five feet, ten inches. She could have been Emory's glamourously, spectacularly attractive big sister, with an athletic build, gleaming smile, piercing blue eyes, and bouncy beach-blonde waves.

Emory did not shake. She did not show signs of discomfort. She was making a life and death presentation in the front of the room. *Rocks don't sweat.*

"Marilee Callahan—"

Mari Cooper, Emory's brain insisted.

"—has even more good news. She's not only starting a lifestyle brand, featuring organic nutrition and health products, and her own fitness clothing line—"

Carrington guffawed. "Isn't that your ex, Emory? That chick that dumped you?"

That left me. That rejected me.

That destroyed me.

"—she's starting a brand-new life! Callahan has announced her engagement to her fellow business entrepreneur and tech mogul—and America's most eligible bachelor—Benjamin Thorston, with the nuptials to be held in Malibu this spring." The screen showed a video of the two of them together at a film premiere. Benjamin Thorston's absurdly pale skin gleamed in the light of paparazzi flashbulbs, but even as strong-jawed and handsome as he was, he couldn't compete with Mari's star-bright smile. She glowed. It was impossible to look away from her.

Emory's ears rang with the unwelcome sounds of immaturity. *Ooh* and *hoo-ee* and *what a woman*. Carrington's whistle was the loudest of all.

"Hey, now," Tim said, grinning at Carrington, who oozed objectification. "Sorry, Emory."

William raised a hand with the benevolence of a man who'd never had to deflect a catcall himself. "That's enough. See if the game is on a different channel."

Tim turned so Emory could see his shit-eating smirk and began flipping through talk shows and infomercials. He avoided her glare. Fortunately for Emory, even the handful of analysts who waited to be dismissed leaned against the back wall and conferred in whispers, or checked their phones, or watched the channel-surfing instead of staring at her. Whatever game they were looking for was a big one.

Emory's phone buzzed in her pocket and she flinched. She thought she'd set it to silent. (Rule eight: Don't interrupt yourself.) With everyone distracted, she pulled it out and pressed her fingertip to the reader on the back. There was a new email from Malibu Elite Weddings, subject line: SAVE THE DATE FOR M... With a shaking hand, she tapped the notification, scrolling through the cordially invited and all the rest to a mid-May date, six weeks in the future.

"We don't get NY Sports Network Four," Tim finally said, pausing on a screen that prompted him to upgrade to a better TV package.

"Then go look on your computers," William said. He didn't use his cell phone for anything but calls, so it did not occur to him that a portion of the room was already tracking down the score that way. "And Emory, you know that actress? Might be the time to get in on the ground floor of her company."

"Yeah, get in with her," Tim muttered.

"I think not getting it in was the whole problem," Carrington whispered to Bryce, who turned his face to the side and giggled.

William either didn't hear or he decided to let the boys be boys. Just like every other time he didn't hear, or he pretended not to hear. "It's a good connection." He gathered his stack of papers. "More importantly, you should connect with Benjamin Thorston. Whatever he's doing next, we want a piece of it. That's the kind of investment that we're looking for. Especially from anyone who wants a promotion." William tucked the papers under his arm and stood to address the room.

"As usual, expect the update on which presentations I'd like to see at the partners meeting by end of day. And, again, Emory, reach out to that"—he nodded his head toward the screen, indicating that he'd forgotten Mari's name already—"woman to get an introduction to Thorston if it's the right time. We're chasing too many mice and not finding enough unicorns." Then he sailed briskly through the double doors of the conference room, officially ending the meeting.

The newest analyst hire, who had the unenviable job of acting as William's executive assistant in addition to his other duties, scurried after. The doors banged closed, which was the unofficial end of the meeting.

"Of course it's the right time," Emory mumbled into the din of scraping chairs and back patting that followed.

Because, despite every cringeworthy comment, despite the long hours and the terrible colleagues, WW and Partners had been loyal to her for twelve years. In those twelve years, WW and Partners hadn't accepted her marriage proposal and then run away to a Hollywood acting career. Mari had done that, eight years ago. *Mari* was the one who didn't want to be partners. Mari was the one who hadn't wanted to fight for her.

It was definitely the right time. The right time to see Mari again. The right time for Emory to show Mari that her heart was *not* still broken.

Not still broken at all.

two

BLISS TULLY WAS LATE TO her appointment in midtown because the F had been stalled between stations for the usual problem: reasons unknown, relayed as a mumble over the loudspeaker. Maybe it was a track fire, or a malfunctioning door, or a broken rail, or a horde of sentient rats. Nobody knew, and that was the fun of it, other than the being late part. She wrestled her granny cart up the stairs and out of the station at Bryant Park, then made her way to a concrete and glass tower that reminded her of childhood visits to her father's office in Connecticut, where she'd sit in a chair in the hallway while he took calls for endless, boring hours and occasionally a secretary would slip her a piece of candy.

At the time, she thought offices were safe places full of good people. She knew better these days.

But that was long ago, and today, she wanted good vibes only. She checked in with the security guard in the lobby and took the elevator up to WW and Partners, the sort of office where a secretary had to buzz you through to a lobby decorated with dark wood and stiff leather wing chairs. And some kind of giant vase that wasn't for flowers, which, in her opinion, was a waste. Waiting anywhere without a good assortment of magazines was also a waste, so Bliss hoped nobody had to wait at WW and Partners very long.

A woman watched her wrestle her granny cart through the heavy glass doors from behind an oversize desk. She had curly dark hair and deep brown skin with copper undertones, and reminded Bliss of a girl she'd had a crush on for a few weeks in fifth grade. Fifth grade, right before everything went to shit. Before her dad—

No. Only good vibes for her today. And for this place, which seemed like it could really, really use a dose of good vibes to combat the *would be comfy like a library if it didn't smell like judgment in here* aesthetic.

That was a meaner thought than Bliss wanted to have running through her brain. She was usually pretty cheerful, but this WW and Partners place was getting to her already. If her new venture was going to survive, she'd have to get over herself, because a lot of offices were like this one.

Like a reminder.

"Are you here for the plants?" the woman asked, setting aside a stack of courier pouches.

14

Bliss groped in the pocket of her green wool peacoat for a silver case and extracted a business card, then handed it over with a goofy flourish she immediately wished she could take back. "Bliss Tully of Bliss Foliage, at your service. Thanks so much for reaching out." She touched a finger to the name plate on the desk. "Beatriz Reyes?"

Beatriz nodded and offered a wide smile. "Nice to meet another girl with a B name." She quickly and efficiently took Bliss in hand. "You're coming in once a week—"

"Tuesdays and Thursdays to start, but only today this week. After the initial setup, and when the plants are more established, I'll be in once a week on one of those days. Regularly, though! I'll swap out anything that's in bad condition, of course. And if you need extra plants or flowers for an event or for a gift, just let me know, and I'll bring those in for you. I'm here to make things beautiful." Bliss took a breath. She hadn't practiced her spiel out loud, or even in her head, and it had come out a lot faster than she'd expected.

Beatriz held up her phone and snapped a photo. "I'll add you to the security list for both of those days as a vendor, and they'll have a permanent pass for you next time you come. Unless you already have another client in the building?"

Bliss shook her head. "Nope." She pressed her lips into a tight smile so that she wouldn't say what Beatriz didn't need to know: WW and Partners was her first, and presently her only, Bliss Foliage client. That the business card she'd handed over so casually was the lone piece of collateral in her inventory and she had printed it at home last night. And all of this was a big, big problem.

Good vibes.

Beyond the wall behind Beatriz's desk, which divided the WW and Partners lobby from a corridor, sharp-suited men streamed by. A few swaggered past importantly while touching a Bluetooth headset and talking a little too loudly, except for one who reminded Bliss of an overgrown puppy. He made the time for a wave as he bustled past. "Hi, Beatriz!"

"Hey Jeff, say hi to the kids! And to Melody!" Beatriz pushed a diagram of the office across her desk and bent over it with Bliss. "Here's where you can hang your coat. Big conference room at the end of the hall, CEO all the way down on the other side. On that far end are senior employee offices and a couple of small meeting rooms, and back down here by the big conference room, there are a few more small rooms, some cubicles for the newbies, and some junior employee offices. In the middle is the kitchen and the supply room. Those don't need any plants." She looked up at Bliss and deliberately tapped the cubicles. When she was sure Bliss was watching, she circled them again with a finger. "Please prioritize the senior employee spaces."

Bliss grinned and a good portion of the tension in her shoulders disappeared. Vibe check: better than expected. There wouldn't be a lot of room in the cubicles for pots, but as a former windowless cubicle dweller, she knew that even a little bit of green could make things feel a lot sunnier under the fluorescent lights. She took the diagram and a pencil that Beatriz offered, ready to make notes. "I think we're on the same page."

Twenty minutes later, with a repurposed art apron fastened over her all-black but not quite *matching* black outfit, she'd had a look at the boardroom, passed by a line of small meeting rooms with no natural light at all, and offered tiny pots of bamboo and pothos to the workers in the block of cubicles that indicated their lowly position in the company. Most of them seemed suspicious until she said the plants were a "Company perk!" and then they claimed their pots immediately.

Out of the corner of her eye, when she was checking her too-pale face in the reflection of a darkened office window, she caught a reedy man in thick glasses whispering softly to his new bamboo. Bringing some small plants along had been a last-minute decision; her plan for the day was to get the lay of the corporate land and then bring in what the office needed.

Her heart was full. She'd made her own good vibe.

Bliss left a few more bamboo pots on empty desks and ventured back down the corridor. It turned a corner, and while the inner side of the hall was more of the small meeting rooms, closets, and HVAC panels, the outer edge was lined with tiny offices that featured both walls and doors, and to Bliss's relief, windowsills. She stepped into each and took notes on the light and which way the windows faced. The offices got bigger as she went along, and though all were nicely furnished, none was so nice as the CEO's— an airy, palatial space, signaling the apex of the company hierarchy.

Her father had had an office like this one, designed to intimidate by its size alone. You thought these kinds of offices were nice at first, but the people who worked in them always did you dirty.

The empty offices were creepy. Time to get moving.

She worked her way back down the hall, dropping off an aloe in one office and a sago palm in another. Her granny cart was almost empty; she'd found spots for almost everything she'd brought along, and she hadn't had anything for more than half of the individual offices. There was a single plant left, and she decided to leave it in a tiny, bright office halfway down the line of seniority.

Unlike some of the other offices, the one she'd chosen didn't have any family photos or golf trophies on the windowsill, so there was plenty of room for a plant for its occupant: Emory Jordan, Vice-President. Bliss had the perfect thing—well, she only had one thing. She gingerly removed a potted cactus, an *Echinocereus stramineus*, from the bottom of her cart. She'd found the strawberry hedgehog cactus at a street fair three years ago, the size of a tiny button, and it had grown into a decent burrito. Twice since then it had outgrown its pot and currently lived in a bright pink planter. It was *cute*.

Two steps into the room, she heard "Excuse me," and she spun to explain herself—and when she did, she smashed full on into an intimidatingly attractive woman. A woman who sent a chill of rightness through her, a woman whose presence stilled the world for a moment.

But not for long enough. Bliss rammed right into her arm.

With the cactus.

The woman stared at Bliss, betrayal etching her features. She clapped a hand over her arm, which was riddled with little spines, and let out a yelp. "What the—"

"Don't touch those!" Bliss cast around and then deposited the cactus on the floor. She wanted to kick it under the desk and pretend it never existed. "You'll make it worse. Let me help you."

"How do I know *you* won't make it worse?" the woman snapped.

Bliss brought her palms together in supplication. "I am truly sorry, and I promise I know how to make it better right now."

There was a particular kind of woman who went to the gym and drank fresh-squeezed juice and ran the world that Bliss had a weakness for, and Bliss was feeling that weakness for the woman with long, honey-blonde hair that cascaded over her shoulders and bright, intelligent hazel eyes. For one perfect moment, Bliss had been sure that she and this towering goddess of a woman were *supposed* to collide. But they definitely weren't supposed to collide like *this*.

"I can't even reach the cactus from here, so I definitely can't make it worse." She patted her apron pocket like it would deliver something to save the day. "Do you happen to have tweezers?"

The woman dropped her suit jacket and a stack of folders into one of the chairs in front of the desk—probably *her* desk, Bliss realized. The good vibes dissipated. "I am so sorry, so, so sorry, I didn't expect anyone to come in, I..."

The woman shouldered past Bliss to sit in the empty guest chair. She pulled a briefcase out from under the desk and searched through it one-handed. Bliss watched her balance the bag on her knees, where her legs stretched long. The woman's pantyhose was a light sand color, the same shade as her skin. Her suit was a terribly boring dust-colored jacket and skirt, and her stiletto heels were matte beige, with only a sleeveless white shell to break up the monochrome palette. Not that Bliss objected. *She looks good in nude.*

She forced the thought away. Most women weren't interested in other women. Especially not when a meet-cute was a meet-mutilation. And a woman who worked in a place like this was part of the hands-off club. She was pretty on the outside, but corporate work practically guaranteed her inside was all asshole.

The woman held up a pair of tweezers and put her bag aside. "Now what?"

Bliss carefully moved the stack of papers and the jacket from the other seat to the desk, watching for any objection, then balanced gingerly on the edge of the chair. She took the tweezers and put one hand under the woman's wrist so she could see the damage.

"Ouch."

There was no missing the eyebrow that arched up. "Yes, I noticed."

"Okay, hold still. This shouldn't be too bad. It would have been a lot worse if the spines had been smaller, because they'd have been harder to see and to pull out." She plucked one as gently as she could and dropped it into the trashcan. "How was that?"

She got a shrug. That was workable. It wasn't enough of a distraction to last through the rest of the spines. Bliss would have to make conversation. "Um, is this your office? You're Vice-President Emory?"

The woman—Emory—nodded warily. Bliss went on. "I'm Bliss. I can be Lissie or Liss. Only my mom calls me that, though. I'm just saying that you can call me whatever you want."

Emory surprised her. "I want you to be whoever you already are."

Bliss extracted another spine. Emory's arm was supple and shapely, and she smelled like fresh air. How anyone smelled like fresh air in midtown Manhattan was beyond Bliss's comprehension. Technically everyone should have smelled like exhaust and garbage juice. "I want to be Bliss, then." Emory opened and squeezed her hand a few times before letting it go limp. Maybe Bliss's nervous talking was working magic. "What do you do here in this stuffy office?" Maybe that was the wrong sort of nervous talking. Besides, she didn't really care what Emory did. The leather and wood and snobby signage told her everything she needed to know about who worked at WW and Partners.

"I'd like to point out that you're also in this stuffy office." The desk phone rang, and Emory hit a button that silenced it. She watched Bliss take out another spine and hissed softly. "I go to stuffy meetings. I pitch businesses to the company, and if I'm

21

successful, I get to help make businesses better. We advise businesses and give them money, and then when they get bigger, they give the money back with profit. Or we keep owning part of the business, maybe. Lots of possibilities."

"Oh?" Bliss rubbed her finger over the spot where a spine had been, feeling for anything she'd missed. "So you make businesses successful."

"Sometimes. Sometimes you fail. A lot of the time, at my level, you fail. And it's one thing when you fail because you got beat, but it's another thing entirely when you fail because nobody believes in you."

A deep frown crossed her face and Bliss held the tweezers still. A look like that didn't come from a cactus spine. There was something else going on. A couple of employees passed down the hall, and Bliss could hear their laughter—a "hur, hur, hur" that eventually faded when a door slammed shut. Emory got her feet beneath herself and pushed herself up straight in her chair. "But that's business."

The phone rang again and Emory picked up with her free hand. "Hello, Clark, can I call you right back? I'm in the middle of something, but in a few minutes, I'll be able to give you my full attention. Thanks so much."

There were three big spines left. Bliss needed Emory to be distracted a little longer. "How do you get into a place like this? Like, how do you start working here?"

"Lucked into it during school." Emory was quiet while Bliss twisted her arm back and forth, examining the angle of the spines so she could pull them out with minimal damage. Emory repeated the question back. "How did *you* get into a place like this?"

Bliss removed the last spine and pulled Emory's arm close to inspect her work. Her own distraction let the truth slip. "I sent postcards to every business in a ten-block radius. Beatriz was the one person who called."

Emory leaned forward. "That's good. Good for you." Her hazel gaze was curious. And seated, without the additional advantage of three-inch heels, she wasn't so intimidating. Her hair slipped down over her shoulder, so close Bliss wanted to touch the soft curve at the end and curl it around and around her finger. "Thanks. You have good hands, Bliss."

The spines had probably hurt a lot, but Bliss was the one feeling tortured. She did have good hands. If Emory only knew.

A second later, Bliss remembered that people like Emory couldn't be trusted. She felt like she was on some third-rate carnival ride, bouncing back and forth while her brain rattled out of her head. She dropped Emory's arm. "If you have anything like witch hazel or aloe, that would be good to put on later. There's an aloe plant in another office down the hall—I left one. I think it said Adam Carrington on the door?"

Emory raised her face to the ceiling and huffed out a long breath.

Bliss didn't know what to make of that. "Go to the doctor if your arm gets puffy or hot, or if it keeps hurting." She scooped up the cockeyed cactus and carried it tenderly to the windowsill. It had been through a lot.

Emory pushed in the extra chairs and settled herself behind her desk while Bliss used a corner of her apron to right the plant in its pot, and when she did, she noticed a tiny prism hung on a metal rod. She'd completely forgotten that was there. When she pulled her apron away, the prism caught the sun and scattered rainbows across her front. "Should I—"

"That's the most fun this stuffy office has seen in a while." A rainbow streak refracted on the wall behind Emory's computer monitor. It was the brightest spot in all of WW and Partners. "Might not be the right accessory for all of the offices, though."

Bliss nodded. *Good business advice.* "I will check on your cactus next week. We can see if you want to stick with it or not."

"Stick with it," Emory repeated. She snorted. An endearing little snort, angry-cute like—like a strawberry hedgehog cactus. The side of her mouth twitched, then twitched again, and the start of Emory's smile disappeared.

Was it the pun? Was that smile a crack in the ice? Bliss edged toward the door anyway.

"Next week. We'll see if I'm feeling prickly then," Emory said.

Bliss laughed.

And fled.

three

THE RAINBOW ON THE WALL faded away too soon. Early April clouds blotted out the sun, followed by a spattering rain on the windows that provided a soothing backdrop to Emory's afternoon routine of research, calls with business founders, and email after email after email. At six-thirty, she started closing out her open tabs, but before she finished, a notification popped up: TODAY'S PROPOSALS. She stretched her arms over her head in an attempt to quell the ripples that ran through her stomach whenever William sent out the post-meeting list. It wouldn't work; she knew that. The fastest end to the feeling was to open the email.

Neighborhood Answering was not on the list.

"Goddammit."

Again. Nine times in the last six months, she had gone into battle. Nine times she'd presented companies she truly believed in, and the sole business William wanted to take to the partners was a small and—in her opinion—highly sketchy crypto and stocks app. That investment hadn't even been her idea, so she didn't count it in the nine; one of the junior partners had a friend who had a friend, but that partner decided to "quit the rat race and live a quiet life," which apparently meant living on a boat in the French Riviera while Emory took over his half-finished presentation deck and played phone tag with a blowhard guy who could only explain step one and step three on the road to profit. She counted herself fortunate that the partners had their eye on a competitor in the crypto space so she could wiggle out of further contact.

But this lost battle hurt, and next year's bonus was looking shakier and shakier.

Emory badly needed a win.

And a win with a women-owned startup was a win she'd wanted—particularly this one, as she remembered again her first apartment after she moved out of her dorm, where even her junk mail went missing because her landlord couldn't be bothered to care about maintaining the front door lock, much less the mailboxes.

The world of venture capital was overwhelmingly white men giving money to white men. That was the way of capitalism, and most of the time, she could put her head down and go to work and not think about the unfairness of it all. Every time

Emory failed to make a case for a business with founders that didn't fit that profile, she got a headache behind her eyes. Every time she heard a yes for the previously lauded winners of the money wars, she had to wonder if she wasn't widening the world, but creating a narrower ladder and pretending that everyone could climb it.

She jabbed the power button on her laptop with a finger and tucked it into her briefcase. In the morning, she'd make the call to Neighborhood Answering. Today had started with bad news; it didn't have to end with it too.

Or, more accurately, it had started with weird news. Emory had closed her door to avoid the whispers from her colleagues who had been around for her breakup with Mari eight years ago, and foregone coffee from the break room to escape the stares of newer employees. She habitually avoided Hollywood gossip, so the news had been especially unexpected. And there were reasons she didn't talk about her romantic life at work, not that there was much of one to speak of.

Enough. Enough spiraling around the ills of capitalism and ex-girlfriends. As she pulled her trench coat tight and took the elevator down into the glossy, wet streets of Manhattan, she vowed that she would let her brain off the hook for the rest of the night.

There weren't any available seats on the subway. That was fine. Emory didn't want someone else's damp city water on her backside. And she could concentrate on finding the hidden pictures in the overhead subway ad and not think about Mari. Except

27

for all the moments she kept thinking about Mari. They hadn't spoken in years. Why did Mari think Emory would want to come to her wedding after all this time?

When the train emerged from underground and crossed the bridge into Brooklyn, Emory pulled out her phone and sent a text. *Dinner?*

The response came back immediately: *yes but im filthy.*

Only your mouth. Take a shower. Omw.

She stayed on past her stop, trying not to breathe the humid reek that accompanied New York, wet or dry, and exited at Park Slope. The streets were quiet. Emory stalled at a corner to take out her umbrella and watched a woman in a leaf-green coat with a slim, sharp build and a granny cart cross on the other side. It was dark enough that Emory couldn't quite see her face, but she thought rain was dripping from the woman's overgrown pixie. She looked like the stabby plant girl from this morning. Bliss.

After the stabby part was over, talking to Bliss had been the best part of Emory's day. She definitely needed a haircut, Emory thought. But her dark brown hair and gray eyes were objectively attractive, and her hands were warm and soft, and that was probably why Emory had wanted her to stay and talk about cactuses.

The light changed and Emory crossed the street, walking as fast as she could without falling in her stupid battle-unready heels, but when she came to the next corner, the woman was gone.

It wasn't a loss. She hadn't been in pursuit.

Emory turned in all directions. There was a bar on one corner, a coffeeshop on another, and—there, that would do. A few minutes later, she had takeout from New Hunan Style under her arm and was buzzing her best friend's brownstone apartment.

Francis opened the door in her bathrobe and bunny slippers. Her hair was tucked inside a towel turban that was printed with ducks and dripping water from her shower. "I love you."

Emory laughed. "Of course you do."

"I was talking to the takeout," Francis replied, taking it into her arms and petting it exaggeratedly like she was soothing a fractious child. She waved Emory inside. "I keep meaning to go check this place out, but leaving the house right now is such a production."

Emory kicked off her heels at the threshold and hung her coat on a hook. "Can I borrow some socks? Maybe black ones? I have a blister and I don't want it to pop and bleed all over your floor."

Francis carried the damp takeout bag to the kitchen. "People who bring me dinner can freely raid my wardrobe. Jackson Pollack this whole place with your hemoglobin if you want." She unpacked and opened cartons, inhaling each one rapturously.

"Francis Yoon, you leave some for me," Emory admonished her, not even waiting for Francis's "we'll see" before tiptoeing into Francis's bedroom. Her infant daughter, Sophie, slept in a bassinet by the window, and Emory leaned over to get a peek at her sweet face and tuft of black hair. She eased open a dresser drawer to grab a pair of fuzzy socks with owls on them that Emory was pretty sure Francis had worn back in their college days, then slipped back down the hall to the bathroom, where she turned on the bathtub tap; also from their college days, Emory knew that Francis never turned down having someone else draw her a bath to follow a quick shower. She balanced on one leg and then the other to pull on the socks over her stockings, because the thought of wriggling out of the latter to put them on again when she went home was exhausting.

Emory was adding bubble bath when Francis came in with an open carton of the house special lo mein. "This tastes like heaven." She handed the carton to Emory, who took a few bites while Francis climbed into the tub, sinking back into the warm water like she'd never experienced such luxury before.

"When's the last time you had a full night's sleep?" The lo mein wasn't anything Emory would have described as heaven, but it was generous with shrimp, and the shrimp *was* pretty good, twice as good as the shrimp at Eight Palace, where they'd had dinner the day before Francis went into labor. Emory and Francis hadn't managed to get together except for brief visits after Sophie was born, so their spreadsheet-enabled, color-coded plan to work their way through the restaurants of Park Slope and beyond had understandably stalled.

"Last week, the night before my mom went back to San Jose," Francis replied. "But really, eleven weeks ago, right before Sophie came. Which is why I'm multitasking." She reached an arm up for the lo mein, which Emory handed back. If Francis was so hungry she was willing to eat in the bathtub, Emory was going to support her in that decision. That was what friends did. They didn't question things when their friends got weird, as long as nobody was getting hurt, and Francis had always been a weird friend. The best kind, really.

Francis closed her eyes. "Tomorrow I'm calling HR and telling them I need another month off. I can't believe I only get twelve weeks of maternity leave. I can't believe we don't all get two *years* of maternity leave. I'm going to need two years off just to nap."

Emory couldn't imagine. She'd never even been a babysitter. "Are you going to have your mom come back to help, do you think?"

Francis caught a wayward noodle before it slipped into the bathwater. "Yike. Okay, dinner in the bath is not a good idea. No. I think I'm hiring a nanny, but I keep putting off looking for one. I don't want anyone else to be with the beansprout all day."

"No word from Buck?"

"Oh, he's sent money like he promised he would. I tried to send it back. After all, I didn't have to buy sperm because he donated it to me for free. I haven't started the custody paperwork either. Kind of hard with him being out of the country." She picked through the lo mein, lifting out a carrot, and inspected it like it held a secret. "My mom won't say his name. We haven't told the extended family yet. Being a single parent can be a mark of shame in Korea, and it's a lot for my mom to wrap her head around. I should have told her I was pregnant sooner and not when I was practically in labor."

Francis piled her black hair behind her nape and tipped her head back against the tiled wall. "Honestly, I'm not sure I've wrapped my head around it. I can't believe I had a fling with a guy named Buck, who didn't want a baby because he was on his way to a three-year contract doing scientific research in Beijing, and now I'm a mom. A job I *more than once* told my mother I never wanted."

Emory wasn't sure she could believe it herself. While Francis did like to try on a new guy regularly, she'd never once mentioned wanting kids. She was the perfect, businesslike managing director at an investment bank by day, and in her off hours, Francis was a whirlwind free spirit who did her own thing, whether it was jetting to Bali for a weekend or exploring hidden corners of Brooklyn. So it had been a complete surprise when Francis decided to go her separate ways with Buck and still have the baby. Emory had met Buck once—a nice enough guy, though maybe not nice enough for Francis. Her best friend deserved better.

They both deserved better than being alone. Except for casual dates here and there, Emory had been alone since Mari chose Hollywood and the unknown instead of New York and Emory. "He can disappear. We're going to hold out for Mr. and Mrs. Right."

"Damn right we are." Francis tossed the takeout carton into the bathroom trash. "I've told you about how my parents don't know what to do with their wild and wayward daughter and now granddaughter, right?"

"Probably a dozen times now, yes."

Francis dipped her hand into the tub and flicked water at Emory, who ducked most of it.

"I'll listen as much as you need me to. Whenever you need me to. Besides, you never repeat yourself unless you're tired. And you have the right to be tired. It's in the constitution."

"It better at least be in the bill of rights." Francis turned on the tap to add more hot water. "Anyway, I'm tired of my drama today. Please distract me with someone else's drama."

"Things are a lot easier when your parents don't care much about what you do." Emory grabbed a tube of the sort of face mask that she never bothered with unless she had a free sample and slid down to sit on the bathmat. Francis squirted creamy pink clay into her palm and applied it to Emory's nose. "Um, so, I do have some drama of my own. Mari's getting married."

Francis swiped the clay across Emory's cheek. "Whoa."

"Yeah. She—she sent me a wedding invitation. Well, her wedding planner sent me an invitation. Mari had to approve the invite list, though, right?"

"That is usually how it is done, yes." Francis sat back and began rubbing the clay mask across her forehead. She didn't look at Emory. "Are you going to go?"

Emory twisted her hair back and tucked it into her sleeveless blouse to keep it out of the way. "No." There wasn't anything else to say. She couldn't go. It was unthinkable.

"Going might provide some closure," Francis said softly.

Eight years since their last phone call hadn't brought any. Emory tugged at a thread on her stocking and watched it unravel down her leg. "I don't want to go alone. I don't want her to think—" She didn't know what the rest of the sentence was. "But at work, William found out, and commented that I should make the connection to her husband. Implied that would be good for getting the junior partner job."

"Who's she marrying?"

"Benjamin Thorston," Emory replied.

Francis raised an eyebrow. "That new age-y tech guy? Who does the—what again? Space cars or AI social networking or robot teachers?"

Emory laughed. "I think it's some business backend software thing where he made his money in the first place. I haven't checked into it because I don't want to go to the wedding, and I don't want to meet him, and I don't want to—I don't want any of it." She didn't want to befriend a tech bro. She didn't want a deal with a tech bro. She didn't want to sit in a pew and watch Mari marry a tech bro.

"But you do want the promotion," Francis said. "It's what you've been aiming for since you were an intern."

Emory rubbed her temples. The clay mask got on her fingers and she scrubbed the drying granules against her palms. "I do. I mean, I think I do. Junior partner won't be as hands-on, but it's more responsibility. Even better pay. It's the natural next step."

Francis snapped the lid of the mask tube closed and spoke with exaggerated cheer. "Well, I can't go right now. And it sounds

34

like you have to. We'll find you a plus-one. Since you've been taking a break, we'll swipe and swipe to find you some arm candy."

She'd tried apps. She'd tried speed dating. She'd tried pretending that she could pick out her soulmate in a room full of chattering women. "You know I don't work that way." Emory pushed the edges of the hole in her stocking together. They never lasted more than a couple of days. Not stockings, not women.

"I know," Francis said. She rubbed Emory's arm with the gentle affection she saved for when she was joking but serious. "When you work right, you work hard. Let's not work hard and have you waste a potential girlfriend on a boring, ungrateful, smelly ex-fiancée's wedding. You just need a warm body. You can hire someone, like you do for tasks you hate, your suit shopping and getting your dry cleaning and driving you to the airport. A wedding nanny."

Emory laughed, and when she did, Francis did too, and their masks cracked up around the edges and flaked off.

———✥———

There was trash to take down to the curb, and laundry to be thrown in the hamper, and dishes to do. Emory worked her way through the apartment, and in twenty minutes, the place looked almost like it was Francis's bachelor pad again. Only the unsorted boxes of baby supplies stacked in the living room gave the game away. Francis had done some serious online shopping. Emory thought that once she fought her instinct and hired a nanny to help, Francis would be glad she had someone else to handle the everyday, tedious tasks. It was worth paying for that sort of thing, in Emory's opinion.

Maybe a wedding nanny wasn't *that* weird of an idea.

After a while, Francis snuggled in bed with Sophie for a nighttime feeding, and Emory stuffed her feet back into her shoes, rolled down the fluffy socks so they wouldn't be so obvious, and saw herself out. The rain had stopped, and the streetlights were reflected in the pavement. She walked up Flatbush, favoring her blistered heel, until she stood across from her building and waited for the light to signal her safely across the busy intersection.

A city bus featuring an advertisement with Mari's face on it pulled up to the curb. She was laughing, with her head thrown back, her blonde hair swept out in a wave behind her, her arms around a muscular man with three days' stubble on his chin. She was happy, or doing a great job of acting like it.

The bus accelerated through the intersection and into a puddle that splashed Emory up to the neck.

"I hate you, bus," she said. "I hate you, I hate this rain, I hate everything and everyone."

She pulled out her phone and opened the email from Malibu Elite Weddings. It had embedded buttons in the shape of little hearts for some replies, and broken hearts for others.

Emory selected the sparkling red heart for WILL ATTEND.

And she also selected a pair of pink lips, animated to cycle between a toothy smile and an exaggerated kiss, for PLUS-ONE.

four

BLISS WALKED DOWN 7TH AVENUE in Park Slope. She should have thrown an umbrella in with the plants that morning, she thought, as it began to drizzle. After leaving WW and Partners, she'd stopped at the library to renew her card and borrowed some business books. In the freezing reading room, she flipped through a half-dozen books aimed at startup businesses. All of them seemed to focus on business plans and business loans in the most confusing way possible, or they were filled with advice about dreaming big and seeking niche opportunities with no actual practical tips. Bliss spent a happy hour going over her notes about the plants she needed to fulfill Bliss Foliage's one and only contract, then laid her head down on her stack of books and flipped her collar up, which turned into an accidental nap that left her chilly and slightly irritable.

By the time she dropped the useless books back at the circulation desk and took the train to Brooklyn, it was dark enough that she tricked herself into thinking someone was watching her. It wasn't all that late, and plenty of people were out and about, so she didn't feel unsafe, but she didn't dawdle.

She pulled her cart across the street in the rain and onward to brightly lit Park Slope Express Floral, a beacon even at this hour. Bliss stepped in out of the darkness and shook the rain from her pixie, which needed a cut so badly, it was almost a bob on one side.

"You gonna let me clean that up?" Selma, Park Slope Express Floral's owner, lifted a pair of shears and rattled them like castanets. She had an immaculate gray buzzcut that she maintained herself, but Bliss never took her up on the offers to trim her side shave.

The question cheered Bliss right up, though. "The hair or the puddle I brought in?"

"That scruff!" Selma rattled her shears again.

Bliss ducked. "Ha! No, I'm here to get other things trimmed!"

"Honey, you're going to have to ask somebody else about that kind of thing."

There was nothing to do but laugh. Selma had a knack for seeing who needed a dose of humor, which was why Bliss had come into the shop now and again over the past year after buying a rainbow floral crown from the store's booth during Brooklyn Pride. She still had it, dried and turned into a decoupage storage box.

And when she'd mentioned to Selma that she had an idea for a plant service company, Selma had been nothing but encouraging, even if, Bliss thought in retrospect, she probably should have questioned Bliss's qualifications.

Selma's shop had a round wooden table and chairs tucked into the front corner under the window display, which was currently themed with baskets and bunnies. Bliss stacked three-ring binders full of bouquet photos and wreath designs until she'd cleared enough space to open the one labeled HOUSEPLANTS and also have room for her Moleskine. "I saw my first client today, and I'm going to need some more foliage for Bliss Foliage real quick or I'm going to have to drop the foliage part of the company name."

"I'm just the person you need to see." Selma stowed the shears and sat down with Bliss. "If you're really doing this, I have to recommend you grow some completely on your own. Do you have some room in a yard or on the roof where you could set up a greenhouse? Maybe some seed trays and other supplies? Or you could start from cuttings. I remember what it was like starting out, and you've gotta save all the money you can."

Bliss nodded. "I do. I mean I don't. I do need to save money, because the startup fee I'm charging to get the plants situated is solid, but the ongoing maintenance fee doesn't let me support myself without more clients. I don't have much more room in my apartment for plants. I guess I'd have space if I got rid of most of mine—"

Selma gasped. "No, no. The poor babies." She shook her head like Bliss had suggested murdering a child. "We'll get you figured out."

There was more to say. "Thanks, Selma. I—I was hoping you'd be able to give me a discount for buying a lot of plants all at once?" Bliss hated asking for money favors. Too much like being a teenager. Too much like watching her mom crumble when her mom found out her father had left them with nothing. She flipped through the pages of the houseplants book so fast she couldn't see anything but green flashing by.

"I've got you covered. I can add you to my wholesale order and charge you cost." Selma put her hand down on the binder pages so Bliss wouldn't tear out the page protectors with her frantic fidgeting. "Some of us need to stick together. And I've got amazing foot traffic and I own the building and everything's good for me. You're new. This is the most interesting thing that's happened to Park Slope Express Floral in a decade. Even if I think it's going to take a while for you to make steady money."

"It's not all about the money. It shouldn't ever be all about the money." Bliss redirected her nerves into clicking her pen rapidly. "I know that too well. Get a lot of money and all you end up with is unhappiness. I also need money to live on, but I'd rather not have to think about that."

Selma rested her elbows on the table and her chin on her fists. "You don't wanna think about it. Do you wanna talk about it?"

"No." Bliss really, sincerely did not want to think or talk about money. She wanted money to take care of itself so she didn't have to. Like back when she was a kid. Before.

"Then let's see what you've got."

Bliss paged through her notebook and unfolded the office diagram from Beatriz. It was covered in miniature doodles of each plant and its exact location at WW and Partners.

"You could have written out a list, but you made the plants a seating chart. That's why I like you." Squinting, Selma touched a finger to each office and made suggestions. "Here, maybe a snake plant? Not the most original, but it'll get pretty big and match the scale of the room. And over here, the chump with the office that doesn't get direct light, I've got a ZZ plant ready to go. In this office, who got the cactus?"

"I found the perfect home for my strawberry hedgehog cactus with the office ice queen." The ice queen who looked like a golden goddess and was the sort of woman whose little hint of nice in the ice would set her to daydreaming about running off to a faraway castle and fighting over who would carry whom over the threshold. Bliss shook her pen. Between the doodles and her notes from Selma, she was running out of ink quickly. Cheap ballpoints did that. She traced over Emory's name in her notebook with the nib, and got it inked as far as EMO. "I...kinda...stabbed her with it."

Selma turned serious. "Did she survive?"

"Oh, yeah. I got the spines out and she didn't seem like she wanted to press charges or anything."

That earned her a gentle swat. "Not the woman. I meant the cactus! Now give me your list and let's get your order in."

Bliss pressed the pen down once more and eked out enough ink to finish her list, then handed the notebook over. Selma took it behind the counter and typed the order into a computer. She turned the old, bulky monitor around for Bliss's approval.

The total wasn't as bad as expected, but still gave Bliss an instant gas bubble under her ribs. She swiped her credit card anyway. Math time. She would give WW and Partners their bill for April at the end of the month for the initial setup fee and weekly service. They'd have two weeks to pay afterward, and Bliss hoped that would be enough, because her credit card bill would be due the next week, and she'd be maxed out. Hopefully Beatriz would get the invoice paid promptly—Bliss didn't trust most corporate types to keep their word, but Beatriz seemed like she was one of the very few good ones, in contrast to Emory, who was stunning and still part of the corporate scam world.

Bliss wondered if she had enough spare cash under her mattress to pay rent on her apartment in Kensington. It was old and cheap because her landlord was an elderly couple that spent most of their time in Michigan visiting their grandkids instead of researching the going rate in the neighborhood or remodeling so they could charge more. Bliss hadn't tried to negotiate last year's increase, small as it was, because she didn't want them to figure out she'd been laid off from her job as a junior-level graphic designer at a Manhattan advertising firm. Even the occasional art classes she'd taught on Saturdays for extra cash had dried up later in the pandemic once people got Zoom fatigue.

Starting over wasn't as easy as Bliss had expected. She was burned out on entry-level positions and the endless hours of busywork overtime, and while she was good at taking a company's materials and making their assets pretty, she didn't love sitting and staring at a computer screen all day. She especially didn't love fielding heinously low-paying offers from freelance sites while she searched for full-time jobs in another browser tab, and coped by collecting plants instead. When her unemployment ran out, so did her patience for the isolation of working from home, and she'd gone on several rounds of interviews to discover she was the first runner-up for positions she didn't really want. She'd waited too long, probably, to get moving on her business idea, because she kept thinking about moving up to Boston, where her friends from college had settled. Moving north wasn't easy without a job waiting there, though.

But if she didn't get her finances in order, she'd be moving back in with her mom in Connecticut. This was her last chance to continue adulting. And it *was* a good chance, so long as she came up with another dozen or so clients for Bliss Foliage. Preferably immediately.

The register started reeling out a receipt. Bliss pushed a relieved hand against her gas bubble. *Down, buddy.* She signed, and it was done.

Receipt in her pocket, Bliss sat back at the table while Selma handled a rapid delivery of supplies from a man with a kind face and white hair. "Ken, this is Bliss. Bliss, Ken Takeda. I don't think I've introduced you yet. You'll be seeing each other around. He works delivery and event setup part time."

Ken, clearly in a rush, waved and steered his hand truck back out the door. "Until tomorrow! Goodnight." He flipped the sign on the front door over to CLOSED as he left.

"Found a place with a good deal on dirt. This looks like all of it. I'm going to put this in the back." Despite being an absolute unit, Selma didn't manage to lift the top box on the first try.

Bliss pretended like she hadn't noticed and started drawing on a piece of loose paper with a pencil that she found balanced on the end of the sales counter. "Can I help with that? I'm not afraid of a little dirt."

Selma brushed off her suggestion. "I know better than to be lifting with my back and not with my knees. I just need to get a cart."

She did as she promised, and shuttled the boxes into the back of Park Slope Express Floral while Bliss sketched tabletop arrangements and sneaked peeks at Selma to make sure she was okay. After a while, Selma peered over Bliss's shoulder and *hmm*ed. Bliss angled the pencil for a better point and filled another piece of paper with petals and leaves until Selma plunked a vase down on the table.

44

It was one of her sketches, brought to life in soft pink and yellow and periwinkle. She didn't know the names of the flowers. Like in her drawing, it was an asymmetrical arc of blooms, graceful and light. Stems tangled together in the bottom of the vase like a reflection of the sweep above.

"You could do this, you know."

"I couldn't," Bliss exclaimed. "This place is all you. Homey and humid and green." She inhaled the leaves, the promising scent of fresh dirt, the water in the bucket that held birds of paradise and was starting to stink a little. She wanted a place that was all *her*. A place like this, a place to make beautiful things and to make things beautiful. A place where she would have enough and not too much. But this was Selma's shop, not hers.

Bliss packed her notebook in silence while Selma put the arrangement in a cooler in the back. She returned with a little sprout in a plastic pot, and said, "Pea shoots. I'm experimenting with vegetable garden supplies. Take it. In honor of day one."

On the way home, shivering in her damp coat, Bliss held the miniature pot in her pocket so it wouldn't get banged around in her cart, especially when she let the cart flop against the stairs while she climbed to her walkup. The fairy lights came on when she flipped the switch—good, she was a little behind on her bills, but the electricity wasn't shut off—and the radiator under the windowsill made the place beyond cozy.

The leaning bookcase Bliss had scavenged a few years ago was out of space. Splitting her bamboo into smaller pots to gift to new clients had seemed like a good idea, but even with all that she'd given away this morning, there wasn't any room for a new plant, so she held the pea shoot in two hands long enough to make a wish and set it on the windowsill. It looked lonely there by itself, but it was green. The color of new beginnings.

Of *her* new beginning.

five

THE NEXT TUESDAY, BLISS HAD to call for a car with her grocery money.

Her granny cart wasn't up to toting the bigger plants she'd picked out for the CEO's office and the boardroom at WW and Partners, so she had to skip the subway and load the pots into the back of a rideshare while the driver grimaced and grumbled about a few *tiny* bits of dirt. In midtown, she rolled the plants on a folding dolly on loan from Selma, hoping that no sidewalk cracks would break her delivery's back. Or her delivery's terracotta. At the front desk of the building, after handing over her building pass as Beatriz promised, the security guard directed her to the freight entrance, all the way around the block in the back—so as soon as he was occupied with a flood of visitors, she swiped through the flap-barrier turnstile and dashed to an empty passenger elevator.

Only one monstera leaf got caught in the closing doors, and only a *little* line of dirt made a trail on the floor. *Win.*

Upstairs, Beatriz was on the phone, touching her headset to one ear. She offered two thumbs up to the dried flowers that Bliss tucked into the ornamental vase in the corner of the reception area. Next stop, the conference room. There had been a meeting in it recently, probably this morning, because a few stapled packets were strewn on the table alongside wet rings from coffee mugs. To Bliss's disappointment, there weren't any leftover pastries or bagels sitting abandoned like there always had been at her advertising job. Of course, smart scavengers knew when to arrive for first pick, and vultures didn't leave anything behind, so maybe she was too late.

She dropped off the mature snake plants Selma had sourced for her and headed back down the other way to leave a couple monstera in the CEO's office. Once the biggest pots from the day's batch were off the cart, she could park it and deliver the rest by hand. On her way past the kitchen, she poked her head in: room to park the cart out of the way, but no lonely bagels there, either.

Beatriz was still on the phone, so Bliss couldn't ask if it was okay to have coffee. Coffee that was 90% milk, 5% sugar, 5% sweet caffeine. Her hand hesitated over a stack of mugs with the company logo on the side (*Fuzzy resolution—maybe they need some freelance graphic design help?*), but Bliss didn't want to *take* anything without asking. Corporate America made people think they could take and take, just like her father had.

Back to work, babe. Most days she didn't think about her father at all, and hadn't even at her design job in an upscale, modern building downtown. Something about the wood and the carpet and the golden nameplates on the doors was getting to her. And this was not the time for wallowing.

Like they'd been last Tuesday, the offices of WW and Partners were quiet, mostly either empty or closed. The heavy pile carpet forced her cart to a stop a few doors down from Emory Jordan, Vice-President.

"I think a spring rollout for the software makes sense. That gives you more time to figure out the marketing, and there's more of a cushion for getting the backend ready. If you're on time and on track, there's room to add a few more features. The financial picture isn't that much different. I know you're going to lead the team to victory and make a big splash."

Yes. Bliss nodded, reassured. She'd have that software ready on time. After a second, she caught herself, both pumped up and lulled by the comfort of Emory's voice. Woman could make you feel like you were a contender, that was for sure. Bliss rattled the cart, but it didn't budge.

Squatting, she looked at the wheels to see what was wrong. Both her Converse had come untied. She fiddled with the laces while Emory got on another call.

This time, she was the ice queen. "Hi, Jim. I reviewed the documents you sent over, and we can't agree to those terms. We've been clear about what you need to do for us to move forward with

49

the deal and without that reassurance, we don't think the chain has growth potential. I'm especially concerned that when I take these documents to the partners, they're going to notice that you don't have the evidence we requested."

She went on, looping through business phrases that meant nothing to Bliss. Bliss felt a twang of sympathy for the failure on the other end of the line as Emory abruptly ended the conversation. Laces tied, she stood up and gave the cart a massive shove, which loosened the wheels along with a puff of dirt.

Bliss sneezed. The sound echoed down the hallway.

Emory poked her head out of her office.

"Sorry to interrupt," Bliss said.

"You're not interrupting anything," Emory replied, and disappeared again.

Bliss took that as a sign. She grabbed an asparagus fern from the cart and slipped into Emory's office. Emory was sorting files at the windowsill. She cleared her throat. "I, um. Hello. Sounds like you're very busy and very stressed, so I'll only be here a minute. I thought maybe a different plant—"

"Are you planning to penetrate me with that one too?"

Oh, no no no. Bliss's horndog hindbrain provided her with a split-second vision of Emory, long limbs stretched wide, waiting, arching— "It's not my implement of choice." Was it her imagination, or was Emory squirming a little? The room deadened with an awkward silence Bliss was desperate to fill. "This is an asparagus fern and it won't hurt anybody. Unless you eat it. Or if cats or dogs

eat it. So if you have dogs that come in to help with stress or anything, don't let them have any."

Emory stretched out a finger and ran it gently along a delicate
frond that spilled over the edge of the pot. "I'm not stressed. I like
my job, actually. Most of the time."

Bliss wished she were a fern. "Was that last call some of the
most of the time?"

"Well, no." Emory went back to sorting through her stack of
files. "I like the part where I get to sit down with company founders
and help them organize things. Get better at their business. I like
when things are hands-on."

Hands-on. Bliss really needed her brain to stop. But what
Emory was saying made sense. She could use someone to organize
her own business. Did venture capitalists do that for people who
had one client instead of a hundred? Maybe Bliss could ask her to
go to coffee and not take up all of her time asking about business
like advice was a freebie? She could ask if Emory liked coffee.

If she liked women.

"And I guess I should disclose that sometimes I'm the one who
needs some business help."

Emory was talking about her job and Bliss wasn't paying attention. She gripped the edge of the fern's pot hard. Her dirty fingernails, her messy hair, her black polo that looked like it had a stain
on the chest because she'd picked off the embroidery on an old
product sample she made at her last job, her paint-speckled

apron—all of it was *bad* compared to Emory's sleek, buttoned-up navy pantsuit.

But then, her rent bill was waiting on the kitchen counter at home. Surely a venture capitalist had enough business knowledge in her pinky finger that a little of it would rub off on Bliss, and with a solid dose of luck, she could get organized and build her own success without resorting to loans. Or to designing brochures for pennies. Or to her personal credit card, which wasn't an option until it was safely under the balance limit again. Bliss didn't want to be the market leader or whatever it was they had called successful companies at her advertising job. People who had too much money started paying attention to their money instead of everything else.

The thoughts that were tumbling through her brain when Emory paused, like she'd asked Bliss a question, started tumbling out of her mouth. "There has to be a way to avoid working late nights to prove I have passion for making web banners for companies that care more about clicks than people. I want to walk home in the evenings at a reasonable hour. I don't need much. I only need enough. I want to live simply and beautifully, and make the world a beautiful place—"

Emory interrupted. "What I need is an escort."

Bliss was confused as all fuck. *Is she even gay or what is going on right now?* She sat down in one of Emory's guest chairs and hugged the fern to her chest. "Are you asking me to find one or to be one? I'm more of a couple of dates before we let things heat up kind of girl, no shade to anybody who likes a hookup. Of course, I'd hook up with you in a hot second—" Had that really come out of her mouth? "And also, sex work is absolutely real work, but not my kind of work, personally, so I, uh—"

Emory's mouth dropped open and a deep red glowed on her cheeks. She held her hands up. "Oh, no. I, you see, I have to go to a wedding in a few weeks and I..." Her open hands squeezed into fists and she walked around the desk to sit down. "I don't want to go alone." Even the tip of Emory's nose was blushing now. "I suppose I'm asking... What you could do is pose as my serious girlfriend for the event."

This was one of the weirdest things that had happened to Bliss since the time she'd found a goat in the science classroom in high school, and at the time, she'd known for sure it was a prank.

Emory rushed on. "I'd pay you for your time, of course. Cover your expenses." She turned to her computer and started punching numbers into the keypad, mumbling to herself. "Retainer for the next few weeks. A few meetings to get our story straight. Trip to Los Angeles—the wedding's in Malibu." She looked up at Bliss, who was speechless. "So time, expenses, and travel needs, and a final payment when the job is complete."

Emory scribbled on a sticky note and slid it across the desk. The number she'd written wasn't huge, but it was more than Bliss had ever had in her bank account at once. It was enough to catch up on her late bills. If Bliss was careful, she could stretch the amount to cover her expenses for about three months. All for the low, low price of pretending she was Emory's girlfriend for one.

There was no question. Or maybe there was, but her mouth beat her brain in the speed contest. "Hell yeah."

Emory groaned and smacked her hands down on her blotter. "Don't you even want to negotiate? You should always negotiate!"

"Okay." Bliss transferred the potted fern to the middle of the desk. "Is a retainer like a deposit?"

Emory nodded. "Yes, it is."

"I need the retainer now. Today." As soon as she said it, a wave of nausea creeped up her throat. She sounded like her father.

"That's a good ask." Emory folded her hands in her lap. "I can't accommodate that. I need to draw up an agreement—"

Bliss's stomach growled at an embarrassing volume. She put her hand there, which made the growl go on and on. And on and on. Dramatically, like the theme from a movie where ships sank and true loves wept at their misfortune.

She and Emory looked at each other. There wasn't anything else for Bliss to say. *Excuse me, I'm super embarrassed, please don't fire me, boss lady.* If she were a comedian, that wouldn't get a laugh.

Especially given the sober look on Emory's face. Bliss expected her to come back with—something, whatever it was that you did when you negotiated.

Emory found her purse. She said nothing as she extracted a silver key that unlocked a file drawer or as she patted the underside of the drawer above. Bliss heard the zipping sound of tape coming loose. The search uncovered an envelope with *in case of emer-*

54

gency written on the flap in loopy handwriting. Emory lined up the tips of her fingers on the envelope's edge.

The phone started ringing. Emory ignored it. "Promise me it's yes. This will be our verbal agreement."

Bliss said the word she'd wanted to say to Emory from the first moment she saw her. "Yes."

Emory handed her the envelope. It was full of cash. Small bills. Bliss could catch up on rent today. And she wouldn't have to eat the dusty can of low-sodium vegetable soup in the back of the cupboard that she'd been avoiding, or grocery shop at the discount store tonight. Was this what people did? Spend their life trying to figure out how to play by their own rules, then break them the minute it was convenient? Stay far away from the one percent until they were horny and hungry?

She and Emory listened to the phone ring, then pause, then start again. Finally, it ceased, and they watched the fern fronds stir under their breath.

There was a knock on the doorframe. Beatriz leaned in. "The folks at Mackenzie Aeronautics are trying to get you. The board meeting started and you're not logged on, but you confirmed, and they don't know whether to wait for you or not."

Emory was back on track. All business. "I'll be right there. My computer decided to update and restart."

See. They all lie.

Beatriz shook her head. "Happens. I can sit in, take notes if you want?"

"I've got this one," Emory replied, smiling. "You're the best, though."

Bliss got up, planning to follow Beatriz. Her bones felt slow, like something big had happened and her body hadn't caught up. "She is the best. I don't know why she works here."

Emory seemed to agree, at least with the first part. "Beatriz is the smartest person in this entire office. If she tells you something, pay attention." She tried to talk to Bliss and type at the same time but gave up. "I have a meeting now, but I'll have the agreement paperwork for you on Friday," she said. "Come back then?"

Bliss knew when she was dismissed. After a beat, adrenaline gave her the strength to haul two monstera to the CEO's office without the cart, and it didn't take long for her to deliver the couple of other smaller plants she'd brought along. Beatriz wasn't at reception when she left, which was a relief. She didn't know what expression was on her face. But by the time Bliss was back on street level, she was feeling good again. A little sassy. Relieved.

Weird.

She weaved through the lunchtime crowd straight to the nearest coffee cart. "I'll have a bacon, egg, and cheese on a roll," she said. Her hand found the envelope of cash in her coat pocket. "Actually, I'll have two."

Bliss leaned against the steel and glass wall of one of the tallest office buildings in midtown. She smushed her two sandwiches into a Frankenstein and took a giant bite. Luxury.

What the actual fuck had she gotten herself into?

six

AT THE END OF THE day, Emory was in the supply room printing financials from Mackenzie Aeronautics on legal paper. She'd told Bliss she wasn't stressed, but that was a lie. Mackenzie Aeronautics was struggling with company culture and retention, so she'd been prepared for a meeting where the management dug in their heels and resisted change. Instead, the board had been hit with the news that there were some financial discrepancies. The words *corporate malfeasance* were spoken more than once. A forensic accountant would be hired. The upcoming initial public offering of stock would be postponed. Emory expected to spend the summer with a massive headache.

The copier glitched. It liked to freeze and wait for attention, but it had an easy fix. Emory turned it off and on again, and waited for it to warm up and finish her print job. Meanwhile, she could practice her cold open. "Hello, Mr. Thorston. Mari and I go way back. Mr. Thorston, we both work in business development. Um, pleasure to meet you. I've heard so much...I've read...no, maybe, hello! Benjamin. Emory Jordan of WW and Partners, venture capital..."

Jeff, her favorite VP and the antithesis of Adam Carrington, came into the supply room. They'd been hired as analysts fresh out of undergrad, and even though Jeff had gone to Columbia and she hadn't, he didn't give her any of the attitude that the other WASP-y Ivy League graduates had. Perhaps that was because his family was well off but not well off enough to bypass the corporate ladder like most of their colleagues, or perhaps because they'd both been hired and mentored by William's name-buddy, a partner named Bill Wheat, who was one of the gentlest people Emory had ever met, and who also didn't care that she graduated from a CUNY school on a Rotary Club scholarship.

Emory had asked Bill, once, why he put his money into venture capital and not into philanthropy, and he'd answered, "Same thing." That had been close enough, she supposed, for someone like Bill. In the years since he'd passed, Emory noticed how rare it was for WW and Partners to invest in what Bill would have deemed "the everyday Joe, the little guy, the gal who can outwork you and outthink you."

She and Jeff had tag-teamed on the Mackenzie Aeronautics deal, and while Emory was their main contact for strategic planning, Jeff had stayed on as their numbers guy. He shook his head when he saw her, and from long experience reading his body language, she knew he would stay awake all night trying to solve their money problems. So it was a no-brainer to agree when Jeff said "Drinks, and we'll deal with our airline issues tomorrow?" after the other copy machine gave him one rumpled piece of paper and blew a fuse. She grabbed her coat and a box that arrived at the end of the day from a company that had reached out to her—something about health and relaxation for women. The mailing box was hot pink and the company name, Bodytime Clarity, was emblazoned in silver foil bubble letters. Emory put the whole thing in her bag to deal with later.

Their regular spot, Kelly's in Havana, was around the corner and down the street. They'd been coming here since their first week at WW and Partners, typically with whomever they could round up at work. Once they'd made VP and their colleagues were mostly people like Adam, they'd stopped arranging group happy hours. Kelly's in Havana was neither Irish nor Cuban, but the sign over the door wasn't as important as its location. There were several high-end restaurants between the bar and WW and Partners that were guaranteed to draw off upper management.

Kelly's in Havana's current iteration was what Emory deemed "mid-upscale": nice enough for a business crowd during the early part of happy hour, then dedicated drinkers and budgeters moved elsewhere. The place was quiet enough for conversation at other times, and not so sought-after a reservation was needed.

Emory kept this perfect spot a secret from all but her favorite people. When she and Jeff arrived, happy hour was over and the candles had come out. Kelly's in Havana would have been a good spot for a date if Emory weren't vehemently opposed to even the chance of running into a colleague.

If she dated regularly.

A few theater-goers were finishing up meals, and the hostess, who knew them on sight, nodded the okay for them to take a half-cleared booth. Jeff ordered a beer, and Emory got her usual bourbon. They ordered potato skins out of nostalgia; when they were analysts, the potato skins at an earlier version of Kelly's in Havana had been a huge platter for $4.

Today had been Jeff's turn to crash and burn, presenting a rocketry company that hadn't earned William's stamp of approval. Carrington had taken up the discussion period with a speech about why no one could or should compete with his heroes, and it had been clear who his heroes were. He called them captains of industry. Emory called them robber barons.

"I can't believe some of the stuff Carrington says." Jeff dipped a potato skin in salsa. "It's like he's got an asshole on both ends of his digestive tract."

Emory wiped a string of hot, gooey cheddar from the corner of her mouth. "An asshole who's probably going to get the junior partner job instead of one of us."

"Gaaaaaah." Jeff took a swig of his beer and said, "I have heard it said, by our certain someone with an extra asshole, and I won't say anything about when or where except that I waited to flush, that we're going too hard on education and tech, and the partners, William especially, want to balance that out with more pharma."

Emory groaned. She hated pharma deals. "Do we have to? It's always either Shkreli types at these companies or people shilling the next weight loss pill. We're lucky we never got in on Theranos."

"I think you're just unlucky," Jeff replied. He brushed his brown hair to the side so it wouldn't fall into his glasses. "And you look for more immediate social good than the rest of us do. You bring in as much money over the long run."

"Either way, William's going to remember the latest and greatest deals, not necessarily the best, when he makes his decision about who he wants to fill the junior partner spot." The six positions for vice presidents had turnover; people left for consulting gigs or to be heads of companies. The four junior partners rarely shifted, and the four senior partners hadn't changed since Bill Wheat passed—and then William brought on his own son, Weston, who was in his fifties and the presumptive successor to William. As far as Emory could tell, Weston golfed, and that was about it. He was hardly ever in the office. "My biggest successes happen when I find something that's a seed or take over a project someone else gave up on and nurture it back to health. William wants to see high-profile deals that make their money back fast. So between us, he'd pick you."

"Or some outsider. That's happened."

True. It was very common everywhere. "As long as it's one of us and not Carrington." Emory was sincere. If she didn't get the junior partner position, she'd be genuinely happy if Jeff got it. But if anyone else did? All bets were off.

"I'll drink to that." They toasted and Jeff downed the rest of his beer.

Emory picked up his glass. "Want another?" He usually had two or three beers to her one bourbon. She didn't know where he put it all.

"Nah." He patted his stomach. "I'm getting dad bod."

"You are a dad, Jeff." Emory sent his girls, both in preschool, balloons on their birthdays. Sometimes she was the tiniest bit jealous of his happiness. How he knew he wasn't going home to an empty house. How he knew he'd wake up next to his wife. "How's Melody? Your anniversary is soon, right?"

Jeff nodded. "June. Like everybody else's. Six years, two kids, one dog, and a commuter rail pass. Worth the dad bod, every bit." He swirled the dregs of beer at the bottom of his pint glass. "Speaking of marriage..."

Emory cringed. There was exactly one thing this could be about.

"So, Mari. That's big news. I remember when she would meet you at the end of happy hour and you'd end up staying longer because she'd start a drinking game. You seemed so in love, even though you were so different. I thought you'd settle down first, as the responsible one of the pair. You doing okay?"

She avoided the question. "I *am* a good catch. And I don't go for drinking games these days."

Jeff's cell buzzed. "Sorry, have to take this." He gave her a flat smile. "Pharmaceutical company that William's bullish on."

He stepped outside to take the call. That gave her the perfect answer, too late. It wasn't easy to settle down when work followed you home. Late nights and weekends were part of the job, and it wasn't until the last year that Emory felt comfortable disconnecting from them. She hadn't managed it entirely, and if she was honest, she didn't want to. Work filled the empty hours when you were single.

Jeff had inadvertently hit on one of the things that had wedged itself into her relationship with Mari. She hated Emory's schedule, completely hypocritically, since she disappeared for weeks whenever she got a part in a show. Mari's appearances at happy hour were timed to usher Emory home, though extroverted Mari couldn't resist a party that she invented on the spot.

One summer Friday night, when the sun stayed up late, Emory had dragged a reluctant Mari out of happy hour and up Fifth Avenue. They'd walked at NYC speed, bickering between calls— Emory had a group project due for her MBA and one of her classmates "didn't use email," and as a pre-MBA associate, she was casting a wide net for contacts, so nothing ever went to voicemail. Emory was used to the constant interruptions. She assured Mari the investment of time would pay off and turned left at Terrace

Drive so they could walk across Central Park to the Ladies Pavilion.

But Mari dug in her heels near Pilgrim Hill and refused to go any farther. She grabbed Emory's phone and threw it into the grass. "I'm trying to talk to you!" she'd yelled.

"And I'm trying to talk to you too, Mari Cooper," Emory had yelled back. She had a *plan*. Mari was being a pain because she didn't know the time was *now*. She grabbed Mari's hand. She looked into her blue eyes, at her stubborn jaw, at her hair blowing in her face.

Emory reached into her purse and drew out a black box that fit in the palm of her hand. "Will you marry me?"

Mari frowned and laughed at the same time.

Emory felt tears welling up—not tears of joy, but tears of embarrassment. Something terrible knotted in her stomach with every second that passed. People were watching them, and what had seemed sure before started to seem impossible.

Mari put her hands on her cheeks and held perfectly still. She closed her eyes. The warm, pink light of the setting sun glanced off her cheekbones. Bystanders gathered and snapped pictures. Slowly, Mari spread her arms wide, like she was soaking in the applause after a night on stage. She took one long-legged step toward Emory, and another, and then she was running. Mari tackled her into the grass, and they were kissing, laughing, crying. Holding hands. Walking back through the park. Stopping to buy a painting from a street vendor. Taking a taxi home. Drinking wine.

Taking off their clothes. Getting into bed.

Deciding when to tell their families. Mari wanted to wait. She had an audition in Los Angeles. She wanted to have a plan for the wedding before telling anyone.

The plans got wilder and bigger and more expensive. Then Mari got cast in a pilot. She stopped returning calls. Returning texts. Stopped flying to New York when she had a long weekend.

Until she called to say the wedding was off. "I hope you'll be happy, Emory," she said.

Well, Emory was going to go to Mari's wedding and show her what happy looked like. Her date was even called Bliss.

Jeff still wasn't back. In the good old days, he could be counted on to split the peanut butter brownie, so she ordered it, dad bods be damned. While she waited, she searched Mari's wedding venue—a guest ranch in Malibu. The hotel boasted extensive property and beautiful views, and was far fancier than the expensive places Mari had floated during her first engagement.

There was a link in the save-the-date email to RSVP for rooms. Emory considered. She could go out to LA for a week and meet with some of her prospects, then head to the wedding and be back in New York the next Monday. Maybe one of her potential investments would pan out, or maybe she'd make some high-profile contacts at the reception, and William wouldn't notice she'd avoided Benjamin Thorston.

She'd spent a few hours looking into Mari's business plans, which didn't seem particularly special or like a good investment for

WW and Partners. In fact, the bland workout gear and health supplements seemed like inferior copies of products that other celebrities had quietly retired when they discovered people were not interested enough to make them millionaires off white label protein powder. Even Bliss Foliage would have better chances with the partners. Of course, that wasn't an option. Too inconsequential for William. Bliss seemed sweet, and naïve, and Emory didn't like the idea of feeding her to the wolves.

Naïve. Funny. A good plus-one for a wedding.

Emory scrolled through the room options at the ranch. The accommodations were pricey, and a part of her wanted to stay somewhere else, like that would show Mari she wasn't super concerned with being around for the festivities. And maybe staying at another hotel would give her the excuse to leave if she needed it.

She was overthinking. Emory opened her frequent flyer app to buy plane tickets. After she picked dates and seats, she realized she didn't know Bliss's last name, much less any of the other personal information she needed to book her flight. Overthinking and getting ahead of herself.

Asking Bliss to be her plus-one was foolish and impulsive and not like Emory at all. What did she even know about the woman? She knew about plants and needed some cash. And Bliss had seemed agreeable when Emory had clumsily asked her to sign on for a month of make-believe. She'd said, "I'd hook up with you in a hot second," but she had probably meant to follow that with "if I liked women," the universal compliment for modern heterosexual women who weren't interested in but weren't bothered by attention from lesbians.

Her hands were soft and precise if you needed cactus spines removed from your arm. Her hair was dark and messy and brushed her rosy cheek on one side and her pale jaw on the other. When she looked at plants, she bit her lip with a look of intense concentration. She saw how things could be beautiful.

Emory supposed she was even cute. *Objectively.*

Maybe this was a bad idea. Emory had meant to call a casting agency, not ask Bliss to be her fake girlfriend. Well, *hire* Bliss to be her fake girlfriend. Bliss didn't seem to have the cutthroat desire to win the part. Was Emory taking advantage of someone who didn't have enough money in her bank account to say no?

But wasn't that business? Everything had been straightforward. Simple. They both had a business problem. Emory had a business solution.

And Emory remembered what it was like to be a scrappy upstart. Most of the people she talked to these days were polished professionals, backed up by family money, looking to sell their business in a couple of years, not trying to build something special for themselves. Living simply and beautifully wasn't part of their business plans.

Why not?

She was scrolling when her phone rang, and she swiped up on the California number accidentally. "Hello?" At first, she thought someone had buttdialed her from a club, the electronica coming through the speaker was so loud. "Hello?"

Boom-tcha boom-tcha boom-tcha boom-tcha. She'd gone to a rave with Mari once. It had been her personal nightmare.

The caller was a man. He had the quintessential valley accent. "Miss Jordan," she heard, and "Malibu Elite Weddings," and more talking, but it was unintelligible over the background noise. She heard "regarding your RSVP" and tried to confirm.

"I'll be there for the *soiree*," she said loudly, hoping the person on the other end could hear.

They couldn't. "RSVP and we need to know..."

"I'll be there for the *big day*, yes." This was so irritating.

"...your fiancée," she heard. "We'll tell Mari you're both coming! She wanted to know." The music drowned out whatever else the man from Malibu Elite Weddings had to say. The line went dead.

Fiancée.

Emory dropped her phone.

And dropped her face into her hands.

seven

THE PEA SHOOT DIDN'T SURVIVE a couple hot nights above the radiator. Bliss thought that was a very bad vibe.

Even if it was her own forgetfulness that created her own bad luck this time.

Who would hire an office gardener who killed her own plants?

No one.

Bliss Foliage still had only the one client. She'd sent another round of postcards. Made a few cold calls. Set up ads on social media, checking in on their performance three times a day because she was worrying about her credit card balance. Totaled her meager freelance income and paid her estimated taxes for the quarter. She didn't know much, but she knew enough to put that payment aside every time and never spend it on anything else.

She sat on a bench at the wood-topped table in the space that served as dining room, living room, office, and garden. There was an outlet for her to plug in her laptop (so long as she unplugged the TV), and one end of the table had accumulated an unnerving pile of paperwork. Bills. A couple of design magazines that she'd bought a year ago when she'd been sure she'd nab a graphic design job again. The form she'd filled out to do business as Bliss Foliage. She needed to figure out a filing system.

Where she'd set up that system in her tiny Kensington apartment, she didn't know. Maybe she could give up the table and swap in a desk, and resign herself to never having anyone over for dinner again. Her bedroom was hardly big enough for a full bed anyway, and the cramped closet was stuffed full. The open galley kitchen —kitchenette—had two stools shoved against the countertop, and she was loathe to give up the one space that was reliably clear of clutter.

Bliss had already slipped her rent money into the landlord's mail slot and sent her mom an envelope with a few twenties. A few more went into her wallet for groceries and emergencies. The rest she'd take to the bank and deposit.

She fired up her laptop. Mornings were a good time to work on her design portfolio. The all-purpose main room of the apartment took on a golden glow, and Bliss had an easy time coming up with little illustrations and ideas for sample brochures. She hadn't been inspired to create much beyond a bare-bones webpage for Bliss Foliage, though. There, she had complete designer's block, and she didn't know why. What held her back made no sense. She needed clients to choose Bliss Foliage because it was reliable and respectable, and you got respect with history and reputation, but not having a history or a reputation meant she needed to fake it until she made it. She should have been able to fake a reputation with her design skills, so that no one would think she was as green as the plants she offered.

It was embarrassing that she'd worked at an advertising firm and never paid close attention to how things got marketed after her designs were done. She felt like a fraud, and clicked the tab closed, taking her scanty website out of view.

The Boston group chat pinged. Her college friends had all ended up in Massachusetts, and they and a few new people had gelled in the years since. Bliss hadn't found a circle in New York that was remotely the same. And her dates, during the pandemic, had been few and far between. Nobody ever stuck around.

Misty, bohemian and blasé, spent a week taking selfies with Bliss's plants, then loaded her bags onto a bike trailer and pedaled herself off to Taos. The selfies sometimes showed up on Instagram, but Misty never responded to a DM or text from Bliss again.

Jayye, with their flouncy hair, decided after two lunches that dating was interfering with their goal of a world's record for length of meditation.

71

Then there was Hema, who wanted to establish a rooftop garden collective and take entire neighborhoods off the capitalist grid, and who'd been enthusiastic when Bliss had lost her job, but turned out to be buying up apartment buildings that were underwater on taxes and letting them fall into disrepair so that the state of New York would designate the neighborhood as unsafe and force it to secede, leaving Hema to take charge as dictator in the fallout. The least Hema could have done was make her diabolical plan clear on her dating profile.

Bliss didn't know how her love life could swing from smooth sailing to category 5 hurricane so quickly. At least her friends were dependable in all weather. Her ports in a storm. Her unscrapable barnacles. Or something like that.

> goofbot2000: what r we doing tomorrow
>
> meowsville: same
>
> meowsville: I mean same question
>
> Erika: Movie?
>
> goofbot2000: again we did movie last week
>
> Erika: Righteous Scorpion is out.
>
> meowsville: ooh, Bradley Davis in spandex
>
> goofbot2000: that the one with clive buster and Marlene callahan
>
> Erika: Yeah. No, it's Marilee.
>
> goofbot2000: autocorrect
>
> blissfulmess: Wish I could be there!

Erika: MOVE UP HERE, BLISS. BOSTON BOSTON
BOSTON.

meowsville: Move in with me and seven rescue cats,
ha ha

Charlize Horse: YEAH

blissfulmess: My lease goes to September :) but I'll
think about it. Who can resist seven rescue cats?

goofbot2000: me 7x

The fun went on. Bliss kept an eye on the scroll of jokes and emojis until her phone buzzed. A text from her mom came in, the same thing she always sent at the end of the week: *Hope you're doing great! I love you!* Bliss sent her usual reply: *I love you too!* And this time, there was another in return: *Are you sure you don't need this money?*

She tilted her head. Her mom didn't know she'd lost her job and run out her unemployment. That was the kind of news that would send her mom into a fit of worry long after the worrying years were over. Technically, with a brochure or a presentation or a business card project now and again, she *was* still working as a graphic designer. And technically, her mom *did* still live in the same apartment they rented when Bliss was in middle school, and her mom *would* clean out the second bedroom, and Bliss *could* move back in with her.

But moving back home would make it harder for Bliss to find something that was hers. The something beautiful she'd never been able to make concrete instead of a vague feeling that plants and art projects weren't quite enough.

And moving home would make it tougher to ever have another date, ill-advised or not.

She texted back: *Of course not. Wanted you to get some good takeout. I know it's spring break next week and I know you spend the whole thing grading!* Her mom replied: *That's sweet. Love you, honey. Recess is almost over. Back to work.*

Work. Bliss printed out an invoice for WW and Partners and folded it into her purse. She'd give it to Beatriz early in case there was something wrong with it. Half the time, there was some company paperwork that didn't materialize until clients saw a bill. Then she logged into the freelance designer site where she'd been making a few dollars here and there, and skimmed the list of open projects. There was nothing with a budget over $50. Bliss put her cursor over the ticky to select all and chose "decline."

———— ∞ ————

Bliss took the *F-this* train from Ditmas to Park Slope. Park Slope Express Floral was busy; Selma hustled from the counter to the back room to the counter again, handing over arrangements for weekend birthdays and parties. Locals wandered in for a bouquet and Selma sweet-talked them into something from the glass display case in the main shop. A class of preschoolers hovered outside the front window while their teachers pointed at the letters painted on the glass. A delivery driver from UPS had Selma sign for a stack of boxes. Ken weaved through the customers with his handcart, loading up the Park Slope Express Floral van with funeral wreaths.

It was organized chaos. She loved it.

Bliss didn't have to deliver any plants to midtown today, but she did have her meeting with Emory, so she'd dressed in what she thought of as her interview outfit: a black sweater and slacks, ankle boots, and a hot pink moto jacket that won compliments from art directors. Her plan was to talk to Selma for a few minutes about next week, since she needed more plants for the mid-level offices at WW and Partners. While she waited, she sketched. A wedding arch. A bridal bouquet. A tablescape of rocks and orchids. A couple of people asked if she was an employee, and she had to say no. Eventually, guiltily, she had to slip out and hope that she could meet up with Selma later.

There was no rain in the forecast, but there were still puddles. Her dead pea shoot had been an omen. Crossing back to the subway, Bliss stepped in one that was way deeper than it looked and the dirty water flooded over the top of her boot. Then the F was stalled underground where she didn't have cell service, "due to *fwissbitternships*," according to the speaker system that was apparently made out of potatoes and masking tape, and by the time she got to midtown, the usual lunch hour was almost over.

In her defense, Emory hadn't picked a time.

At the office building lobby, Bliss swiped her card at the turnstile. Nothing happened, and she realized the pass only worked on the days she'd specified for Beatriz. She wasn't an employee.

Emory also hadn't given her a number.

Building security had to call. Upstairs, Beatriz buzzed her into the lobby. "Wasn't expecting you today!"

"I stopped by to drop off this invoice." Bliss handed it over. "And fill out any forms. I was...in the neighborhood. It's easier to do this separately from hauling everything else."

Her lie backfired. Beatriz did have forms—lots of them. And she checked over every detail, handing them back to Bliss for corrections. "You won't want to do this twice," was Beatriz's reasoning. "And everything will be ready for me to submit at the end of the month, right away." The saving grace was that it took so long, Beatriz didn't even raise an eyebrow when Bliss asked if it was okay to use the restroom before she left. That made it a lot easier to wander the halls of WW and Partners without a watering can.

Emory was on a call. She put her hand over the mouthpiece. "I'm almost done here. Meet at four-thirty?" She handed Bliss a sticky note that read *Kelly's in Havana*. "Down the street."

Ah. Meet there, not go there together when the call was over.

"You're quick," Beatriz said when she reappeared.

"Like the wind!" Bliss replied, waving as she left. Beatriz was the smartest person in the whole office, she remembered. She probably should have loitered for a more believable pee-break length.

Kelly's in Havana was for fancy people, but not the fanciest people, Bliss decided. In a couple of hours, it would be packed. This time of day, it was still quiet. She was glad she'd worn the moto jacket and the black silhouette. The hostess told her to sit any-where, and she chose a booth halfway along the wall.

"How did you know this table was my favorite?" Emory slid in opposite her and pulled a manila folder from her bag. "The barten-der makes a really good soy latte with cinnamon. It's great on a chilly day like today. Could I grab you one?"

Bliss nodded her agreement. As it turned out, Emory *did* like coffee. And Bliss supposed she probably also liked women, given the circumstances. Bliss watched Emory lean over the bar, texting while she waited. Always working.

Soon enough, though, she was back. Emory handed her a mug, and Bliss had to agree: soy latte with cinnamon was a good drink for a chilly day. "There isn't a good coffee shop right around here. Everything for a few blocks is cramped and noisy, and I thought we should do this outside the office." Emory blew on her steaming drink. "Plus I can't be away long. I am trying this—" Her lips twisted to the side while she came up with the word. "*Lifestyle* where I'm constantly available during business hours so that I can be less available when it's not business hours."

Bliss traced a finger along the bottom of her mug, where it left a damp ring on the table. "No, it's fine. I can understand why you'd want to separate your business and"—she pointed between them—"your business. No problem."

"All right, then." Emory opened the manila folder and gave Bliss one of the stapled packets inside. "Here's the agreement I drew up."

The document was only a couple of pages and laid out in neat blocks of text. *There are so many better fonts.* Probably not the feedback Emory was looking for.

"The flag stickers are the places where you can fill out your full name and address, and where we fill in our phone numbers and preferred contacts." All business, Emory tapped a finger on the blank lines, and turned the page to show Bliss more. "When the contract is up, at midnight after the wedding is over, we'll both destroy our copies."

Bliss wasn't paying attention. She was looking back at the first page, at the part that said *scope of services*. She was supposed to act as Emory Jordan's girlfriend, but that wasn't what the contract said. "Wait, this isn't right. It says I'm going to be your fiancée."

Emory read the first page of her copy of the contract, almost like she'd never seen it before. "Yes."

Oh. Oh what the flying— "So I'm getting fake married, no, fake engaged...." *To an Amazon goddess.* "For thirty days."

"The terms have changed a bit since we discussed them due to...reasons. This contract lays out my offer in full. The changes are semantic. I also thought that we should have some formal, scheduled meetings ahead of the wedding." Emory picked up her mug and put it back down again without taking a sip. She sat up very straight and spoke in a tone that reminded Emory of a radio announcer. "With my business clients, we go over plans and strategies in preparation for any big presentations. The presentation this time is the wedding, and we'll need to collaborate on our back-story, obtain appropriate formal attire, and so on."

Emory wasn't wrong. They *did* need to get their story straight. And Bliss had some cool dresses. Nothing that would be appropriate for a wedding, though.

"The rest is laid out on subsequent pages. I thought we should go to Los Angeles together a week before the wedding. For efficiency, of course. We won't be caught out if there are travel delays. I'll need to work, but after hours, we can finish any tasks that are incomplete. In the daytime, you can do whatever you want. Consider it a vacation, perhaps.

"And remember, I'll be paying your sexpenses." Emory heard her own flub, and her whole demeanor fell apart. "I meant *sexpenses*," she said, repeating the mistake. She covered her mouth with her hand before trying again. "*Ex-pen-ses.*"

"You can pay for those too if you want," Bliss joked. While Emory looked good in nude, blush pink was also a flattering look on her. She tried another joke. "But I'm not sure you're very good at this whole business thing. I've never had a relationship last an entire thirty days. I go on dating apps and hardly anybody messages back."

Suddenly, it all went sideways. "You didn't decide to swipe on me. I was just the profile you saw first." Emory wasn't the one who'd responded to her marketing postcard for Bliss Foliage, even. "You thought I'd agree to all of this because—I'm—" She didn't want to say *broke*.

Broke. Broken. Like when her dad left. And then her friends left. And everyone she'd known disappeared on her except for her mom. She didn't want to think about it.

She *had* to think about it. Emory was beautiful, really absolutely disgustingly gorgeous, and she'd been kind enough so far, but Bliss couldn't trust her. Not when she was part of the business of making money and screwing you over in the end.

Emory was stricken. "I have to be honest—I didn't mean to spring this on you. Like I said, the situation is more complicated than I previously understood." She put her copy of the contract back in the manila folder and reached for Bliss's as well. "You don't have to take every deal you're offered, you know."

Bliss's phone vibrated in her pocket. She didn't have to check the notification. Her online bill payments had gone through and her bank was disclosing the overdraft fee.

"Wait."

She closed her eyes. *We're not getting married. It's only a game of pretend. It will be fine.* Emory needed a warm body and Bliss was a warm body. Except for her feet, which were still cold and damp from the puddle incident earlier.

A week in Los Angeles sounded fun. Her plants at home would be fine for a week, as would the plants at the office. And in thirty days, her bank account would love her.

What could go wrong in a month's time?

Bliss blinked. "You told me I'm supposed to negotiate."

Emory was quiet. She took the contracts out again and spread them on the table. "If you look at the payment schedule section, you'll see that I added some funds to offset the additional time I'm requesting from you in Los Angeles. I intend to compensate you fairly."

What was it like to throw money at someone because you needed a date? What was it like to have so much money you could buy one in this miserable economy? Bliss put her hand on her purse, intending to find out if there was a pen wedged underneath her wallet and half-empty packets of gum and miscellaneous receipts.

Emory must have thought she was playing hardball. "Stop! Here—" She added a line at the end of the payments list and held her copy out for Bliss's approval.

Bliss took the second copy and ran her fingernail over the new ink, which smudged, but not unreadably. The figure was enough to last an extra week.

"Approved."

Emory took the contracts back and penned matching amounts. "If you date and initial here, we don't have to print this out again. We'll keep these copies instead. Until the destruction date at the end of the contract, that is."

Bliss finished filling out her information. Emory sat next to her and they compared the pages, side by side. It didn't take long. "We have a deal," Emory said, and she held a contract out to Bliss, who tucked her copy away.

"And now we're engaged," Bliss added. The absurdity of it all washed over her and she felt her toothiest grin cracking through her mixed feelings. "Let's toast."

Emory picked up her mug and tapped Bliss's. Instead of drinking with Bliss, she held the mug close to her chest. "Are you sure you're sure?"

Bliss slammed the mug down and pointed her chin up haughtily. "I'm going to be the best fiancée you've ever had. Pinky swear." She stuck her little finger in front of Emory's face like a sword.

Emory flinched.

"It was supposed to be a joke." Bliss dropped her hand on Emory's shoulder. Time to flirt. The engagement was fake, but the fun didn't have to be, as long as Bliss remembered not to catch any feelings. She winked.

Emory finally got it. She nodded and winked back, stiffly.

Bliss walked Emory out to the curb. "What subway line do you need?" There was an entrance next to Kelly's in Havana. The sound of a train's squealing brakes floated up from the tunnel below.

"I'm breaking my new rule about not being available in the evenings. I have to get across town for a drinks and dinner meeting with a potential investment." She raised her arm for a taxi, but the cab was occupied and passed her by. "I guess I should get a ride-share. Before you go, can we confirm our meeting tomorrow, for shopping? And please look over the schedule in the contract and let me know right away if you have any conflicts with the dates so we can reschedule."

"I'll do that," Bliss answered in her best business voice. Her flirty business voice. Her throwing caution to the wind voice. Her "I have *two* business ventures" voice.

Emory was committing for thirty days. For thirty days, Bliss would commit too. She would commit so hard, Emory wouldn't know what hit her. She'd show her what *real* commitment looked like.

"Thanks again for coming today." Emory held her hand out. Their meeting was clearly at an end.

Bliss clasped Emory's hand tightly and shook her head. "That's not how an engaged couple says goodbye." Without letting go, she pulled Emory forward.

And realized she wasn't a little shorter than Emory, she was a *lot* shorter than Emory. She had an excellent view of her collarbones. Bliss craned her neck up.

Emory's hazel eyes were wide. Close. Bliss's heart was beating funny. She tried to smirk, hoping it didn't look like a grimace. She leaned in and waited. Emory was going to have to bend her way.

The view of Emory's collarbones became a view of Emory's chin, and then, her mouth.

It was enough.

Bliss brushed her lips against Emory's. Soft. Another.

Again.

And Emory finally, finally kissed her back. The tiniest, gentlest kiss.

Bliss stepped away. "Pleasure doing business with you." She turned and ran down the steps into the subway while the warm air of an arriving train rushed past her, back up the stairs, back to Emory.

eight

ON SATURDAY MORNING, EMORY WOKE up later than usual. Her drinks-and-dinner appointment the night before had droned on and on about some theoretical business law and not nearly enough about their company's prospects. She'd had one too many bourbons, then missed the sleepiness window and ended up sorting through her backlog of analyst reports while some of New York, though certainly not all of it, was quiet.

That meant morning was somewhat unwelcome. There was a slight headache ringing around her hairline. Her eyes were dry and gunky. Her mouth felt...buzzy. Like she'd put on a lip-plumping gloss. Had she? That didn't make sense.

Oh. She remembered.

Bliss had kissed her.

It was nice. Not part of their deal. Emory would need to make that clear.

But nice.

She hadn't expected the kiss, and that was probably why she was still feeling it. Bliss had stopped her in her tracks with those clear gray eyes, with that twitch on the side of her full mouth that Emory had leaned down to see better, wanting to know the joke.

Then Bliss's mouth had been exquisitely—

Mari's kisses never haunted me the next day.

What kind of a thought was that? Emory had never compared Mari's kisses to anyone else's. She'd had so few kisses in recent years. Quick goodbyes on the cheek, brief, obligatory first-date enders. There wasn't a lot to compare to, and maybe there was nothing to compare to at all. It had been so long since Emory last kissed Mari that all she remembered was being happy. She couldn't conjure up a physical memory, except for the feeling that it was her job to cajole Mari into the bedroom, to initiate, unless they'd fought and Mari wanted to kiss and make up.

Emory rolled onto her side and curled into a ball.

From her new angle, she could see the box from Bodytime Clarity that she'd carried home. She sat up and opened the garishly pink mailer. Inside, it had several nesting layers of boxes— overkill—and each darkened the packaging until she was holding a matte black box the size of a grapefruit and labeled in script: SUPERSQUISHLOVER. She supposed that was the product name. Instead of a brochure or a personal note, the packaging referred to "men's power of post-coital clarity, but for women" and "breaking free from the haze of love." Well, product messaging could always be tweaked. She tried to reserve judgment.

She opened the last box. The object inside looked like a cross between an oversized beauty blender and the branded stress ball that her crypto app guy had sent when they were discussing his undeveloped plans for how crypto would make money for them both. Like the outer box, the Supersquishlover was hot pink. There were no visible buttons; the only thing that broke up the expanse of soft foam was a charging port.

Emory turned it around and over. There were no instructions. At the bottom of the final box, there was a charging cord and a plug that appeared to be the same size as the charging port. She pushed the plug into the port, gripping tightly.

That made the whole thing vibrate. She nearly dropped the— well, it didn't say, but apparently "breaking free from the haze of love" required a vibrator.

Vibrators didn't tickle her fancy, not that she'd tried more than a couple to see if there were some that *would* tickle her right in the fancy. More importantly, sex toys were not WW and Partners' thing. She recognized that wasn't fair, but there was no universe in which she stood up in the Tuesday meeting and successfully sold the room on women's pleasure, not even using the phrase *some people are saying*. She squeezed the vibrator in frustration. It made its presence known.

A trial run couldn't hurt. Best to inspect the offering before making any decisions. Emory preferred to send sample products back with a supportive note and general referrals to other financing options when she knew for certain she had to refuse the opportunity. But surely Bodytime Clarity wouldn't expect this particular item to come back in the mail. She unplugged it again.

The Supersquishlover was silky smooth. Emory tried running it down her arms and underneath the tank top she'd worn to bed. Not unpleasant. Of course, she needed to clear her head if she was going to give the vibrator a fair shot. *Silk sheets. Sunset. A glass of wine.* The poster of Xena that graced her wall throughout high school.

Emory pushed the vibe lower, concentrating on the image of a tall brunette with incredible arms. The harder she gripped the vibe, the harder it worked. Long hair. Rippling ab muscles. Swords. Things were definitely moving in the right direction.

Xena faded away, replaced by a shorter woman in miniskirt body armor. The dark hair stayed the same, but instead of a sword, the woman wielded a cactus. She wielded it very sexily. Then the cactus was gone, and the vision was her soft, soft hands, her smile, and... Emory tried to push Bliss out of her mind as the vibration increased, rumbling beyond her hand, beyond the juncture of her legs, shaking the entire bed—

Wait. No. That was her alarm—another product sample from a home tech company. Their only good idea had been one very noisy clock.

Emory swung her free arm over the shelf-slash-headboard to hit snooze and managed to turn the whole thing off instead.

She made a half-hearted attempt to get back to work, but guilt plagued her. Furthermore, the trajectory was shot. The promises made by the Supersquishlover would not come true today.

That was probably for the best. She had no business letting business creep into her fantasy. Emory put the vibrator on her bedside table to deal with later and checked her phone. A notification popped up regarding the very person she was trying not to think about. SHOPPING WITH BLISS TULLY AT BELLWORTHY'S, MIDTOWN LOCATION. Time left: two hours.

Shit. How had her date with Bliss fallen off her radar this morning? She corrected herself: her *shopping* date with Bliss. What had happened was she never got to the post-orgasm clarity, and all that remained was confusion.

———∞———

Emory took the fastest shower ever. Hot water and citrus body wash cleared her mind in ways the vibrator hadn't; by the time she was spraying dry shampoo into her hair, she had identified the problem and found a solution. Emory didn't go around kissing people she hardly knew, and Bliss had unnerved her. Therefore, she needed to let Bliss know that there was no part of their deal that required physical contact anyway, and adhering to that rule would keep their relationship on a fair and even keel. The obvious next step was to prepare a contract amendment spelling everything out.

That would have to come later. Emory clutched a towel around her middle and ran from the bathroom to her walk-in closet, though her light-filled apartment in a high-rise in Brooklyn was situated so no one could easily spy on her. She'd rented it for that reason, and also because she liked the bird's-eye views. It was calming to look out her window at New York Harbor and the Brooklyn Bridge when she wasn't running so far behind schedule.

Thankfully, the gloom and drizzle of early April was absent this morning, and sun peeked through clouds that swept across a blue sky. Emory dressed in navy blue wide-leg slacks, a muted pink blouse with a floral print, low-heeled Oxfords, and her spring trench coat. She wished she could spend the day in yoga pants and a hoodie, but out of long practice, she reserved that look for exercise only. Her business casual outfits had become her casual outfits. The day she wore a primary-colored blouse under her blazer was probably the day William would invite her to find another employer. William didn't play by the rules, exactly; the firm ran on his sense of what needed to be done over any standard structure. That didn't mean Emory got to break the unwritten dress code rules, and she didn't want him to spend any time thinking about how she wasn't another one of his boys.

Saturday mornings were the busiest times for people coming and going in her building. Emory let three elevators pass her by, checking her watch between each. Finally, she was able to squeeze on with a load of strollers, puppies, and gym- and grocery-store-goers. She waved at the doorman as she exited to the street.

Outside, the breeze was chilly. She pulled her collar high. She was so, so late. She hated being late. Even when she didn't want to go to a meeting at all. Her usual subway line didn't run on the weekend, and the alternates ran with long gaps, so she hurried down the block to another line, which was roped off. A service change notice was posted. She'd have to go back to her local stop, ride the wrong direction, and switch lines to end up on the east side of Manhattan, and between construction and needing to transfer, there was no chance of being early to meet Bliss.

Frustrated, Emory opened a rideshare app on her phone with one hand and held the other up toward passing cabs. No dice, either in the cars or in getting picked up. Beyond the views, Emory's reasoning for living in downtown Brooklyn was the convenience of being close to Manhattan without being directly in it, and today, everyone else was taking advantage of the weather to get errands done, so she had to wait her turn among those holding grocery bags and bulky boxes of new household items from Target before she was in a car and on her way.

The driver sped over the Brooklyn Bridge. Emory wondered if she should have offered to pick up Bliss. Bliss didn't live terribly far—in Kensington, past Prospect Park—and it would have been polite. Given her improper thoughts about Bliss earlier, and how irresponsible she'd been with time management, Emory was quietly glad she'd left it to Bliss to get to Bellworthy's on her own. She needed the car ride to settle back into business.

There was no small talk as the driver avoided a stalled box truck on the FDR Drive. Emory checked her watch again. She wasn't keeping Bliss, not really. They exited at last, and wordlessly, the driver dropped her off outside Bellworthy's.

As she shut the car door, Bliss came around the block. She looked like Saturday—that is, she looked comfortable in jeans, a navy peacoat over what Emory guessed was a band t-shirt, and a yellow knitted hat that Emory strongly suspected was homemade. Emory tried to think of what to say first. *About last night. About that kiss.*

Bliss saved her. "So, dresses? Do we hate shopping? I hate shopping."

Maybe Bliss had forgotten the kiss entirely. Emory laughed despite herself. "Yes, we hate shopping." That was one thing they had in common, then. She could bring up the PDA later.

She led them inside. Emory had scoped out the floorplan in advance, since she shopped at the Bellworthy's in SoHo instead of heading north from the office. Shopping for Emory meant getting a personal shopper to select outfits based on her past purchases and stopping in at the store to pick them up on her way home.

She really hated shopping.

And she really, really hated shopping for a dress to wear to her ex-fiancée's wedding. She hadn't done it yet, but she knew she hated it already.

The other Bellworthy's location in Manhattan hadn't had any appointments yesterday when Emory put together her plan of attack for attending Mari's wedding. So Emory had compromised, both on going to the unfamiliar store and going in at all.

Their appointment was on the fifth floor. Emory headed toward the escalators but turned back when Bliss didn't follow.

"I kind of like this one," Bliss was saying. She draped the skirt of a ladybug-patterned retro dress across her front. The rack she was looking at was all sundresses, most in floral pastel prints. They'd be cute with a crinoline underneath and a pair of vintage sunglasses. "What do you think? Hot or not?"

"Maybe not," Emory said. The sundress was perfect for a day in Montauk, not a night in Malibu. She hadn't explained any of that to Bliss, and meant not-hot to the dress for the occasion rather than not-hot to Bliss, but Bliss was undeterred.

"With a hat and sandals?"

They needed to move along. "Will that fit?"

Bliss considered. "Possibly." She looped the hanger over her head so she had two hands free to hold the waist against her own. "Might need some tailoring." She stuck her arm down the bodice, searching for the price tag.

"Bring it and come on." Emory didn't look back. This time, Bliss followed behind; she heard her humming softly as they were swept from floor to floor. Halfway up, she noticed that Bliss had left the sundress behind, but decided not to ask questions. She didn't want to miss their appointment.

On five, a very tall Black woman with a heart-shaped face and braids piled elegantly atop her head waited with a much shorter, medium-toned, curly-haired man in a casual suit paired with designer sneakers. "Emory, I hope?"

"Yes!" The word came out far more excited than she meant it to. Nerves. She glanced at her watch for the millionth time. "Sorry we're—"

"Very prompt. Nothing to worry about at all. I'm Miss Dana—you can call me Dana—and this is Enzo." She held her palm up to introduce him, and he gave a bow with a little flourish of one hand. "Right this way, please."

Dana escorted them to a private suite. The walls were covered in ornate gold-framed mirrors and white satin, and a cluster of purple velvet ottomans held court in the center of the room. A plush carpet extended to the walls.

Enzo took their coats and served champagne from a bar in the corner. Bliss accepted a flute, biting her lip against a grin before she drained her glass. She seemed amused as heck. Enzo said, "My kind of girl," and refilled Bliss's champagne.

Emory wished she was having half that much fun. The bubbles in her glass fizzed over the top and sprinkled the back of her hand. She wiped it on her slacks.

Dana had a clipboard stashed at the bar, a perfect red lip, and a suave presentation style. The cut of her black suit balanced her broad shoulders with a peplum that highlighted her trim waist. A heart-shaped brooch, striped pink, white, and light blue, graced her lapel. She was sleek, stylish, and consummately professional with a hint of action hero. Emory wondered if she should change her preferences to this Bellworthy's location for her personal shopping. The Bellworthy's in lower Manhattan fitted her out with perfectly boring suits, and seeing Dana pull off one with flair as a taller woman made her wonder if she could too.

Mari would have encouraged her. William would probably frown. And that would be the least of it.

"Emory, based on what you told us when you made your appointment, Enzo and I have gathered a few items to start us off. We'll use these to get to know you and your style, and we'll use that knowledge to refine our picks so you go home with the perfect outfits." She checked another page on her clipboard. "To confirm, you need dresses for a black-tie wedding—"

"Mmmf!"

They all turned to look at Bliss, who held her glass to her mouth. She recovered quickly. "This is...really great champagne. Where did you get it?"

Enzo topped up her glass. "It's Dom Perignon. We have it on three, if you're interested, but you can purchase it at any fine liquor establishment."

Dana shared a raised eyebrow with Enzo and went on. "Sorry. Dresses, as well as all accessories, and any necessary lingerie?" She looked between them and rested her chin playfully on her hand. "Black-tie wedding guest dresses. Now, I might be imagining things...are you two sure you don't need a pair of wedding dresses?"

Emory was horrified. Getting Bliss down on paper as her fiancée was a lot different from the reality of acting like they were engaged in public. Her stomach cramped. She needed to get used to this before the wedding. "Um, no, not yet, but this is my—" Her tongue was two sizes too big. "F-f-fee...fiancée."

Bliss stifled a giggle in her fist.

All she'd said was *fiancée*. It wasn't *that* funny. Emory insisted, "Just formal dresses today. We're going to my ex-fiancée's wedding."

This delighted Dana. "I see. We'll make sure you look like you're living your best life."

"Best life." Yes. Emory needed perfection. "And, well, it's a celebrity wedding, in Malibu. We should probably seem like we fit in—"

Enzo gasped. "Malibu! Who? You must tell us."

"We can keep a secret." Dana leaned in.

Bliss sidled closer to hear. She put a curious hand on the small of Emory's back.

Emory took a swig of champagne. There was nothing that could relieve the apprehension that had doubled since the wedding invitation arrived. She squeezed her eyes shut.

"Marilee Callahan," she whispered into the huddle.

Bliss spilled her drink on everyone's shoes, and the gossip party ended.

nine

CHAMPAGNE TRICKLED DOWN BLISS'S ANKLE and into her Converse. Her feet were hardly dry from yesterday's puddle disaster.

But she wasn't sorry she'd dropped her drink on purpose.

Dana blotted her hot pink stiletto heels with a monogrammed handkerchief while Enzo layered towels on the floor. "It's no problem at all. This is why we don't get out the red wine! Nothing to stain." She tucked the cloth away and helped Enzo by stepping on the pileup of Bellworthy's finest bath sheets. "If I'd had a glass when you said what you said, I'd drop it too. I used to daydream I'd marry Benjamin Thorston—that man is *fine*. And rich. We'll find you something extra special to wear to this wedding."

"And as you can guess, it's not even the first time a spill has happened." Enzo lowered his voice to a whisper. "This week."

Their shoppers kept up a lively banter about things that had been spilled in the personal shopping suite while Emory used the corner of a towel to wipe off her shoes, head down and face obscured by a sweep of honey-blonde hair.

Once the floor was recarpeted in bleached-white terry, Dana and Enzo split them up and started measuring. Bliss's shoulders. Her chest, waist, hips. Back length. Wrists. Neck. Earlobes. Enzo noted down the circumference of her upper arms, her elbows, her ankles. The process was extremely thorough so that, as he told her, he wouldn't bring her anything that was "out of whack." He handed her a satin-lined robe that made her think of a spa ad and asked her to change while he and Miss Dana stepped out.

They were alone. She realized, then, that she and Emory would be changing in front of each other. Emory scrutinized the collar of her robe and didn't speak. After a long moment, she turned around, dumped the robe on one of the ottomans, and started unbuttoning her blouse.

Bliss turned away too. She gratefully removed her damp shoes and shucked out of her jeans. One foot got trapped in the hem and she hopped sideways, trying not to accidentally sneak a peek at Emory in one of the multi-panel mirrors.

Once she had her soft-as-kittens robe on and had kicked her clothes into a pile in the corner, Bliss listened for Emory to be done changing. The snapping sound was probably Emory folding her pants. *Of course* she was folding her pants. A muffled thump was probably a padded clothes hanger going back on its hook behind the door.

Bliss waited another thirty seconds for Emory to fuss with the robe tie and backed toward the middle of the room. When her feet touched the wet towels there, she spoke.

"Yesterday, when I said I was going to be the best fiancée ever, I didn't know...I didn't mean to—"

Emory cut in. "It's nothing. We broke up eight years ago. It's still weird."

"I can understand that." Bliss took another step backward, and her clammy, damp foot found one of Emory's. "Oh, sorry, sorry."

"You can turn around now."

Bliss did. Where the robe was glamorously long on Bliss, Emory's arms and legs stuck out awkwardly. She held her robe closed at the chest. This was as out of sorts as Bliss had seen Emory since the great cactus incident. She tried for funny. "On the maybe or maybe not the best fiancée front, it's a little weird this is my first time seeing you in your nightie."

Emory ran her free hand over the front of her robe. She didn't laugh. Bliss hadn't expected her to, necessarily, but even though she didn't know Emory well, she knew Emory was smart.

Maybe a different distraction would help. "These are soft like kittens, huh?" She imitated Emory's motion. The robe was so soft, Bliss could have melted.

No answer.

Bliss wanted to ask *who hurt you?* That definitely was not the right joke, because the obvious answer was Marilee Callahan. Bliss had seen the star's face on billboards and movie posters. She'd seen her in movies and forgotten her afterward. How in the world was *Marilee Callahan* Emory's ex? And—why? Emory was the whole package. She was beautiful, smart, successful. Even when Bliss stabbed her, she hadn't been awful. She had her shit together.

Bliss was far from having her shit together.

Then again, if you looked fine on the outside, that didn't mean you were okay underneath. Appearances could cover up nasty currents under the surface. She knew all about that. Her father taught her that lesson early. She didn't know anything about breaking off an engagement, however. This wasn't a heartache she knew. But she did know what it was like to be sad.

Emory sniffed, once, and sat on one of the overstuffed poufs. Bliss found a tissue in her coat pocket. It was a little ragged, but didn't look dirty. She offered it to Emory, who clutched it in her hand without changing her stoic expression.

There was a knock and Dana and Enzo came in, rolling a garment rack between them. "Let's talk color!"

"And silhouettes!" Enzo added. He parked the cart as a divider and beckoned her to the far side, and the shopping began in earnest. Before he let her browse, he asked, "All good for me to help you dress? One or both of us can step out if you want."

Bliss nodded assent. "Stay. And I've been meaning to say—your guyliner is on point."

Enzo favored her with a smile. "Thank you so much for noticing! It's Bobbi Brown. And confession, it took me three tries to get it on this morning, so it's nice of you to say something."

Making people feel good made Bliss feel good. She had a feeling that a small, genuine compliment wasn't going to be enough to make what was going on with Emory better, though. Bliss caught a glimpse of Emory's hair over the top of the cart and the flash of skin as she raised her arms. Mostly, she couldn't look, because Enzo had plans.

The first plan was a lavender ballgown. It had a full tulle skirt and a halter neck. "I'm trying to get a feel for what your dream dress would be like. You can style this with rhinestone heels or a leather jacket."

Too much fabric. Too much like a doll. Fun to swish the skirt and twirl around in. Probably not fun for a whole day. She couldn't find her legs. "I have a rule—I can't wear it if I can't pee by myself."

"Fair." Enzo held up other patterns and Bliss faithfully tried them all. A floral, matronly midi gown that wasn't improved by boho accessories. A shimmery bottle-green slip dress that was the color of her summer dreams, but wouldn't fasten in the back, and there wasn't enough material in the seams to bother with tailoring. Reluctantly, Bliss took off the strappy punk heels and chandelier earrings Enzo had picked out to accessorize the green option. She'd almost, *almost* been a secret assassin or something.

There was a sleek white pantsuit that gaped open to her belly button. Bliss pushed her overgrown bob into a pompadour. "I look smokin." She gyrated her hips from side to side and hummed into an invisible microphone. "Maybe a little too Elvis?"

"Verily, I am shooketh up, yes," Enzo said, tugging the jacket's lapels into place. "Let's rewind your fashion a little more. Trust me."

He offered up a gown with a vintage flair. The fabric was golden, lustrous, but not garish. Bliss slipped it over her shoulders and Enzo zipped it for her. She swung her arms in the full sleeves. "I'm good lookin', yeah?" Bliss wasn't sure if the dress was her style, but who was she kidding—she was still figuring out her style. She wouldn't be embarrassed to be seen in the dress, at any rate. If she had to walk down a red carpet, she could hold her head up. Pose for the camera. She stuck one leg out and accidentally stepped on the hem.

Dana popped around the side of the rack. "Don't worry about that. We'll take it up half an inch."

"I need shoes for this one—I didn't think this would be it, but she looks good," Enzo told Dana.

She nodded. "I need a bracelet and different heels for Emory. We'll be right back."

In the calm after their shoppers left, Bliss posed for the mirror. Okay. Hopefully Emory was okay as well. "Did you find something?"

Emory's voice came from the other side of the rack. "I think so. Will you—will you tell me what you think?"

Bliss was around the rack in a flash. Emory's column dress was blush pink—quickly becoming Bliss's favorite color on Emory—and it had a plunging back that revealed an expanse of inviting skin. Even though she could take in all of Emory with the mirror's help, Bliss said, "Let's see."

Emory tucked her hair back. Her face was unreadable.

Wow. Bliss's legs were shaky, like she'd had too much champagne. Like she'd swallowed the whole bottle instead of pouring her share on the floor. Barefoot, without accessories, Emory made her jittery in a way that went far, far beyond butterflies.

It was freaking velociraptors in her stomach.

"You'll be the most beautiful woman at the wedding," she said. "No one will look at the bride." Bliss took a step toward her. "I wouldn't. I'd only look at you."

Emory's eyes went wide, and a tear rolled down her face, trailing mascara and a hint of brown eyeliner. She pressed a hand to her cheek and sucked in a shaky breath.

"I made you cry," Bliss said. "I didn't mean to do that." Emory needed to know that she was good enough. Beautiful enough. Everything else more than enough. People deserved to hear that, over and over. "But I meant what I said. You're so beautiful, Emory."

A terrible, gurgling chortle came out of Emory's mouth, and she sniffed back an impressive amount of snot. "Iiiii-iii-it's not polite to upstage the bride!" She laugh-cried again, and Bliss pulled them onto an ottoman. "Oh, wow, oh, this dress is actually comfortable to sit down in. I wasn't expecting that."

Bliss scooted close to Emory. They sank back into the ottoman, fused together from shoulder to hip. She could smell mint in Emory's hair. "We can take care of that problem. I think Enzo is coming back with shapewear." She twined her fingers around Emory's, and Emory didn't pull away.

Emory. Emory who ran the world, and Emory who sometimes cried. Bliss remembered a discussion from an art class she'd taken, about how imperfections were part of authenticity and charm. With sniffles and raccoon mascara and a self-conscious laugh like a goose, Emory was Bliss's kind of charming.

Out of Bliss's league, too. But for now, she wanted to enjoy their game of pretend. Soon enough, Emory would be back to business. Soon enough, their contract would end.

Bliss ran her thumb over Emory's knuckles. "Let's get out of here. The schedule says we have lunch next."

Emory favored her with a watery smile. "Yeah."

Then Emory's stomach rumbled, rivaling the time when Bliss had been hungry in her office, and when Dana and Enzo returned, they were in the throes of a giggle fit, one starting up again as soon as the other stopped.

ten

EVERYTHING WAS SO BLURRY. Emory could feel Bliss's hand in hers, warm and a little sweaty. That was real. In her other hand, she could feel the sharp handle of the shopping bag cutting into her palm and the serrated top edge of the bag scraping her knuckles. That was real too.

Her knees wobbled more than they should have, like they were on a different street from the rest of her body. Blink, and the memory of tears swam in her eyes. Blink, and she was squinting in the sunshine.

She hadn't felt this way, not even a little bit this way, since—

Bliss turned the corner at Lexington, tugging on Emory's arm gently. Emory managed to get her uncertain legs beneath her and stumbled along behind. They dodged open cellar doors where workers hauled supplies to basements and sidewalk sandwich boards that pointed them at stores and restaurants. Sometimes, Bliss squeezed them to one side so others could pass, and Emory acknowledged a tiny pinch of guilt for committing the New York crime of taking up room on the sidewalk to walk side by side.

But she never did that normally. And it was so nice to have someone else lead the way for a few minutes. Nice to have someone else to share the job of maneuvering through the weekend crowd. To see how Bliss did—anything.

Bliss stopped in front of a café: September, which displayed a menu outside that promised *fine European-style cuisine*. "How about this?" There were tables on the sidewalk, nestled into temporary booths with plants at the top of the dividing walls. The sun was high enough to filter down to street level, and they'd be as warm there as they would be if they went inside the midday darkness of the restaurant.

Emory nodded her agreement. She remembered to take back her hand. They really needed to talk about physical expectations.

They found seats at an empty booth next to the sidewalk. Emory picked up her menu—it was damp from a recent wiping—and prepared to confront the public display of affection she'd participated in, to her disgrace. She should have said something as soon as she saw Bliss this morning. Bliss wasn't responsible for acting like her fiancée beyond the wedding, and Emory would not put Bliss in the position of holding her hand—or kissing her—to fulfill their contract.

Bliss got there first. "We need to talk about some of this."

That was instant relief. Emory slouched into the bench on her side of the booth.

But Bliss meant something else. "I want to know what's going to happen at the wedding, with Mari."

Their waiter brought water and pointed out the specials. Her spiel went on and on, and Emory's mind raced. She had deliberately tried not to think about the actual wedding part of the wedding invitation.

As soon as the waiter stepped away, Bliss continued. "I know we have a schedule, and I know there is time set aside in it for exchanging stories. I think—it sounds like this wedding will be a lot for you, and maybe you should talk about some of it now. A friend of mine says that thinking about something and talking about it aren't the same thing."

Bliss was calmer and more serious than Emory had seen her be. How much did she know about this woman who made rainbows on her office wall, and stabbed her with a cactus, and called her beautiful when she was a complete disaster? How much did she know about this woman who'd fallen into her life out of nowhere?

When Emory had told Bliss she needed to negotiate, she hadn't expected her to get so good at it so quickly. Without any instruction, Bliss was using the tactic of silence. She didn't say more to Emory. She put her finger into the pot of the nearest plant on the booth divider and gave it a drink of her water, then removed dead leaves from its trailing vines while Emory's silence spooled out.

The words started tumbling out of her mouth. Emory realized she'd been bested, and she let it happen.

"Freshman year, I came to New York City from upstate and started taking classes at Baruch, and I knew nothing. I lived in this private dorm. It wasn't school housing, and my roommate, Francis, was going to Fordham, and at first we were pretty—it's not that we didn't get along. We didn't know each other, and we were both busy and trying to cope with a new school, and a new life, and being away from home."

She rubbed her thumb along the side of the menu as the memories surfaced. This part was the easiest to remember. "We're best friends now, but then, I was so...lonely. Lonely in the way you are your freshman year when everything is different."

"I remember that," Bliss said. She stacked her dry leaves next to the salt and pepper shakers.

"One day Francis was out somewhere, and a girl came down the hall, knocking on all the doors. Mine was open—I must have been coming back from doing laundry, maybe—and she asked if I wanted to go to this LGBTQ student meetup she'd heard about. I said yes."

Emory had been surprised to hear herself agree. She hadn't joined any LGBTQ+ clubs in high school, not that they had any. She hadn't ever let herself think about what those letters meant. But what did it matter? None of her classmates from upstate enrolled in college in New York City, so she wasn't going to run into anyone she already knew.

"We always walked to those meetings together, rain or shine." Rain was her favorite, with Mari's arm around her waist and Mari's umbrella bumping against the top of her head. "Afterward, we would find a diner, and we'd split toast and bacon and talk. About going to college, and which movie stars were cutest, and what we wanted to be someday. We'd stay up all night in the hallway—Francis would study to midnight on the dot with her headphones on, then throw us out very nicely—and sleep end-to-end in my bed until the sun went down the next day."

Being together then had been everything. "Winter break at my parents' place was torture without her. So when we came back in January, I asked her if we could go on a real date. And that time, she said yes to me."

A line formed on the sidewalk next to their booth. September was bustling, even as the lunch hour slid away. Emory waited for the host to clear the backup, swirling her water glass and avoiding Bliss's gaze.

Once there weren't people looming over their table, Emory continued.

"We were together through college, on and off. Sometimes Mari would want to take a break. She'd date other people. I waited it out, and she'd eventually come around." It sounded bad, put like that. And sometimes, it had been. They'd break up for the summers and Emory threw herself into internships, waiting for Mari to come back from camp jobs covered in mosquito bites and faded hickeys. She'd go on dates with guys she met in the library and girls she met at the bar, and Emory would pretend she didn't care.

"You're not supposed to get serious in college," Mari said, right after they spent their junior year spring break curled up in bed watching movies. Francis was gone, visiting her parents in San Jose, and it was just the two of them heating up mini bagel pizzas and drinking powdered lemonade. "It's not that I don't want to be with you, Em. I feel like I'm not letting you explore the world. I'm holding you back."

"I'm a serious person," Emory had said, holding back the tears for once. "I'm serious about you." She wrapped an arm around Mari's shoulders, and Mari shrugged out from underneath, insisting that they both needed to learn how to be apart.

"I'd believe you if you'd tried anything else, Em. You can't know what you want if you've only been with one person."

That wasn't fair. Emory no longer remembered what she'd said. It didn't matter. They were back together by finals.

"We moved in together after graduation," she told Bliss. The sun was in her eyes, and she squeezed them shut. "I worked and started an MBA. Tried to figure out how to do my job. You know, people often thought we were related." She had stories about that, funny ones. "The first time I got a solid bonus at work, I picked out a ring and I asked her to marry me. She said yes that time too."

Bliss had patience—Emory had to give her that. She waited a good minute before asking, "And then what happened?"

It was the sunshine and the success of finding a dress in one afternoon that loosened her tongue. "And then it started to hurt." Enough. She whipped out her phone and scrolled to her frequent flyer app. "Right now, while I have you, I should buy plane tickets."

"Okay," Bliss said. "I think there's more to that story."

There was. Emory decided it would have to come in installments. Well-redacted installments. Emory double-checked that she was searching for the Sunday ahead of Mari's wedding and selected two seats in first class. She had so many miles banked from years of crisscrossing the country to meet with company founders that she could probably count on a complimentary upgrade for herself, but hell with it. If she had to go to this wedding, they could fly in comfort and style.

The app wouldn't let her finish without Bliss's information. "I'm going to need you to put in your birthday and frequent flyer number and that sort of thing."

Bliss was still looking at her with a calm assuredness that was unnerving. It was like the worse Emory's story got, the more Bliss dug in her heels. Maybe Emory was projecting. Her own defense against pain was stoicism, and maybe she was scaring Bliss off.

"Here, I'll let you type it in." Emory handed over her phone.

The corner of Bliss's mouth tipped up. She started typing in her details with one finger. "I don't have any fancy-flyer numbers. I haven't been on a plane since I was a little kid. We went to Florida, to the beach, before everything—"

Emory had a lot of questions about that *everything*. "Well, sign up for a number in case the plant business...takes off." She was very proud of the pun, and of the way Bliss closed her eyes and shook her head hearing it.

Bliss gave the phone back. Emory checked that the form looked okay, scrolling up and down. She calculated in her head. "You're twenty-seven. I usually date within five years of my own age."

"My birthday is in July! I'm practically twenty-eight now."

"And I'll be an ancient thirty-four," Emory teased her.

Bliss pretended insult. "Pssh. That's hardly robbing the cradle, and I'm not a baby."

"I suppose it won't matter once we're married," Emory said. What was she thinking? Being with Bliss got her off track. They weren't getting married. They weren't even really engaged.

Their waiter showed up at last. Emory ordered boring grilled chicken and vegetables. Bliss ordered a cheeseburger. "I should be asking more about you. I think I assumed that because you're into plants, you'd be a vegetarian."

The game was still on. Bliss gave a mock gasp. "We don't eat *plants*. Plants are our *friends*!"

A shadow stretched across the table. William Wils stopped next to their booth with his wife, Ellen, who recognized Emory at once. "Emory! How are you doing, dear?"

Ellen was a fixture at the company holiday party, and occasionally tagged along to certain dinners following the closure of deals between the company and old friends of William's. Where William kept his employees at arm's length, Ellen was cheerful and warm. "Hello," she said to Bliss. "I'm Ellen Wils. And you're—"

"Emory's fiancée," she chirped.

William must not have paid enough attention during the Tuesday hell meeting when Mari's engagement had been announced, because he seemed unclear on the concept. "So, you live together."

Ellen moved her round, black-framed, oversize glasses to the top of her head and gave her husband a nudge. "Lesbians do that when they get married, you know."

"Actually, I'm attracted to all kinds of people," Bliss mentioned. She smiled Emory's way. "But to Emory the most. So I guess you could call it a lesbian wedding. Sapphic works too, poetically."

Emory was going to die.

Though, Bliss: not heterosexual. Confirmed.

Ellen leaned over the booth. "Have you ordered? You should stay out here, it's such a nice day, but the service, so slow. And girls—" She patted Emory's shoulder. "I don't see any rings! Darling, what's the name of that place you go to get fancies for me?"

113

"Bartholomew's. On Madison." William didn't seem inclined to go on until Ellen prompted him with another nudge. "They have new pieces and estate jewelry."

"See, there's a recommendation. And William is a big fan of marriage, right, dear?"

William nodded. "Of course."

The host approached with menus. Clearly, the Wils were regulars. "It's too chilly for these old bones, so we'll go inside. Lovely to see you."

Ellen followed the host, and William added, to Emory, "Stop by Monday. I have a few leads from old friends at the club that you might look into for me. Most won't be anything useful. We'll review as favors to old friends." He took a step to the side and his arm swung up, almost like he'd thought to offer a handshake, then followed Ellen into the dark cavern of September.

Bliss looked at her, puzzled.

"William Wils." That didn't seem to ring a bell. "The initials in WW and Partners."

"Oh. *Oh no.*" Bliss rose half out of her seat. "I didn't mean to make your business *his* business. I've never met him before. His office is always empty—"

That was when Emory realized that William and Bliss probably hadn't been in the office at the same time, not that he paid much attention to anyone besides the circle of partners and junior partners except to evaluate the vice-presidents for future promotions.

114

It was her turn to be stoic. "He's not very social at work. He comes to meetings and then goes back to his desk and shuts the door. Most days he's either locked in his office or taking meetings at his club, and Ellen likes him to be home for dinner. She tells me so every year at the holiday party."

She leaned back over her seat. William and Ellen were out of sight. "William knows about Mari's wedding, and he thinks I should approach the groom while I'm there for business reasons. He doesn't usually suggest deals to me. He occasionally gives me half-baked business ideas from his friends to investigate, and I come up with a reason or two he can use to put them off with. It's never anything big. I don't impress him."

Bliss laid a hand on her wrist. "That can't be true. You're incredibly impressive."

"Not in WW and Partners terms." Emory drew her hand away.

"If he likes people to be married, the engagement will help," Bliss insisted.

Emory had to point out the obvious here. "But the breakup won't."

And then there was the less obvious: she doubted she would be roping Mari, much less Benjamin Thorston, into a deal with WW and Partners.

When their meals showed up, Bliss went straight for her cheeseburger. Emory's chicken was as bland as she'd expected it would be, and she chewed distractedly. Fire trucks and an ambulance lined up in the street, sirens blaring, and then there was a traffic backup complete with honking and swearing. There was no opportunity for more conversation before the waiter came with their check, much more prompt to have them leave than to see them fed.

The afternoon was getting late. Bliss checked the time on her phone. "I should go, but I'll see you soon. I put all our meetings in my calendar and set reminders and everything." She took out her wallet.

"Put that away. All expenses paid, remember. We have a contract," Emory said. "See you soon." She slipped a credit card under their bill, hoping the transaction wouldn't take long.

Bliss gathered her shopping bags. "I'm sorry about telling William. I thought—you know what, I'll let you tell people about the engagement yourself if the subject comes up in the future."

Emory answered her with her most formal business voice. Habit. "I'm sure we can handle it."

Bliss looked at her shoes. "All right. Goodbye," she said, before Emory could ask her if she needed a ride. She slipped out between the tables, and Emory watched her walk away until she couldn't see her bright yellow hat anymore. When she left, the April sun succumbed to clouds, taking its warmth with it.

eleven

THE NEXT WEEK PASSED QUIETLY. When Bliss went to WW and Partners on Thursday, a temp greeted her, and she slipped through the empty offices like a ghost with her watering can. *Did everybody quit?* she texted Emory.

Annual company retreat in Montauk, Emory texted back. She sent a picture of a drooping bouquet at the resort reception desk. *I think this place could use a little of your magic.*

Ha ha, maybe, Bliss sent back. Then she spent the rest of the day going in circles about what she should have texted instead and checking to see if Emory replied. Eventually, she realized that whether it was Emory's job duties or her uninspiring text, the conversation was over for the time being. They didn't have any contractual preparation meetings scheduled until next week; her assignment for the weekend was to come up with things they should know about each other. Bliss hadn't expected to go so long without seeing Emory, and the hours ahead suddenly seemed empty.

After leaving WW and Partners, Bliss went directly to Park Slope Express Floral to order the last couple of plants she needed for the office. She waited at the round table at the front of the shop, scribbling figures in her notebook. Emory's engagement offer was merely a reprieve. She needed to figure out a workable budget for Bliss Foliage. The numbers swam before her eyes. How did Emory look at this kind of thing all day long and make sense of it?

Selma finished with her line of customers. She followed the last one to the door, locked it, and flipped the hanging sign to CLOSED.

"I'm sorry, I can go—"

"Good news, I need you," Selma cut in. "Closed for the rest of the day for an emergency." She carried a sheaf of papers to the table and handed them to Bliss. "You left these here. In fact, you left them in my wedding designs binder."

The sketches. She remembered. "I didn't mean to leave my scribble trash. Sorry about that, Selma."

Selma raised her hands to the ceiling. "You are killing me."

Bliss was mightily confused. "What?"

"I booked a last-minute wedding for this weekend—all kinds of rush fees to go with it, I can tell you—and they want the flowers to be based on your design. I couldn't talk them out of it."

She couldn't help clapping her palms to her cheeks—it was unfamiliar, lately, feeling absolutely *pleased*. Somebody, two somebodies, saw what she could do. And they chose *her* designs to make their most special day beautiful. "Selma! Really?"

Selma mimed shaking her by the shoulders. "Yes, really! We should talk about you doing more designs, Bliss. You've got a fresh feel and I..." She sat down at the table. "I've been in this location for a long time and business is stable, but still goes up and down. I haven't booked a wedding in a year. So I have you to thank."

The couple's choice was enough for Bliss. "And you wouldn't have booked a wedding if they didn't know this is the best florist in town. Don't blame this success all on me."

Selma didn't laugh. "We should discuss money, especially since I should have discussed with you first. Because of the rush, there won't be much profit, but I'd like to give most of it to you. And then talk about more designs. But first, the emergency is that I have a staffing issue. I had a girl coming in half days and she got another job yesterday. Are you interested in picking up some shifts here at the shop? Do you think you could work today and tomorrow to get the pieces ready? Saturday for the wedding itself?"

Bliss couldn't get a word in edgewise. She'd never seen Selma so serious, or seen her look so tired.

"I can't get it all done alone. Ken's great at delivery and building stuff, but he doesn't have the patience for arrangement work and he doesn't like it. He doesn't want anything more than some part-time hours to keep him from being bored in retirement, he says." Selma's shop talk rolled to a stop.

"This is—this is amazing," Bliss said. She meant it. "I'd love to help with the wedding, and I can't say no to picking up some shifts. You know I need the money. I feel happy when I'm here, so I'm sure I'll feel happy working here. Except—" Her calendar was going to be blocked. "I'm going to Los Angeles soon, and there will be a whole week when I can't help out."

This confused Selma. "Is it plant business? They have a big flower district. Hon, you don't have to spend money on travel when you're broke. We've got plenty of plant business right here. I'll take you to the flower district with me sometime, we'll go early before they open to everybody else—"

Bliss wriggled uncomfortably in her chair. "It's something else. It's a secret."

Selma leaned in. "I love secrets. I'm pretty good at keeping them. Have a history of hiding my teenage relationships and all that."

"Well...I have a contract." She owed Emory her privacy. On the other hand, she was going to a wedding and even Emory's boss knew that there was an engagement.

"And does that contract say you can't tell anybody?" Now Selma was concerned. "Honey, are you in some kind of trouble?"

Bliss tried to remember whether the contract had a non-disclosure clause. It had a lot of stuff about what was going to happen for the thirty days of her engagement with Emory, and when they would meet, and when she'd get paid, but she didn't think it said anything about what she could or couldn't *say*. The secret was implied. "Can you not tell *anybody*?"

Selma got up and checked that the front door was locked before responding. "Okay. Shoot. I've got you."

Bliss scooted her chair around to Selma's side of the table. She didn't want to say what she had to say very loudly. "I'm going to pose as Marilee Callahan's ex-fiancee's *new* fiancée and get paid to do that by a venture capitalist named Emory."

"Wait, who's on first?" Selma slapped a hand to the top of her head. "I'm lost here."

They went behind the counter and Bliss searched for Marilee on the computer. The top result was a gossip site story about the fashionable businesses contributing to a gift bag for those attending the "massive" wedding. There was more news about the wedding plans than about the actress, so Bliss switched to an image search.

Selma recognized the woman at once. "Oh, yeah. I used to watch her on that show—what was it? Ran for something like two seasons and got canceled. She was an assassin or a cop, maybe. Lots of shooting and rappelling. I liked the woman who played her mom better. Now *she* was a real looker."

Bliss shrugged. She didn't have cable and she'd had to cancel her streaming subscriptions. She had seen Marilee in movies, and while Marilee looked a lot like Emory—who had grabbed Bliss's full attention from the start—the actress wasn't on Bliss's radar.

"Well," Selma said, after Bliss didn't reply, "I know you're short on funds, but a job is just a job in the end. Don't go getting your heart broken for money."

"I know," Bliss replied. Selma wasn't referring to the present. The second time she'd come in, looking for a new pot for her overgrown pothos, Selma had asked her a question—Bliss couldn't remember anymore what it had been—and Bliss had ended up spilling the story about how her dad had ruined her family. How she'd built a protective shell around herself forever after. But shells could crack. As usual, Bliss wanted to think about something else.

Selma provided her with that something else. "You can be the right person for somebody, but they gotta be the right person for you too. Bring a weird contract into the middle of things and it's gonna be easy to get confused."

The brick wall behind the register was covered in framed photographs of all sizes. Selma pointed to one, viewed best from behind the till, that Bliss hadn't noticed before. "That's me and my wife. Rosie Takeda."

Bliss stepped closer to look at the faded photo. Selma was younger, thinner, but recognizably Selma. Rosie was dark-haired and sweet-faced. Her hair was permed and she wore a windbreaker, so Bliss guessed the picture was from the 1980s. "Around the mouth, she looks a little like—"

"Yeah, she's Ken's big sister. Look at the two of us, a burly Swede and a skinny Japanese girl. You think people don't like lesbians these days, you should hear some of the stuff they said to

122

us back then, even when we thought we were keeping our own secrets." Selma took the photo off its hanging nail and handed it to Bliss. "We both rented shops in this building about the same time. Rosie started a stationery business next door. Later, she wasn't doing so well, and we bought out the third storefront and the apartments upstairs, the whole building. Things used to be cheap around here, if you can believe it."

She had to laugh. "Liar. I do believe you two were soulmates, though." Bliss gave the photo back to Selma, who hung it back on the wall with practiced gentleness.

"I don't know about that. But if I got to pick a soulmate, I'd have picked her." Selma stood back to check if the frame was level. "When I first knew Rosie, I dated everybody, but Rosie kept turning me down. I had to see all of her and she had to see all of me before we got along." She patted the frame, like she was sticking it to the wall. "We were married twenty years. Said we were, that is. Wasn't legal then."

Bliss didn't know what to say. The world wasn't always as beautiful as she wished it would be. "That's a good long time."

Selma sighed. "She got lung cancer. Smoking. Bad habit. The only bad habit she had. She ate vegetables and exercised and meditated and stuff like that." She found a piece of gum deep in her pocket and popped it in her mouth. "I can feel a cigarette in my fingers sometimes and I quit thirty years ago. Rosie started smoking in secret when she was ten and she never did kick the cravings. Tough thing to accept you can love someone from top to toes, but

123

you can't change them. They have to change themselves. I'm still trying to accept that. If I could have another day with her, I'd nag her to quit, thinking I could turn one more day into two if I did."

Bliss closed her eyes. Twenty years. What was it like to love someone that long, and have that someone love you back?

"Don't be sad. If you're said, I have to be sad, and Rosie wouldn't like that. Miss her the same either way." Selma came back around the counter and rummaged in a drawer. "What I want to say is wait for the right person. Some of the ladies like to jump the gun. Back in the day, some of them liked to jump *my* gun!"

Scandalous. Bliss burst into surprised laughter.

Selma laughed heartily with her. "I didn't ask Rosie to marry me until we'd known each other for five years, and we were engaged another five. She was worth the wait." She tapped her nose and pointed at Bliss. "You're worth the wait too."

———✖———

Bliss got out of bed at an unwanted hour on Saturday. She met Selma at the bar at eight, and a half hour later, Ken arrived with the Park Slope Express Floral van. His grandson, six-year-old Ethan, jumped out of the back. "Great-auntie Selma!" If Selma hadn't been built like a linebacker, Ethan's enthusiastic hug would have sent her flying.

Selma, Ken, and Bliss carted the floral arrangements through the bar and to the back patio while Ethan kept up a running commentary about the video game he was playing. The adults nodded along, and Ethan didn't seem to mind that no one else was obsessed with capturing one of the many dragons that were apparently lurking around every corner, completely invisible to anyone without the game.

Out back, Bliss helped Ken assemble the pieces of the wedding arch that once had been nothing more than an idle sketch on scrap paper. Selma used a handcart to place sprays on a pair of plinths, and eventually, she cajoled Ethan away from his game to tie garlands on the backs of folding chairs. After the patio was in place, Selma and Bliss moved inside to prepare for the after-ceremony lunch while Ethan showed Ken how to add the game to his phone, then pulled his grandpa along to the street for his first battle in the quest to capture a dragon. As Bliss understood it, there were a great many kinds to catch, and one aspired to complete the set.

Selma was deep in discussion with the head server, deciding where to place the low bouquets that the bride wanted among the place settings, so Bliss wandered out to the patio again. Her arms and back ached from the lifting and turning, holding and twisting. The mild pain was satisfying. And it was satisfying, too, to see the flowers from the shop turned into wedding decorations that she'd designed herself. The arch was triangular, woven with ivy and tweedia, and the same flowers were twisted through the rest of the arrangements.

Bliss hadn't been sure that the arch would be the right size—she'd never been to the bar, and they'd taken the owner at their word on the dimensions of the space—but it was perfect. She hoped the bride and groom would agree. Chances were good, in her opinion. And last-minute planners couldn't complain.

Bliss thought she would like a wedding like this one. Small, but big enough for everyone she loved. Maybe a ceremony on a back patio with a meal together afterward—no big ballroom where she and her new spouse ate alone on a dais.

After telling Selma about her engagement contract, Bliss had gone home and looked up Marilee's wedding details. Five hundred guests expected at a swanky Malibu ranch. The groom was some kind of bazillionaire. What was it like to turn your wedding into a publicity event?

Sort of like the business of being engaged for thirty days, she supposed. She couldn't condemn Marilee. But what did show-casing your love do to you? What was it doing to Emory? And wasn't eight years long enough for Emory to be over Marilee? Too bad Emory was stuck in the past instead of living the present.

She snapped a selfie of herself with the bride's bouquet of sweet peas. This was the showstopper: a mix of flowers that would spill out of the bride's hands and wrap around her like a train. She'd made it almost all by herself, with a few assists from Selma, who'd helped her figure out some structural points and what tools to use to bring her idea to colorful life. Bliss texted the picture to Emory.

Emory sent back a heart, and Bliss couldn't bring herself to swipe the notification away.

Too bad they couldn't mix business with pleasure.

twelve

EMORY GOT OFF THE SUBWAY at Bryant Park at 7:27 a.m., like she did every Tuesday morning (barring delays), and walked right past her office. She made a beeline three blocks south to a sterile salon that she started patronizing when she made the jump from analyst to associate. Mondays were for hair in a twist because it was too hard to get out of bed early enough to style anything else, and being late was worse than having frizzy hair. Tuesdays were for WW and Partners' biggest meetings, so Emory got a blowout and a simultaneous express manicure first.

Before Emory completed her MBA, before her salary started to match her skills, she spent her Sunday nights and Monday mornings on her hair and short, buffed nails, sensing that this was

the equivalent of shined shoes and a fresh cut on her colleagues—
and much more time-intensive and expensive.

Her present Tuesday morning routine was part of playing the
game. That didn't mean she didn't resent it. But it made it easier,
she hoped, to do her job. She loved sinking into numbers, loved
ruminating on the best hire for a company's C-suite, loved
learning about new technologies and careers that she'd never be
able to experience. It never—or, to be accurate, rarely—seemed
like the clock had ticked into the evening when she went home,
not even in the earliest days at WW and Partners.

Mari had noticed, though. She resented waiting for Emory to
come home at night, after work, after classes. Emory wasn't
allowed to miss Mari when she was in a show and her late-evening
stage doors turned into late-night drinks with the rest of the cast.
When Mari left for Hollywood, Emory threw herself into her
work. Her fiancée was gone, so why go home?

Maybe Mari was right to warn her away from working so many
hours. For the past few years, Emory had been feeling...sluggish.
Less than excited. Like there had to be something else. She went
to her appointments and blocked her calendar on evenings and
weekends as often as she could; she hired personal stylists and
dry-cleaning services and grocery shoppers. She guarded her time
with hard-earned money.

That was why Emory liked this salon so much. They let her
trade luxury for results and didn't try to be something beyond a
practical service that catered to all the women in the midtown rat

race. Early morning or pre-event night, someone met you at the door to take your coat and purse. Another person wrapped you into a cape. A manicurist cleaned the old, neutral polish off her nails while her head was tipped into the sink at the shampoo station.

"Short nails, miss?" she was asked, like always. Familiar. Predictable. She was buffed and filed while two women attacked her head with hairdryers. The assembly line had her out the door in forty minutes. She didn't even have to sign; they had her card on file. And then she went to work, refurbished for the week ahead.

Emory had even come in the previous Tuesday, dragging her carry-on bag. The WW and Partners annual offsite retreat was scheduled for three days in Montauk. While it was timed to fall after the end of the company's fiscal year, Emory suspected that William chose the off-season so that no one would be distracted by the beach. He chartered a bus from the office to force everyone to ride together; sneaking in or out with a rental car was frowned on, though employees had occasionally been known to slip away on the LIRR.

Not everyone loved the three days of the partners' review of financials, prospects, and goals, or the inevitable need to work all of the next weekend to catch up on everything else. Most years, Emory enjoyed the retreat, if "took an interest in and really didn't mind" could be considered a synonym for "enjoyed," but this year, the meetings were numbing, and she found herself resenting the idea of using Saturday and Sunday to clear her email instead of doing something fun. Something like...she didn't know.

When had she last had *fun*?

She texted Bliss a photo of a wilted flower arrangement in the hotel lobby. Bliss probably spent entire weekends doing nothing but having fun. Emory tried to imagine what that was like.

And tried not to imagine what it would be like to spend an entire weekend with Bliss.

Beatriz passed her a plastic glass of champagne. Emory held her hand up to refuse—she'd had some last weekend, only half a glass, between trying on dress after dress—but Beatriz was firm. "Ellen called," she whispered.

Emory looked around the meeting room. The employees of WW and Partners all had a glass of something. Even William, who stood and raised his. "Our congratulations on your engagement, Emory. To you and...to your fiancée."

William usually had more to say, but it didn't surprise Emory that he didn't have an anecdote or special words for her. Jeff was the one who saved them all by wiping the baffled expression off his face and saying, "Cheers!"

Other employees followed on, and eventually a break time buzz—golf games, sports playoffs, cars—filled the room. Emory drained her glass in one gulp, and Beatriz poured the last drops from a bottle in. She swallowed that too.

"Ellen wanted to know when you would be free for dinner. She says she and William want to schedule something at La Grenouille to celebrate." Beatriz opened her laptop and started the company calendar. "Could have said something, Emory. I'd have written a note for William and he could have told us all her name."

"Huh, that's you ghostwriting his speeches?" Emory pretended to be distracted by a thick packet of printed spreadsheets. "We're planning a long engagement. Really long. Like years, maybe. I'll have to get back to you."

Beatriz wasn't the smartest person at WW and Partners for nothing. She bent over her screen so no one would hear her question but Emory. "Are you for real? There's no fiancée, is there?"

She calculated. If she said no, but William was in the office and ran into Bliss, it was possible everything would fall apart. The engagement was going to fall apart anyway. In the meantime, it would be easy to get caught in a lie. A lie about another lie. "I'm engaged to Bliss Tully."

"What?" Beatriz heard how loud her voice was and brought the volume down. "The plant girl? I didn't even know she, *you know.*"

"It's corporate plant care and office beautification," Emory interjected, defensive. "Yes, the plant girl." She pretended to type something to avoid saying that she hadn't always known *she, you know.* That it was luck Bliss was oriented toward *you know*, and how being around Bliss made her impulsive. Impulsive enough to hire Bliss as her fiancée.

Beatriz closed Emory's laptop over her hands, very slowly. "That was fast."

Option one was to agree: *Women sometimes move fast. Ask U-Haul.* Option two was to say that they knew each other before Bliss started coming into the office, which looked shady upon closer examination.

Option three was to tell the truth, and that was no option at all.

Option four: deflect. "We're very happy," Emory said. "Opposites attract."

Beatriz did not look convinced.

———❧———

On her way up the elevator to her office, Emory should have been focused on the junior partner role and how she was going to get it. About Benjamin Thorston, the business catch she knew William wanted so much, who would secure her position at the company. About the business referrals William had passed on for her to review, all of them imprudent and ill-conceived ideas from his contemporaries and his contemporaries' kids. She needed to finish her writeup for him.

The elevator opened on a random floor. No one was waiting to board. What if this round of referrals was a test? What if she was supposed to come up with brilliant transformations to show William that she was a creative thinker? She pushed the button to close the doors and chipped the fresh polish on her index finger. Maybe that was a metaphor.

Emory hurried past reception because Adam Carrington was there, standing in a circle of business bros and guffawing about something one of them said under his breath. Maybe there was no future for her at WW and Partners. She didn't have boots on the ground experience or an MBA from an Ivy. She'd only had the mentorship of Bill Wheat, who sat next to her at the summer intern mixer and said she reminded him of his daughter in a genuine way, not in a creepy one.

Would it be so bad if Jeff got the junior partner job instead of her? She was comfortable. Safe. She got to spend lots of time hands-on with companies, and her impression was that William discouraged that approach in favor of running them by influencing their boards of directors. On the other hand, she could pay back Bill's favor, mentor new analysts, perhaps, if she moved up.

Mulling over the possibilities, Emory brewed coffee in the kitchen and made her way back to her desk. She spent the morning catching up on business news and blogs, trying to find the underdog that would be her big investment prospect for the year. After lunch, her calendar reminded her to start setting up meetings for her week in Los Angeles.

That was what she was doing when Bliss came into her office holding a watering can and wearing a shoulder-length red wig.

"What are you *doing*?" Emory hissed.

Bliss startled and slammed Emory's door shut.

"No, no, open it!" Emory put her work aside as Bliss fumbled with the door. When it was propped open again, she beckoned Bliss into a seat. "What's going on with your hair?

"Um." Bliss leaned back to check that the hallway was empty. "You, um, work here. I mean you work here and William works here, and I'm kind of like the help and I know I'm not supposed to say anything but also he's your boss—"

Emory cut in. "Beatriz already found out we're engaged. I had to tell her because she would have figured it out and lying would have made things worse. Ellen—the woman we met when we had lunch at September, William's wife—had Beatriz set up a company toast, so the rest of the office knows too. Halfway knows. They don't know I'm engaged to you specifically. Not yet. But they might find out."

"I'm sorry again," Bliss whispered. "If I'd known...I don't want you to get in any trouble here."

She considered this. "We have a no-fraternizing rule, but—well—you're not exactly... If we were going to come in on your business, or if we already had, I'd run afoul of the rule. I take my ethical obligations seriously."

That was true; it was also true that she'd never wanted to date a coworker or any of her business associates. "But—"

"But I'm different. Not part of the one percent." Bliss crossed her arms.

Emory touched her temple. A twitch was running back and forth under her eyebrow. "William won't remember he met you."

The thought that he might be in his office down the corridor didn't keep her from the truth. "Like a lot of men here, he doesn't...he doesn't see the people who keep things running, especially if they're women. If you walked in to water his plants and said hello, he probably wouldn't recognize you, with or without the wig."

When Emory went to group meetings with new company founders, she noticed that the other side always remembered Adam Carrington's name. Or Jeff's. Or everyone else's but hers. Being invisible took its toll.

"To be fair, he's not unique." She focused on the chip in her nail polish. "People used to ask me if Mari and I were sisters. Sometimes cousins. One time, I was going home on the train. I was in a suit and Mari was in sweats and this tourist woman from Iowa asked if I was her mom. We were both twenty-two."

Bliss didn't laugh like Emory hoped she would. She asked, "Why do you put up with this?"

That wasn't a question Emory could easily answer. "I love my job?" She didn't want to admit that she had asked herself that same question over and over. "All I want is for William to file me with the family men in his brain, but I don't fit into the cabinet. And he's been reminded of that lately..."

Was that good or bad? "With you on board, I'm not completely invisible."

For now.

Putting on fake cheer, she added, "And Bliss Foliage technically reports to Beatriz, and not in any way to me, which is a good thing." She shuffled together a pile of loose junk mail to discard along with all these serious thoughts. "But if Beatriz ever grabs your cute little butt, you let me know, because that's *definitely* not allowed."

Bliss burst into surprised laughter. Finally. Emory didn't like Bliss's sad, defeated face.

The giggles faded faster than Emory wanted. There was no denying it; their engagement was messy. They were going to break up—fake breakup for a fake engagement—in a little less than three weeks. Eventually, everyone would know, and if Beatriz spread the word about Bliss, Bliss could get pulled into the office drama. That bruised Emory's sense of fairness. Bliss was a person. She didn't deserve that.

But then, Bliss had agreed to be her thirty-day fiancée, and they couldn't have planned for everything. Their agreement was a way for her to help Bliss, and Emory was paying Bliss well. The whole scenario was simply a job. Sometimes jobs had tricky parts, like Jeff and Emory's ongoing financial investigation of Mackenzie Aeronautics. Like the expectation that she was going to charm her ex's fancy, rich new husband into a business deal.

And what other options did she have for a plus-one? She hadn't been on a date in a year. If Francis had been free to travel, and Emory had tried to drag her along as a fake girlfriend, Mari would have seen through their pretense in a heartbeat. Plus, Francis was a bad liar. No, Bliss was the easiest charade. And their charade would end. Soon.

"You're coming over tomorrow night, yes?" Emory asked.

"No, I texted you—"

"That's right, you did." Emory checked her phone, flustered. "I remember."

"I'm not trying to break our agreement. I'm helping out a friend and I thought we could move to Friday." Bliss's defensive posture relaxed as she retrieved her cell phone from her apron pocket. "Could we also swap the Saturday brunch to Sunday? I have a shift at my other job. I won't miss anything else," she said, sincerely. "I've made it clear I have a commitment to you."

That made one person. "Those changes are okay with me," Emory answered. "I don't know if you were able to come up with getting-to-know-you questions, so I've been making lists of things we should know about each other." She opened a file on her computer and printed a copy for Bliss. Emory was proud of the way she'd formatted it with spaces for them to write in their answers.

Bliss read the double-sided page of questions. "Of course I've been brainstorming!" she said, in a way that made Emory think Bliss was behind on her homework. "I'll get it done, scout's honor."

Emory held up three fingers. "Were you a scout?"

"Well, no." Bliss shrugged, and smiled. Her smiles lit up Emory's brain. "But there are some things I want to know about you."

"Me neither," Emory confessed. She handed Bliss a spare pen to write down this new knowledge.

Their hands touched, and Emory thought again about the softness of Bliss's skin. "And there are some things I want to know about you too."

Because Emory took ethical relationships with her business partners seriously, and the weight of their contract was heavy, she refrained from detailing exactly what those things were.

thirteen

THE END OF THE WEEK was the quietest time at WW and Partners. Even the newest analysts usually left early for drinks and networking. Emory liked the peace. She could return calls and emails without people poking their head in her office or pinging her for a last-minute meeting.

The single welcome interruption was Beatriz. Emory sat down in reception with a fresh cup of coffee. Beatriz had commandeered the coffee table and couch to sort a snowdrift of receipts. She, unlike Emory, hated Fridays, because it was the day she set aside to handle expenses, and more than a few people at WW and Partners tossed their crumpled records at Beatriz without further explanation.

"Look. What *is* this?" She smoothed out a receipt that was mashed into a spitwad. "Two hundred at the Hilton for movies in his hotel room? He has to pay for personal charges himself. He *knows* that. I have *told* him and *told* him. Next time he tries to sneak one through, I'm going straight to William."

Emory set down her cup and started a series of hand and wrist exercises that were supposed to relieve the pain of too many emails. "Let me guess."

"Of course it's Carrington," Beatriz grumbled. "That lambón could at least sign and date like he's supposed to, and he could do me a favor and total up his personal charges. I hate math."

"You don't. You hate jerks." Emory's thumb was a little tingly. She wiggled it. Thank goodness it was Friday. Her brain was doing fine, but her body needed a break. "Math is a tool that helps you draw conclusions. Predict the future. Solve problems. It's two plus two."

Beatriz tossed Adam Carrington's receipt onto the pile on the coffee table that looked the most like litter. "See, I'm no good at it. I didn't put two and two together about you and Bliss."

True. But she hadn't been meant to.

"And two is better. I'm glad, Emory, even if it's weird. You need something in your life besides this place. Me, I have Pedro, and my dog, and my family. People make things easier and better. You need more people."

Emory agreed. WW and Partners wasn't the most important thing in the world. Unfortunately, for the moment, it was her only thing. "Like I said, you're good at this. You should apply to be an analyst. I heard that Mark what's-his-name turned in his notice, isn't that right, so we'll be hiring."

Beatriz scrunched her nose in doubt. "I don't know. I've seen our payroll."

"See!" Emory sat forward in excitement. "You know the going rate and you can ask for more because of what you bring to the table. You can do the math, literally and figuratively, and the math matters. So does research, initiative, and a nose for a deal. You should get a piece of this place."

The hard sell prompted Beatriz to roll her eyes. Emory truly believed Beatriz was wasted at reception. Hiring an analyst with her kind of savvy would be good for the company. WW and Partners had a surfeit of Carringtons and not enough Beatrizes. Emory would have to keep working on her.

Plus, for the short term, Beatriz would be distracted by her application and interviews and wonder less about Emory and Bliss. *Ugh*. Emory didn't like admitting her ulterior motives, but she had to be honest with herself.

Just over two weeks left. Then it's done.
All of it.

———— ✎ ————

Emory paced her apartment. Bliss was coming at seven. It was six fifty-eight. Fifty-nine. She checked the intercom panel. No missed messages. Twenty steps past the open kitchen to the wide windows, squinting against the intense orange sun sinking beyond

141

the harbor. Twenty steps into her bedroom, twenty to pace around the king bed where she liked to stretch out across the down comforter.

She double-checked that the Supersquishlover was hidden at the back of her sock drawer in the walk-in closet. Five more steps into the tile-and-glass bathroom, scrubbed spotless in case Bliss peed sometimes like other people did. No stray bras drip-drying in the shower. No long blonde hairs hanging out in the sink.

The intercom chimed and Emory sprinted toward the apartment door. She let its high-pitched song repeat twice more so she wouldn't seem overeager. Emory pressed the green button to answer. "Yes?"

A split screen showed the doorman on duty and Bliss waiting at the desk. "You have a visitor, Bliss—" There was no microphone facing into the lobby. Emory watched Bliss mouth her name. "Tully," the doorman finished. "Should I send her up?"

"Yes, please," Emory answered. The screen went dark. She smoothed her hands over her hair, checked that her blouse was buttoned correctly. Took three breaths and named the things she could see and feel to settle herself down. After a few seconds, she walked over to the living room so that she wouldn't be hovering at the door.

When the knock at 37B came, though, she hurried back. "Hi!" she said, flinging the door wide.

"Hi yourself." Bliss held out a hot pink flower Emory was fairly certain was a daisy. "For you."

Emory stepped to the side so Bliss could enter. She accepted the flower, wracking her brain for what to put it in. A spare highball glass would have to do. Bliss followed her to the sink in the quartz-topped island and used the kitchen scissors that Emory kept in a utensil holder to trim the stem.

"You didn't have to," Emory said, admiring the pop of color on the counter of her mostly monochrome space.

Bliss laughed. "I think I did. Which is not to say I don't like your apartment up in the sky. It's like a little nest."

The walls were white. The couch was white. The table was glass. Emory's khaki chinos and white linen blouse blended with the scheme. She hadn't thought about the palette before. "Decorating is not really my forte. I'll eventually get around to hiring someone. In the meantime, I appreciate that you brought me something pretty." She opened the fridge. "Beer? Wine? Pop, or soda if you prefer the term, or seltzer?"

"Water? I walked."

Emory filled a glass with water and ice for Bliss, who leaned against the island, then returned to the fridge for a small box. "So, I got this kit for us to make for dinner. I thought the activity might be a good way of getting to know each other a little bit." She tore off the tape and opened the flap. "It's pasta and tomato-basil sauce with garlic bread. I thought that sounded easy enough. Of course, if you decide you'd rather hang out on the couch while I cook, that's something I would know about you for our backstory, and not a problem at all."

143

Bliss reached into the box for a sprig of basil, which she crushed and held to her nose, inhaling. She...just *did* things with enthusiasm. "Mmm. You can never have too much basil. Or garlic," she said, smelling that next. She held the basil under Emory's nose. "It's so fresh."

Emory thought most herbs smelled alike, but she played along. "All the better for us to eat it." They read over the recipe card. Dinner in twenty minutes.

The meal took much longer to prepare than the recipe card indicated because they took the instructions point by point. Bliss opened a can of tomatoes and emptied it into a battered saucepan Emory bought at a thrift store right after college. She had a better pot for boiling the pasta water. Emory reached into a high cupboard to retrieve it. "You can probably tell I don't cook much. My mom didn't have a lot of different recipes in her repertoire. She could turn any kind of leftovers into a casserole, so reheating those is about the extent of my culinary skills."

"I cook. I had to," Bliss said. She didn't elaborate. Instead, Bliss whipped a pen out of her pocket, along with a paper that Emory recognized as their questions sheet, and posed like a reporter. "What's your favorite casserole?"

"Wait!" Emory's work bag was slung over a chair at the glass-topped dining table between the kitchen and living room. With her own question sheet in hand, she came back to the island. "Huh. I think cheeseburger casserole. It has rice and hamburger meat and cheese and tomatoes and probably other stuff. I've never made it myself. My mom wrote down the recipe on an index card and gave me a box of them when I went off to college. The whole thing's in the entry closet, and I don't think I've looked at it in the last ten years." She jotted that down before finding a cutting board and knife to chiffonade the basil, whatever that meant. "You? What's your favorite casserole?"

Bliss came close and leaned around her shoulder. "My mom didn't really—well, I suppose it would be rakott krumpli. It's sliced potatoes and sausages and eggs all baked with cream."

Huh. "Is that Irish?"

Bliss didn't answer for a second. "Oh, Tully! I mean, no, it's not a recipe from the Tully side of my family. My great-great-great grandmother passed recipes down to my mom. The family thought she was German, but a cousin of my mom's was doing research and she probably was from Austria-Hungary when that was a thing." She reached past Emory for a ragged slice of basil, careful to take it from the edge of the plastic cutting board, far from Emory's unskilled knife work. "Something I've been wondering about you—tea or coffee?"

Emory could feel the jut of her hip, the soft curve of her breast. The heat of Bliss's palm at the small of her back, right through her blouse. She glanced at her copy of the questions, which had a bit of basil clinging to the corner. "Both. Bath or shower—wait." She put the knife down and reached behind herself to clasp Bliss's hand and put some space between them.

She should have dropped Bliss's hand right away. But it was so soft, so warm, and her fingers were long and agile. Instead, she was talking, looking at Bliss's knuckles. "I meant to say something already, and you startled me before, after the contract..." There was no easy way to say what she needed to say, what she was *supposed* to say. "I meant to tell you that you—you don't have to touch me. That's not part of the contract. Even at the wedding, I am not asking you for public displays of affection. It's not—I wouldn't—"

Bliss squeezed her fingers. "Did you touch Mari?"

Emory fixated on Bliss's hand. Her soft, soft hand. "I did."

"Don't you think Mari will notice if you don't touch your fiancée?" Tighter. It didn't hurt.

"That's not the point." Emory tried to untangle her fingers, but Bliss held her in place.

"I'm touchy. I like touching things. People. I like touching you. And—" She put her free hand over hers and Emory's. "Nobody's forcing me. I think we should practice." She ducked her head down and moved into Emory's line of sight. "If you're okay with it. Just—practice."

Acting, then. Not Emory's favorite. She couldn't argue. Bliss was right: if she was going to go to Mari's wedding with a fake fiancée, it would be senseless to fail at the very end of the charade. "Okay," she said, reluctantly. "As long as we're clear."

Bliss nodded. "All clear." She released Emory's hand and picked up the recipe card. "I think we need to preheat the oven, and the pasta water's not boiling." Bliss took care of adjusting the appliances while Emory found a baking pan.

A few minutes later, the loaf of bread was halved (equally, if not neatly) and spread with garlic butter. Bliss wandered over to check out the wide windows overlooking northern Brooklyn and the waterfront. "I would never get tired of this view." As she turned away, her foot caught on a cardboard box that Emory had tried to stash behind the couch for the evening. Bliss searched inside and found a onesie and a plush elephant. "What's this? Emory, do you have a secret baby?"

Emory laughed. The oven came to temperature and she put the bread in, telling Bliss over her shoulder, "Not in this all-white apartment, I don't! It's for Francis. I think I told you about her. My best friend from college. She had a baby a couple months ago." Emory joined her in the living area. On impulse—no, for *practice*—she offered her hand to Bliss, and when Bliss took it, she sat them down on the sofa. They lost their spectacular view. In Emory's thinking, it was worth it to be cozier. "We used to get together once a week. After she had the baby, I gave her some space to be a new mom, and she had family staying with her." She squeezed the elephant's trunk. "She has everything she needs, but I want her and the baby to know I'm there for them. Francis is going it alone. I don't know if I ever want to be a mom, much less a single mom."

"Yeah, I don't know either. My mom did okay with me. In some ways she was a single parent before she was officially single. My dad worked in"—she waved a hand dismissively—"finance or

147

something, and he was never home, so it was her and me, most of the time. After he was gone, that part was still the same."

Bliss went silent. Emory slid close and put an arm over the back of the couch, then rested her hand on Bliss's back. *Practice.*

"What about your parents?" Bliss asked. She shifted on the cushion so that her leg was tight against Emory's thigh.

Practicing. She was practicing paying attention. "My parents... I'm an only child too. My dad works in construction, building and remodeling houses and offices, and my mom does bookkeeping for a grocery store. They came to graduations and awards ceremonies, but we were never really close." She scooted backward, and Bliss came with her, tucking into her curved arm. "I last saw them over Christmas. They do their own thing, I do mine."

Bliss twisted toward her. They were molded together on the couch. "What's your thing, Emory?" she whispered.

"Work," Emory said. She could think about work. Work did not crawl unexpectedly into her arms. "I wake up. Get dressed. Take the train. Go to my desk for emails and phone calls. To the boardroom or out for meetings, drinks, dinners. Then I come back here and work some more."

"To make a lot of money."

Emory shrugged. "That happens in my career. And I've been lucky."

Bliss turned her head away. The view out the side window was mostly another building, and she looked at it longer than Emory expected. "It's not all luck. Not for some people." Whatever she meant, she didn't want to talk about it any longer. She turned back and rested her temple on Emory's shoulder. "How did we meet?"

"Painfully," Emory replied, laughing a little.

"No, like—we need a story." Bliss snuggled into Emory's side.

Emory decided she didn't need practice. She was an expert at displays of affection. Distracting, frustrating displays of affection.

Business wasn't supposed to mix with pleasure. Not in her world.

"I was walking across the Brooklyn Bridge. Oh, I was taking pictures. The sun was out, and it was also a little misty, and the light—the whole world was so beautiful."

"We both live in Brooklyn, so it wasn't a complete coincidence," Emory added.

Bliss snaked an arm across Emory's waist. "You walked out of a cloud and into the viewfinder, and it was love at first sight."

"No," Emory said. That would never happen to her. Not in a million years. "I...Mari would never believe your story. I don't fall in love like that." She untangled herself from Bliss. Because since Mari... "I don't fall in love."

That was the awful, burning truth.

No, it was the garlic bread that was burning. "Shit." Emory dashed for the oven and turned in circles in the kitchen. She needed something to use for a hot pad.

"Turn it off," Bliss called, cranking open a window.

Right. That was first. She found a towel, which turned out to be a good hot pad substitute, since it could be waved at the cloud of smoke that wafted out of the oven's open door. "The bread is actually okay," she said, setting the hot pan on the separate stove-top. It was golden brown, crispy, and steaming. "What—"

Bliss peered into the oven. "Something was spilled in here. When did you last cook?"

Emory was legitimately embarrassed. "I don't know, but it didn't set off the smoke alarm!"

Between the two of them, they finished preparing the meal kit. Bliss cooked and drained the pasta—Emory *did* have a strainer—and Emory scooped thickened tomato sauce and burrata over the noodles and fresh basil. It took far less time for them to demolish their dinner than it had to make it, and for Emory to smear a line of tomato sauce across her shirt when she took the dishes to the sink.

"Argh. Give me a minute to change before this stain sets." Emory went through the bedroom to the walk-in closet. She was too warm anyway. Did she have any thinner, cooler blouses that weren't ratty weekend t-shirts with their sleeves cut off? She settled on a blouse in a marled gray a little darker than Bliss's eyes.

When she went back into the living room, she didn't see Bliss there, or at the dining table, or in the kitchen. Had she left? They were only supposed to meet for two hours, not the three that had passed already. "Bliss?"

She found her in the foyer. Or, rather, she saw the box of reci-pes her mother gave her on the floor next to the front closet. And she saw Bliss emerging from the closet with a hammer in one hand and a framed painting in the other.

"Emory, you have a design solution right here!" Bliss turned the painting around so Emory could see it, but Emory knew the rich, jewel-toned abstract piece by the back of the frame alone. She hadn't seen it in years.

She didn't want to see it now. "No."

"Yes!" Bliss was ecstatic. "You can hang it between the windows, and you'll see it when you come in. It will make everything more cheerful—"

"*No.*" The word came out harsher than Emory intended, and exactly like she felt. It bubbled up from inside her again, louder. "No. Don't you fucking dare."

Bliss set the painting down carefully, leaning it against the entry hallway, and dropped the hammer beside it. "I was suggesting a way to add some more color to your place, like you said you might enjoy. I see I've crossed a big line. I'm sorry."

She had. That painting was in the back of the closet for a reason. It was the one she and Mari bought from a vendor in Central Park after Mari accepted her proposal. It was supposed to hang over their bed. "That's Mari's. Actually, *you* take it." Emory picked up the painting and tried to hand it to Bliss. "Take it home with you."

Bliss sidestepped her. "You should keep it. Or give it to Mari."

"No." Emory slammed open the front door and tossed the painting into the hallway, surprising herself with her brashness. The glass cracked in the frame, broken lines making tangible the old, cracked parts of her heart. "If you don't want it, the painting can go in the trash. It's fucking garbage. She never came back for it." *She never came back for me.*

"I should go," Bliss said hurriedly. She patted her pockets, checking for keys and phone, and Emory thought that would have been endearing if she hadn't been—

Unreasonably enraged? Depleted? Both? "You should," Emory agreed. "Go." She didn't want Bliss to see her this way. The last time she'd been so *angry*, so ripped apart, was when Mari had called to say that Hollywood was her home, and she wasn't coming back, and Emory had torn the painting from one wall and thrown it at the other. And it hadn't had the good grace to break into a thousand pieces that time.

And Emory didn't hate anyone so much as she hated herself.

Not then. Not now.

Bliss didn't look at her as she left. "See you soon. Goodnight."

When she heard the elevator doors close, whisking Bliss away, Emory made herself a promise.

Their relationship needed to be solely business, as she'd said before. Bliss didn't need to know everything. She just needed to know enough to fool Mari. And with a little bit of handholding, they'd pass as fiancées well enough for a weekend. Bliss could do that for two weeks at Emory's rates.

That is, if Bliss was willing to be in her presence ever again.

It wouldn't be the first time she'd been left. Or the first time a breakup had been all her fault.

Practice makes perfect.

fourteen

THE LAST DAY OF APRIL was unseasonably warm. Emory didn't need a jacket, or even a sweater, when she walked down Flatbush in the overcast early morning gloom to Truly Outrageous for doughnuts and coffee, then the last few blocks to Francis's. Francis was sitting on the steps outside with Sophie in a stroller, which she rocked back and forth with one foot. Emory found a dry spot next to her— it had rained earlier that morning and drops of water clung to the sides of the steps—and handed her a decaf latte and a chocolate doughnut with raspberry glaze and sprinkles, which Francis tore into immediately.

Francis beamed up at her. "My favorite! If I liked girls, I would like you best," she said, mouth full.

Emory wrapped her hands around her iced Americano. It made her fingers numb. "Thank you, but I am perfectly happy having you for a best friend." She blew a raspberry at Francis and leaned into her shoulder. The sun peeked through a cloud, and they turned their faces up to the welcome light.

Then Sophie made her own raspberry sound.

"I thought you were asleep!" Francis exclaimed. "Sophie!"

"Apropos, babe," Emory added.

"My baby's first word was *pttthhhbbbt*," Francis called out to an elderly couple that was passing on the other side of the street. They didn't hear her. "That's my girl. Tell it to the world."

Emory picked up Sophie and held her above her head, bouncing her gently. "Hoo-*ah*. Kiddo, I am going to enjoy being your auntie."

Sophie responded by opening her mouth and ejecting a stream of puke down Emory's front. Emory did the most prudent thing she could think of, which was put Sophie right back in the stroller. "Now what?" She was no longer in the mood for her custard-filled Long John.

Francis handed her a cloth. "You give thanks to the holy boob, giver of sustenance, occasionally purveyor of a post-meal barf. And you mop up."

"I *do* give thanks for the boob, the holy boob, but maybe the next milestone to work on is learning not to projectile vomit." Emory swabbed at her blouse.

"Wait until you find out about diapers." Francis squeezed one of Sophie's feet. "I could go away to a spa for the weekend, and you could stay here and be mom. By Sunday night, you'll adjust your expectations about bodily fluids."

"Hmph." At least it wasn't bird poop, she supposed.

Francis pulled out her phone while Emory finished blotting away the splatter. "According to this, Sophie's a little young for raspberries. You're precocious, beansprout." Sophie was nodding off, uninterested in her mother's assessment. "And according to this gossip site I've never heard of, Mari and Benjamin Thorston are getting married because she's pregnant."

Emory had to laugh. "Nah. Mari hates kids. Plus, the other gossip sites all say they're going to break up because she's spending so much money on the wedding, which would be believable if Thorston weren't richer than Midas." When she and Mari had been engaged, Mari's plans evolved from eloping to a sunset wedding with a water view to hiring an entire circus for entertainment. Whether or not Mari had been serious, they'd had more than a few arguments about their wedding budget. There was no reason to believe she couldn't afford whatever she wanted now.

Francis pulled down her sunglasses. "You're reading up on Mari on gossip sites? Since when?"

The Long John was calling her name again. She tore the doughnut bag along its side to make an envelope so she wouldn't have to touch it. No need for things to get messier. "I was trying to find out if there would be other guests to potentially connect with

besides Benjamin Thorston. William wants me to pitch him, but..."
She shrugged. "I think it's a long shot even getting a chance to wave
hello from a distance at a wedding with five hundred other guests.
I've been practicing my introduction in front of the mirror, for
whatever it's worth. I don't know that there's any point. That man
has more money than god and he doesn't need ours."

"But you're still going to see—her? Alone?"

That was trickier. Condensation dripped from her iced drink
onto her slacks. One disaster led to another, every time. "No, I have
a date. Someone I'm seeing."

Francis looked suspicious, and rightly so. "You're not seeing
anyone."

"I am. This plant girl from the office."

"And you never date at the office."

"The office is mostly men, and I don't want any!" That was
true, if not the sole reason Emory didn't fraternize. Ethics aside,
the terror of an office breakup was real, and Emory's office wasn't
big enough for a breakup like the kind she'd had with Mari. "Bliss.
She's a vendor who comes in to take care of the flowers. It's per-
mitted. Things progressed and we got engaged. I know you've had
a lot going on with the baby and your mom being in town, so I
didn't say anything, and here we are."

Francis's look of shock was everything Emory deserved, but
short-lived. Sophie was awake. And squalling. Francis resumed
rolling the stroller back and forth to no effect. "Can we meet up for
dinner tonight so I can hear the whole story?"

"We're not meeting today," Emory said automatically. But that was her schedule with Bliss, not her personal schedule. She didn't want to tell Francis about Bliss, how she was only Emory's escort—*fiancée*—because Emory had taken Francis's less-than-serious advice to hire a date. There was a worse truth, though, that she could share. "I meant, I'm not meeting with Bliss. We had a fight last night. I—it was my fault. She found that painting that Mari and I bought, the one I had you keep for a while, and...I banged some things around. There was a little yelling. I was the one doing the yelling."

"I see." Francis, ambidextrous, patted Emory's arm with one hand and Sophie's tummy with the other. She waited for the rest, though Emory was sure she was holding back a slew of questions about the speed of the engagement.

"I didn't know what to do when I saw the painting, and then—it felt like when I fought with Mari, and I didn't know what to do even more." And things always got worse when she and Mari had tried to talk them out.

Hadn't they?

Or had their talks been another way of fighting things out, and when the fight was over, neither one of them had left the ring? "I know. Yelling at Bliss wasn't okay. I can't believe I acted like that. I'm so embarrassed."

"Yeah. I won't lie to you. I also won't judge you." Francis picked up Sophie and held her baby close, rubbing her back. "I wish you'd told me about Bliss, but sometimes things happen fast.

157

When someone you love comes along, goddamn it, hold on tight."
She laid her cheek on Sophie's head and sniffed back a tear. "You
know what to do."

Emory was clueless. Bliss and Mari—both of them moved
unpredictably. "Do I?"

"The opposite of what you did with Mari. You talk it out." She
kicked the toe of her sandal gently against Emory's foot. "Go, right
now."

Bliss could not possibly want to see her in person. "No—
please, Francis, I think I need to let her have a little time. She's probably still freaked out."

Francis turned Sophie around and bounced her on her knee,
transforming Sophie's fussing into squeals of delight. "You already
know you're wrong and you're stalling. Go, now, or there's going to
be more puke. Do you want there to be more puke, Emory?"

"All right, fine." She slurped the last of her coffee and leaned
forward for a baby hug and kiss. "You would never. Never never,"
she said to Sophie.

Sophie disagreed. Emory got a new splotch of puke on her
other shoulder.

"Tell you what," Francis said. "I'll loan you a shirt."

———✎———

In the end, Francis loaned her a sweater. Emory was quite a bit
taller, so she'd settled on one that was oversized on Francis and
more form-fitting on her. She'd had to; Francis only had one top
that fit, which was how Emory entered Park Slope Express Floral

158

in a yellow sweater with white pom-poms arranged in the shape of a heart over her chest.

She hadn't planned to stop at the florist. Emory had passed the shop dozens of times on her way to Francis's apartment but had never gone inside. A bright display of flowers—labeled gerbera daisies—in the front window brought her to a halt on the sidewalk. Those were a match for the flower that Bliss had brought her, so it was logical Bliss might like the same for herself. A peace offering that acknowledged last night and that color was not a bad thing.

Good. Businesslike with a personal touch. It wasn't too late to save the arrangement.

A bell clanged a deep, round tone as Emory stepped inside. The shop was bigger than she expected, with room for a table at the front and shelves that stretched toward a back work area that she glimpsed behind a half-drawn curtain. There was no one at the wide counter that backed up to a brick wall covered in framed photos.

A purple pot overflowed with vines next to a workstation and register. Fresh bouquets filled a glass display case, and houseplants and gardening supplies clustered on every surface. Emory didn't see any other daisies to purchase. Maybe Bliss would like something else? She didn't know where to start. "Hello?" she called softly. This was a job for: someone who knew literally anything about plants.

The curtain that separated the front of the store from the back fluttered and Bliss, of all people, appeared. She wore all black except for an oversized pair of rainbow-striped gardening gloves and held aloft an impressively sharp-looking tool that Emory hoped was for cutting plants and not for stabbing her. "You work here?"

Bliss didn't look happy to see her, but neither did she look unhappy. Emory supposed with the snipping tool-thing, Bliss had the advantage. After giving Emory's fuzzy-snowball sweater a confused glance, she slowly replied, "Yes." She moved behind the counter and set down the tool. "Can I help you?"

Formal. Polite. Businesslike.

More than Emory deserved, probably.

Emory straightened the hem of her ugly sweater and pulled the wrists flat against her arms, stalling. This would be so much easier if Bliss was one of her business partners. She'd know how long to give them both for a cooldown. They'd focus on their shared goals. Apologies would be made and accepted; needs for future interactions would be asserted. Everyone would carry on.

But—Bliss *was* her business partner, technically, in this foolish business of weddings and connections and capitalism. That professional line between them would *stay* the line between them. "I didn't know you'd be here, but I'm glad you are. I'd like to apologize for blowing up at you last night. We have a professional arrangement, and I should have acted professionally." She stuffed her hands in her pockets and clutched her keys until the metal bit into her palm. "And behaved better."

"I should have done that too," Bliss said. She mirrored Emory, hands in pockets, the counter between them.

She'd gotten comfortable with Bliss, and with her guard down, Mari had slipped between them. But Emory could hold the memories at bay for two more weeks. The wedding would be over. She'd show Mari how she was living her pretend-best life.

Then maybe she'd start working on her real one.

"My behavior was one hundred percent uncalled for. I'm sorry. It won't happen again." She was done with feeling like she had back when she was twenty-six. Boorish, blazing anger had bubbled up from distant memories that she refused to relive, from a time and place—and maybe even a person—who could bring out the worst in her. Emory vowed, then and there, to find another way out if she reacted that strongly again.

Bliss could hold very still. She could be so quiet, so calm, that Emory could barely breathe herself. This was where Mari would have started screaming, and Emory would have held her feelings inside until she broke and screamed back, where their fight would have spiraled into other unfinished fights, the kind that kept reappearing no matter how many times you swatted them down.

But Bliss simply said, "Thank you. I accept your apology, and I look forward to continuing to work with you."

There wasn't any yelling, which was very different from what happened in the fights Emory was used to. Her knees were shaking. She angled herself into one of the chairs at the round table, relieved to let it hold her upright. Of course. Bliss *couldn't* quit. Emory didn't know what else to say.

Which meant she had to stop talking and start doing.

Bliss shuffled some papers at the counter. Emory took a moment to collect herself. The table was smooth, no splinters. The front right leg of her chair was a little wobbly. The open three-ring binders on the tabletop—with pages that were labeled DESIGNED BY BLISS at the top—

Emory was entranced by the sketches. Some were bridal white with restrained hints of color; others were a riot of hues. She didn't know the words for the shapes and angles, the flowers and themes. She only knew that if she could live in a world where these pictures came to life, she'd never leave it again. "These are amazing. How did you learn to draw like this?" she whispered, not realizing Bliss could hear her.

The best thing happened. Bliss came to sit across the table and her shoulders relaxed. Light came into her eyes again. "I loved coloring. I had pastels and crayons and colored pencils. Watercolors. Oil paints. I had more art supplies than any kid needed. More than I could use." A cloud passed over. "I, well. I sort of said—when I was little, I lived in this gigantic house in Connecticut. I had my own art studio instead of a playroom. It was obscene. My dad worked in—finance, I guess, like I said before. I didn't know exactly."

"Sounds nice," Emory said.

"It was." Bliss leaned on her elbows. "Until toward the end of elementary school, when my dad died."

The hurt was clear on Bliss's face, though she tried to hide it with nonchalance. Emory wanted to hug her better for real, not for practice and pretend. "I'm so sorry."

Bliss shook her head. "That's not all. He had been embezzling from his company and gambling, and he left us with a mountain of debt. I think he left the company with a giant pile of even more debt, and there was money missing that belonged to other people in our neighborhood. I don't know what happened. I was too young to know and now I don't want to know. We had to sell the house, me and my mom, and move into a rented apartment. My mom went back to work. Nobody would sit with me at lunch or talk to me at all. I hated school and everyone in it, so I drew in class all the time, and when I hit high school, I worked late nights under the table and napped or sketched instead of paying attention. I guess that was what helped me level up."

"Bliss—" *I'm sorry* seemed so insignificant against the world that had crashed around her. Emory wanted to reach her, to touch her, but she knew her apology wasn't enough to allow for that yet. Not enough to prove to Bliss she was going to be different.

"Nah!" Bliss's demeanor changed. "That's backstory. I went to UConn and studied digital media and branding and stuff like that. I took as many art classes as I could fit in around working full time, and my style went from copies of things I'd seen to ideas that came from the artistic milkshake machine inside my head." She shot Emory a wistful smile. "I even made a few friends."

163

The bell over the door rang. A sturdy, graying butch woman came in carrying a bag from New Hunan Style. "Lunch is here." She took in the scene. "Those designs are Bliss's, if you're interested. She's really good."

Emory smiled at Bliss, who basked in the praise. "Your lunch is going to be good. *She* is fantastic."

"I'm Selma. Are you finding everything you need?" Selma hobbled over to the counter and deposited the takeout bag. It looked like her knee was bothering her.

"Actually..." Emory didn't want to throw Bliss under the bus. Not when she was starting to seem like herself again. She swiveled in her seat, trying to talk to both Bliss and Selma at once. "I need a new mom gift—and I need an apology gift."

To her credit, Bliss didn't bat an eyelash. Emory wondered again about the stillness she was able to display on demand.

Selma didn't notice; she was pulling selections from the display case. "Flowers have meaning, so we'll keep that in mind. Of course, flowers in season are best. I have tulips in red and yellow for great love. Hyacinth, for when you're wrong and you know it. Daffodils for starting over in the springtime. Which one do you think says you're sorry best, Bliss?"

Bliss tilted her head, considering. "Daffodils. They look like kissing and making up."

Selma laughed heartily. "I'll wrap up whatever you choose. For the new mom, I like a sunflower—doesn't take a lot of work. A mint plant is another cheerful option."

Emory considered. "The daffodils, of course." For Bliss, who deserved to set the terms of what came next. "And the mint, I think. I can smell it from here, and I think my friend will enjoy making tea out of it."

Selma bustled behind the counter to ring up the order. She printed the receipt and said, "Thanks," and glanced at the name on the credit card. Her eyebrows shot up. "Emory Jordan." Selma held the paper and card in her hand, glancing at Bliss.

Bliss nodded, and a strange look passed between them that Emory couldn't interpret. If there were sides, Emory put her money on Selma being on Bliss's. But Selma packaged up her flowers without further comment and ushered her out with a polite goodbye.

———⟋∾⟍———

Emory dropped off Francis's mint plant first, using the key she kept on hand in case Francis got locked out, and left it at her apartment door quietly, in case Sophie was having a nap. Then, dodging the intermittent spots of sun and clouds, she made her way to Bliss's address in Kensington. She passed it twice before figuring out that Bliss was upstairs in a detached house, and she had to walk along the side and up a set of stairs to where a screen door displayed the house number. Emory tucked the daffodils in the swirling metal and hurried back to the street in case Bliss didn't get many visitors. She had spent so many years living in secure buildings that walking right up to someone's door felt intrusive.

The morning warmth was slipping away, and a bracing breeze made her shiver. It wasn't too cold to walk, though, and she decided to keep walking. She needed the air, the motion. The wind whipping her hair back as she cut across Prospect Park.

Her phone rang, and her thumb swiped the little icon to answer before she took in the caller ID photo of her mom. "Hello, Emory?" Her face popped up on the screen, and Emory could see the kitchen in her childhood home and her father in the background.

"Hi, Mom," she said. They hadn't spoken in months. Her mom was good about checking in from time to time, even if they didn't have much to talk about. Emory couldn't remember if she'd missed her turn in the quarterly rotation of who called whom.

"We were watching the TV and we saw a story, and I got out the photo album."

Her dad broke in, voice distant. "Your mom saw an actress and thought she looked familiar." Emory heard the refrigerator open and the familiar sound of him cracking open a beer.

"Is that Marilee I saw on TV the same as Mari who was your friend in college? The one who came to Thanksgiving once? We got some congratulations flowers from Mari—I don't know why—and then I saw a movie trailer. Wasn't she your friend?"

The obvious thing to do was to say that the card was a mistake, and Mari was sending flowers to all her old friends and acquaintances in celebration of her marriage. It was the kind of lavish gesture Mari would have loved.

Emory chose to do the less obvious. Because she was tired. Because invisibility wasn't her superpower anymore. "Yes. She was my girlfriend." She dodged a jogger coming at her head on and fumbled the phone before turning it upright. Her mom was turning her phone around like the strange view was being generated on her end. "Mom. She was my fiancée."

Her mom stared into the phone. Dad edged into the frame and cupped his ear. "Say that again, honey?"

Emory turned away from the walking path, toward the trees. "She was my fiancée. We were engaged, after college. We broke up a long time ago."

Something rattled in the background. Emory couldn't see what her parents were doing. The phone was pointed at the ceiling. She could hear her mom's voice, saying, "Why didn't she tell us?"

It hurt so bad, and I couldn't make it stop hurting. "I didn't know how."

The phone tilted. She could see her mom's shoulder and her dad's beard. Her dad must have helped, because the view pulled back, and she could see them both, concerned. Her mom went on. "Honey, we love you no matter what. I know we don't...we don't talk a lot—"

Her dad interrupted. "But we always want to know when you need help. What do you need right now? You can come up here if you want. Stay with us for a little while."

She didn't know what she needed. "It really has been a long time since we broke up. I'm okay." What she *wanted* was to go back to the flower shop and sit at the table in the window and watch Bliss make beauty out of thin air and graphite, and have a—*feeling*.

A feeling she almost couldn't remember. The dizzy, wide-awake feeling of *feelings*. Warm ones. Like cuddling. Like cuddling *in bed*.

And she'd only felt that way a few times. For Sanna in third grade, out of playing foursquare every recess, and loving the way her braids fell on her shoulders.

Out of discussing boys in tenth grade with Luisa, who kissed Emory after a volleyball match and started going out with a soccer player on the boys' team the next day.

Out of watching the back of Cameron's head in physics her senior year, her curly short hair, and never speaking to her because small-town upstate New York wasn't into girls dating each other.

Out of long walks under umbrellas with Mari.

"Thanks, Mom. And you too, Dad." She realized that she'd started walking again and was almost at the edge of the park. Emory held her phone close. "I—I should go. I'll be inside and will lose service in the elevator." That was a lie; she had another half hour's walk home ahead.

They exchanged *love you*s and promises to talk soon. Emory hung up. She wished she could tell her parents she was getting married for real.

Emory imagined it for a brief second. Bliss in a long veil and those little tiny white flowers that Emory couldn't name. Someone saying *you may now kiss the bride*.

Laughing. Dancing.

Telling the world.

But that was a fantasy. Her reality was a lie.

Two more weeks. She put her chin down and headed into the wind.

may

fifteen

BLISS LET HERSELF IN AT Park Slope Express Floral. Selma didn't expect her before ten, and the shop didn't open until eleven on Sundays, but she'd woken up early—too early—and Selma trusted her with the key and the alarm. That meant Bliss could attack some of the less glamorous store tasks without anyone, Selma or customers, looking over her shoulder. Because Selma's longstanding wholesaler relationships loved her enough to deliver, there hadn't been a need to rise before dawn to hit the flower district yet, but Selma had been hinting that they should make a trip there soon.

Yesterday, she'd helped Selma pick through flowers that were lovely but wouldn't last long enough to sell—not many, as Selma knew her inventory and sales well—and Selma was out delivering those to a cancer center and a nursing home. Some of the leftover flowers from the cull were fine to combine into discount bouquets, some she hung on a pegboard to dry, and others she disposed of. Bliss hauled buckets of smelly water to the utility sink for a scrub and refill; if she ran this zoo, she'd put in a floor-level drain and hose. Not that there were any infestations that could be referred to as a *zoo* other than a few fruit flies from a banana peel that she'd inadvertently left out the night before. Whoops. That went into the compost bin.

Her final morning task before opening was to sweep up the leaves and stems that were always escaping her projects, and then mop the pollen that found a way to coat the floor no matter what precautions she took. Another good reason to install a floor drain. She could pressure wash the crap out of the tiles.

Sweeping and mopping only occupied a little corner of her brain. The rest of it needed something to think about, and what it ended up doing was fixating on Emory.

The last thing she'd expected was to see Emory at the shop, coming in after her blowup. Bliss had been completely unprepared for her, not to mention unprepared for her charmingly hideous sweater. And the other last thing she'd expected was for Emory to apologize unprompted. She wasn't supposed to do that. Business-people didn't apologize; they held their ground. They were right every time.

Emory had been wrong and she knew it. Maybe it was the yellow in the sweater, which didn't suit her at all, but she'd looked—scared. Pale. Not Bliss's favorite pink.

Bliss wished she'd had an apology from her father that simple and direct. Emory's was sincere. And then they'd moved forward.

When Bliss replayed the unhappy memory of what happened at Emory's apartment, what she came away with was that Emory had been hurt by Bliss's inadvertent reminder of her time with Mari. And then she'd lost *control*. That wasn't an excuse for her outburst. But deep down, Bliss understood the emotion. She'd taken years to find her calm when thinking about her dad, when she could think about him at all. Letting go wasn't easy. And Bliss wanted to let go when she could—including letting go of the other night.

So now they'd see what was next. Emory had promised: not again.

Bliss would give her one chance to make good on that promise.

At five to eleven, Bliss walked through the checklist Selma had written on a sticky note and taped to the counter, adding to the list as she went along. Computer on, register on. Find the bag of cash for change that Selma sealed in a plastic bag and hid at the bottom of the bucket of asters. Make a mental note to talk to Selma about safes again. Turn on the lights. Unlock the door. Rub salve into the places on her hands where she'd snagged her skin with thorns and branches. Check for bucket sludge on her shoes.

No line of customers was queueing to get in. Bliss took out her phone to snap pictures. Four discount bouquets. A Mother's Day arrangement that was going in the window with a poster about ordering for the holiday. A look at the "goodies" in the compost bin. Park Slope Express Floral had a growing Insta, thanks to Bliss, so it was the work of a few minutes for her to edit and upload the photos. She added a few lines of text, typed in hashtags, and posted the discount flowers first.

The bell over the door rang, but it wasn't an avalanche of customers; it was Selma, beaming and a little sweaty. "Deliveries done! How's business?"

Bliss spread her arms wide at the empty shop.

"Things will pick up. You'll see. Meanwhile, our favorite task." She lifted her arms like a conductor. Then, less dramatically, she turned on a stereo that she kept hidden behind a rack of greeting cards, starting a CD of 1970s hits. "Accounting."

"Nnnnhgh." Numbers were not Bliss's favorite. "How about more social media?"

"Accounting," Selma insisted, which was how Bliss found herself dancing and jiving, staying alive, hustling, and shake-shaking her booty. She found her groove turning printouts and receipts and invoices into graphs, which turned the sea of numbers into pictures that she could understand. Selma only had to help her find one data-entry mistake. Bliss shifted a pile of papers to the side and grabbed the next. This was *almost* fun, even with Selma bumping her elbow because she was...

Checking out a line of customers who were cleaning them out of discount flowers.

Her phone rang, the old-fashioned jingle cutting through the tunes Selma was spinning. Emory. Bliss stuck a finger in one ear and put the phone to her other. "Hello?"

She heard, faintly, "Are we still on for today?"

"Oh, fuck." Good thing Selma didn't care about her language. Her rescheduled appointment for brunch with Emory was half an hour ago. "I'm so sorry. Got distracted—concentrating. Should I meet you there?"

Selma *tsk*ed and put her hands on her shoulders, moving them both toward the front door conga-line style. Bliss almost let the door hit her in the butt on the way out, trying to keep the phone to her ear. "Say that again?" she asked as soon as the disco bass faded. Bliss headed toward the restaurant. "Hello? Are you there?"

There was a crackle and a thump, and background conversation, and Emory answered her. "They can't seat us for a while, so I'm looking up wait times nearby."

Bliss came to the end of a block and darted across the street while the crossing sign blinked a red hand. On the other side, she picked up the pace to a jog. "Come over. I make a mean French toast. So mean it'll make a joke about your momma." It sounded like Emory laughed, but it was hard to tell. The brunch crowd beat the disco florist crowd on decibels.

One more corner and she came up behind Emory, who was waiting in the restaurant standby line dressed in dark jeans and a button-down under a cardigan, and tapped her shoulder. "I'm very sorry I messed up my date with my wife to be," she said, injecting as much humor into her voice as she could.

177

That got her a laugh from Emory. She switched her purse from one arm to over her shoulder. "Apology accepted, wife." And after a beat: "To be."

They stood on the sidewalk awkwardly. Their talk in the flower shop after Emory's apology had broken the ice, but there were still a few cubes floating in the cocktail.

"Sooooo...French toast? Family recipe. I don't have a kit or anything."

To Bliss's surprise, Emory nodded.

They took the F to Kensington. While Bliss knew Emory had found her apartment the day before, she guided them past Uzbek restaurants that already smelled deliciously of kebabs, under the neighborhood trees trading the last of their blooms for spring leaves, and up the stairs at the back of the house where she lived. "It's not so fancy as your place."

"Not my current place, maybe," Emory replied. "But fancier than some places I've lived."

Bliss thought about what Emory was seeing. A creaky door that she had to shoulder open and closed. A cramped, open kitchen and a laminate countertop with two stools. A wooden dining table that clearly doubled as workspace, with a bouquet of fresh daffodils in water leaving a ring on the polish. A pair of threadbare barrel chairs that had lived in the apartment longer than Bliss had. A wide window that illuminated the leaning shelf full of plants. Two doors: one to a cramped bathroom, the other to a bedroom inches bigger than its queen bed.

Emory peered into the bedroom. There was just enough space to edge in beside the sliding closet doors and for there to be a little gap between the bed and the radiator. "This is the same size as my first real New York bedroom!" She repeated Bliss's compliment about her luxury apartment back to her. "Like a little nest."

"Peep," Bliss said, laughing. She eased past Emory to flop onto the bed, which was piled high with pillows of all sizes, most in blues, greens, and purples, with a few silver mixed in. That was her nod to luxury. "It's more like a bouncy house."

Emory crossed her arms. "My assessment is that you didn't send any pillows up when you went down, so I'm still thinking nest."

Bliss rolled toward the window, leaving a strip of bed wide open. She patted the nearest pillow, a swirly green-patterned and blue-beaded rectangle with tassels on the corners. "Better test your theory."

"Oh, I couldn't." Emory stepped back and toed off her shoes anyway. She swung the strap of her purse over her head and put it on the kitchen counter.

"My first night in this bed, I jumped up and down while playing air guitar on it, so you'll have to work hard if you want to do some damage." Bliss moved the pillow from under her hand to behind her head. She kicked one ankle over the other. "I'm going to count to three. One—"

Emory flopped, sort of. She slowly tipped over face-first into the pile of pillows, and Bliss obligingly tossed a couple into the air. "This is really, really comfy," she said, muffled.

179

"It took a while to get here," Bliss said, meaning the whole apartment, but also the bed. "When I moved in, another girl lived in the bedroom, and we put a screen up in the living room. I had a futon where the table is and that meant zero privacy. I've moved up in the world and don't have to share." She stretched one foot up toward the ceiling, which she'd ringed with twinkle lights. Then she rolled onto her side, and the pillows dipped her down, close to Emory's shoulder. "This place gets really great morning sun." *And if you stayed over, you could wake up to it.*

Emory peered through her honey-blond hair, which had fallen across her face. Bliss's bones were turning to water, to streams that would seep through all the pillow-spaces to float them up together. If she rolled a little more, they could become a river.

Bliss's stomach decided to growl in a very loud and unwanted way. "Uh, I'm noisy when I'm hungry, as you might have noticed." Getting out of her squashy bed was a challenge, but she managed it by applying a lot of will to her abs and leaping from the end of the bed into the main room. Where Emory was *not* splayed invitingly on her pillow collection.

Probably safer.

While she searched the cupboards for ingredients, Emory joined her in the main room, hair messy and collar askew, and sat at the counter. Emory watched her stir together eggs and milk and cinnamon, which she didn't measure, and pour the whole mixture over half a loaf of bread.

"I like making it this way instead of dipping bread in the batter. Soaks everything up and I don't have to stick my whole hand in."

"I have actually seen people make French toast before, so I knew about that part. No objections to any delicious methods of construction." Emory put a foot on the rung of her stool and pushed herself back on the seat so that her other leg swung free. For a moment, she was quiet, then she burst into action, digging in her purse for a wrinkled, folded paper Bliss recognized as their questions. She looked it over. "Since we're making a habit of cooking together, I guess, what's your favorite breakfast?"

"In bed," Bliss answered automatically. She plugged in an electric kettle to boil water for pour-over coffee. The coffee maker she'd thrifted a couple of years ago had started emitting a mysterious burning smell the day she'd been laid off, so she'd spent some of her free time learning how to make it the old-fashioned way, and in her opinion, she was highly successful. She rummaged in the fridge for blueberries and maple syrup, and on a top shelf for coffee. "If you were a ghost, what kind of ghost would you be?"

Emory turned her paper over a couple of times. "That's—I don't see anything about—should we add that question to the list?"

"Not if you don't want to." The pan was hot. There was only room for her to cook one slice of bread at a time. "I wanted to know something *not* on the list." Something that wasn't prompted by anything to do with Mari.

There was a pause broken by the sizzling of eggs and milk in a hot frying pan. "I think... Hmm. I'd be a mystery ghost."

Eggs, maybe? Bliss flipped a slice of toast, worrying there wouldn't be enough food. She was ravenous enough to eat Emory's share of breakfast too. Emory didn't make her thirsty; she made Bliss hungry. Bliss groaned internally at herself. "A mystery ghost?"

"Yes!" Emory got more enthusiastic as she went along. "I'd haunt people and leave them clues so they could solve crimes. A detective ghost! There'd be a TV show inspired by me."

That made sense. Emory did seem to like helping people. Weird that she wasn't in some other career field instead of venture capital. "The scary, writes messages on the mirror in blood kind of ghost, or a nicer kind, who moves clues into position?"

"Ideally the second kind," Emory said airily, "but you do what you have to do."

Bliss snickered, imagining a bulleted list of tasks scrawled in neat, red writing on a mirror. The organized, businesslike approach to murder mysteries. "I'd be a poltergeist. All the noise, none of the work."

Emory noted this down in the margin of her paper. Bliss had to make a mental note, as the hot pan had become a *very* hot pan and the toasts needed her full attention. Once she had stacks on two plates, she turned out a scramble in no time. Another few seconds and she had Instagram-worthy plates of French toast topped with blueberry-maple syrup and fluffy eggs, and mugs of coffee ready for both of them.

"You—you let me cook pasta out of a meal kit and you never said—I mean, I could have opened a can of Chef Boyardee and that would have probably tasted better than my cooking—" Emory spluttered.

Bliss laughed. "I loved that pasta because you made it for us. Because *we* made it for us. I should confess I suck at making meals except for breakfast, anyway." She slid onto the other stool at the counter, closer to Emory than she ought to have been, but experience had taught her that there were only so many spots on the floor where chairs sat level. Her elbow brushed Emory's cardigan with every bite. She ate faster to feel the sweater against her arm more often.

"This ish so, so goo," Emory said, mouth full, swiping the last of the syrup on her plate with the back of her fork and licking it clean. "I'm so glad we had this instead of the other brunch. Thanks for being late."

On barstools, they weren't so different in height. Bliss stretched up, with Emory's elbow pressed into her stomach, and kissed Emory lightly on the cheek. "Thank you."

Emory turned her head. And Bliss kissed her on the mouth, where she tasted like sour berries and sweet syrup. Her hair didn't smell like mint anymore, but like vanilla and oranges. Bliss reached an arm across Emory's waist—steady, she needed to hold on—and Emory turned her way, legs dangling.

Bliss slipped down to stand in the space between them, in the space between Emory's bare feet. She found Emory's lips again, warm, soft. Her tongue swiped across the bottom one and Emory made a sound like *nnnn*. The reverberation shivered down Bliss's neck and into her spine, and she wrapped her arm tighter around Emory, bringing her closer. Her free hand trailed a line up Emory's thigh, along the delicious curve of her hip, the muscle of her arm, the slope of her shoulder, and stopped at the back of Emory's neck, where the skin under the fall of her hair was hot.

Emory leaned in. Closer. Bliss smoothed her mouth across her jaw, down along her collarbone. Her hands dipped to Emory's ass, and she levered them together, Emory arcing forward to the want that echoed between them.

And then Emory turned away. Placed her hands on the counter, on either side of her plate, and took a long, ragged breath. "Again. I am so sorry, again. It's more than I asked you for. This isn't part of the deal."

A world without Emory under her hands was washed out, grayscale. "Look, I'm not being coerced." Tentatively, she lifted a finger to tuck a strand of hair behind Emory's ear. "Are you?"

Emory looked down at her empty plate. "I'm not sure what I'm doing."

Me. You were doing me. You were wanting me. "I do. Isn't that enough? For these thirty days?"

Emory squeezed her arm in a friendly way that lacked the heat Bliss was sure she felt. "That's right. Thirty days. Two weeks left. Thanks for brunch." And she tucked her purse under her arm, and slipped into her shoes, and was out the door.

Nobody ever stuck around. They left Bliss. Left her aching and wanting and bereft.

184

sixteen

THE NEXT SUNDAY, EARLY, BLISS's phone buzzed. Emory had shared her location and the car was moving quickly. Bliss grabbed her travel bags and hurried downstairs into the drizzly, gray, too-humid, too-sweaty day. She waited at the curb, breathing in the damp air, running one hand over the freshly shaved undercut on one side of her head, smoothing down the hair that arced under her chin on the other. The motion calmed her internal frizziness.

A sleek black car pulled up to the curb, and the driver helped Bliss put her carry-on and dress bag in the trunk. She buckled in next to Emory and they were on their way.

Since their French toast kiss, Bliss hadn't had a chance to speak to Emory. Her office was empty when Bliss made her weekly visit to WW and Partners, with no sign she'd been there that day.

Bliss had sent a text—*hope you're feeling okay*—and received a brief one back—*all good, off-site meetings*. Today Emory wore soft, slim pants and a cashmere wrap sweater, and looked the very picture of a sophisticated woman having a leisurely travel experience, but her heel bounced up and down while she stared fixedly out the window. Bliss wanted to cup her hand over Emory's knee, hold it there, until the shaking stopped. That was what *she* would have needed if she were flying across the country to see someone who made her as emotional as Mari made Emory. After Emory's blowup, and her rapid flight from their kiss, though, Bliss knew she shouldn't. Emory was going to have to say what she wanted.

If she wanted anything from Bliss at all after their contract ended.

One week left.

At the airport, Emory's stress energy transformed into a take-charge attitude, and Bliss realized she was seeing full-on Vice-President Emory Jordan for the first time. Head high, heels clacking, Emory parted the seas of travelers without any need to ask a pardon, and Bliss jogged along in her wake. They went to a counter with no line—apparently Emory was a very fancy person—and Emory took her ID and got them paper passes. She led them to another line that circumvented the main security wait, and they were through in under a minute. Bliss considered the sea of people waiting for the metal detectors, and Emory noticed her bemused expression. "I fly a lot, so they let us cut. Don't worry; I got us here in plenty of time anyway."

Bliss hadn't thought to be worried about being late when she was with Emory. "I haven't flown since I was a little kid, remember. I thought that line was at least three hours long that day."

"It probably was." Their bags piled up at the end of the conveyor belt. Emory checked that they had everything in hand, and Bliss followed her down an escalator and through a corridor lined with shops. "Where did you go?"

"We took a big trip to Florida—" Bliss dodged a young couple running in the opposite direction. "Not long before my dad died. I always wonder if he knew it would be our last trip or if the timing was a coincidence. That's kind of a downer and I'm not feeling down," she added. "I'm excited to be off exploring the world." She felt a smile flit across her face. She *was* excited to see Los Angeles.

Bliss tailed Emory into the line for coffee. Thank goodness. Some of Emory's nervous energy must have transferred to her. A headache was budding at her temples and a shot of caffeine was sorely needed. She ordered a latte with caramel and mocha, and Emory had a flat white. They found a place to stand against the wall while they waited. And waited. And waited some more.

Emory glanced at her phone. "I hope they hurry up. We're boarding—there's time, but we need to go soon. Was that the last time you went on a trip? The plane to Florida?"

"No. My mom and I took the train once in a while, or the bus. I take the bus up to Boston to visit friends sometimes. The train is better." She rolled her spine into the wall. Bliss didn't have any reason for the tightness in her shoulders. *Her* career wasn't riding on an introduction to some tech guy. *Her* ex wasn't getting married and expecting her to bring a date. "I've been on a budget, but last fall, I took the train to Boston and spent the week. Most of my friends from college moved there, so they see each other a lot, and when I come up, we have a—slumber party, I guess, and spend the weekend watching movies and catching up. That time they let me play tourist, and I walked the Freedom Trail most days."

It had been a good trip for Bliss. Unregimented. Lots of nooks and crannies to explore, and she wasn't locked into a schedule. She could stop and sketch or linger over lunch.

"What did you see? I haven't been to Boston since a class trip in high school. Well, not for tourist activities. Only for business." Emory turned her way, and the barista called Bliss's name, so she darted forward to retrieve the cup. After passing it to Bliss, she went back to the counter and stayed there until their order was complete. Then she grabbed her bag and, Emory-style, influenced the masses to move the heck out of their way.

Bliss held her cup level at arm's length so coffee wouldn't slosh out through the lid. Emory was in New Yorker mode, moving at a clip, and Bliss's clip was slower because her legs were shorter. She was panting a little when they made it to the gate. Emory was sleek and unruffled, of course.

Once their boarding passes were scanned, they went down the jetway. They weren't as late as she'd feared; a line of travelers was leaving bags near a door at the end. Bliss sipped her coffee. Despite the wait, it wasn't very hot.

A flight attendant's voice carried out of the plane. She caught something about the doors closing. Emory craned her neck to see, then looked quickly back over her shoulder, checking for Bliss. "I— good. Still there. The trail?"

"Oh, right." Bliss hitched up her dress bag. Slippery thing. Probably because she'd stored her heels in the bottom. "Boston Common, Old North Church, the USS Constitution." She shrugged. The line moved, and she fumbled her cup and bags before catching up to Emory. "A whole lot of graveyards. That spooked me a little— it's hard not to be haunted by the past."

Emory stopped in her tracks and Bliss smacked right into her. Fortunately, she only got a few drops of lukewarm coffee on her own hand. "Sorry. I got caught up."

"My fault," Emory said, turning around. She held Bliss's wrist and dabbed at the spill with a tissue that she conjured as if by magic.

"I see we're touching again," Bliss said wryly.

Emory took a full step backward. "We don't have to—"

"Like we practiced," she responded firmly. "That's all." Bliss lifted her chin toward the end of the jetway, where a pair of flight attendants waited for them. "Let's drop off our stuff and go."

"No, bring it," Emory said. "There's room." She squeezed Bliss's hand briefly, recovered. Then she took their boarding passes and headed to the door.

The plane was huge, with seats on both sides and in the middle. Every seat she could see from the threshold was filled. Bliss

189

looked down the aisle—it went on and on. But instead of heading to the right, and the back, Emory pivoted. Bliss followed her through an airier section of the plane, with fewer seats in the middle, until they stopped near the cockpit. One seat on each side and two together in the middle. *Holy crap.*

Emory parked her carry-on next to one of the window seats and pointed to the one behind it. "That's you. I thought you might rather a window instead of sitting in the middle with me interrogating you the whole trip. Besides, I have to work."

Bliss was sorry not to be sitting with Emory, but she had to admit she was excited to have her own window. She hefted her bag into the overhead bin while Emory took their dress bags to the galley in front along with miniature boxes of fancy chocolate. The flight attendants greeted her enthusiastically and found a place in a closet to hang the bags.

While Emory chatted with the flight attendants, Bliss got settled in. The window revealed workers busy with last-minute preparations, reminding her of ants with harder work to do than dismantling a picnic. Eventually, Emory came back and perched on the wide armrest of Bliss's seat, searching through her giant work bag.

"So you know the staff?"

Emory nodded distractedly. "I didn't stop traveling during the pandemic, so I got to know a lot of them during that time. On a couple of flights, I was alone in the cabin. No one else to upgrade." Whatever Emory was looking for in her bag must have been all the way in the bottom. "The routes from New York to Los Angeles have a lot of jerks on them, trust me, so I try to make sure the flight attendants know there's at least one passenger on their side. Some people think rules don't apply to them. But just because customers have money doesn't mean they're right."

"I like your style." Especially because Emory's world was about power and money, and about who had it to throw around. Being nice wasn't about money at all. "I wish I were that thoughtful."

Emory paused her searching. "Thanks," she said softly. And, "You are." Her lips were unpainted, pillowy and pink. Bliss could have watched her talk about anything with those lips. Jerks in first class. The way of the world. The price of toilet paper and orange juice.

Another passenger came up their aisle, and Emory stepped into Bliss's seat, bending to fit under the bins. Her hair slipped off her shoulder and brushed Bliss's face. Her mouth was so close. Bliss could feel Emory's warm breath in her ear.

Unfortunately, the other passenger was already gone. Emory reseated herself on the armrest, her legs still tangled up with Bliss's, a reminder of their closeness the day she'd come to Bliss's apartment. Bliss was hard pressed not to touch her.

If you were my real fiancée, she thought, *I'd be all over you.* She considered this, and added, *In a respectful way.*

"Aha." Emory was triumphant as she pulled a box out of her purse at last. She handed it to Bliss. "Here you go. For the wedding. It's rented, so don't lose it."

A flight attendant tapped Emory's shoulder. Emory extracted herself from Bliss's seat, following the instructions to sit down and buckle up.

As the plane pushed back, Bliss opened the box. Inside, there was a ring. A sparkling, transparent jewel, bigger than Bliss would have expected, but tasteful, was set in a slim silver band that wrapped around the stone in a way that suggested, abstractly, leaves on a vine. *Surely that is not a diamond.* She didn't know how to tell. Frankly, she didn't care what it was. Bliss slipped it onto her ring finger. The setting caught the light, splintering it into rainbows.

They accelerated and angled toward the sky. She couldn't have chosen a more perfect ring for herself. Any future engagement ring would have a hard time living up to this one. She held her hand over her heart, holding it—holding everything—in place. Bliss tilted her body toward the window, sending rainbows to the bottom of the bin above. She saw Emory stretch toward the colors before they banked and swung away from the sun, and the rainbows flickered and disappeared.

———❧———

Bliss snuggled into her blanket, a glass of white wine in hand, and leaned her forehead against the window. She couldn't get enough of watching the world below. First, they'd flown over the ocean, and around lower Manhattan, and then over some low, wrinkly mountains. She wasn't sure which ones. Then over a patchwork of different colors that slowly changed from green to golden brown. *Don't get used to this.* What would it be like to go on trips with the same person every time, someone to pass you your snacks in the middle seat in the back of the plane, to be your non-relative emergency contact? She dozed off, wine drowsy, until someone used their call button and the *ding* woke her up. When she came back from the bathroom—which was a lot smaller than the last time she'd been on a plane, or she was a lot bigger—the front galley was empty, and she sidled up to the door to look out its miniature window.

Far below, the patches of green and brown had morphed, like a painting crumpled in one hand while the acrylic was wet—not that she'd ever done that in frustration—and a deep shadow wound through the folds. The sight was breathtaking. A world vaster than she'd imagined, more beautiful.

In the cabin, Emory was hunched over her laptop, frowning and muttering to herself, something about "Perhaps in a few weeks, when things settle down, we could discuss a partnership."

Bliss bent over and whispered in her ear. "You're missing it."

Emory disengaged from the laptop screen. "What?"

"You're *missing it*." She leaned all the way across Emory, balancing one hand on the far armrest, and whipped the window shade open. "Missing it," she repeated, and made sure Emory was looking outside before she hoisted herself back to standing. "The Grand Canyon."

The corners of Emory's mouth raised up, fractionally, and she closed her laptop with one hand. Satisfied, Bliss returned to her seat, and it wasn't long before their final descent. The plane had to circle for a while. Bliss caught glimpses of the Hollywood sign, of clusters of skyscrapers, and at last, the Pacific Ocean, vast and blue. Eventually, they glided to a stop at the gate, and soon they were walking out of the terminal into air that smelled like jet fuel and wavered with heat radiating from the asphalt.

There wasn't a lot to see once they were in the car; mostly, Bliss watched other cars passing by while Emory answered her cell. "Jeff gets to call whenever he needs to, even on the weekend," she explained afterward, "because he knows when something is truly an emergency, as opposed to a manufactured emergency."

"Is everything okay?" Bliss asked as they pulled off in a neighborhood her maps app said was the financial district.

"News on a company we both work with. Aerospace. We think—" Emory stopped speaking abruptly. She looked troubled. When her phone vibrated, she shook her head and answered the text, typing furiously.

Emory's expression grew more and more stark. Bliss waited until they were deposited outside a glass-windowed, high-rise hotel to press her. "What's wrong? Are *you* okay? I'm starting to get worried here."

"Sorry." Emory lowered her phone and gave Bliss her full attention. "I—my colleague Jeff and I—work with a company, and...I'm not sure you—"

"Tell me," Bliss insisted.

Emory pinched her shoulder with her free hand like she was trying to work out a stress knot and rolled her arm. "We think there's some embezzlement and mismanagement going on, and we're trying to fix the problem. Not only because it's an investor problem, or a reputation problem, but because it's cheating, and I don't do that. We have to figure out what's going on and how to make it right, and...it's not easy. People who weren't involved will be caught up in whatever happens next. I know this is sensitive territory and I didn't want to upset you."

Bliss's bones were cold in the baking heat of Los Angeles. After a few seconds, she started to warm back up. "It's all right." It was. The bad feelings she associated with money, with her father, dissipated faster than they ever had. Maybe because she trusted Emory to act professionally. Her probation after the painting incident was still in effect, in Bliss's thinking, but Emory had said that she was a woman who kept her word. And so far, she had. But Bliss didn't want to think about Mari or financial shenanigans any more today. She wanted to move on. "So—is this us?"

Emory caught on to the change of subject without a bobble. "Hear me out," she said, breezing through the automatic doors of the hotel into a lobby that seemed to stretch up forever. "This isn't the most happening neighborhood, but you can walk to some things that I thought you might like to see. Though—" She lowered her voice as they got in line at reception. "People don't really walk here. And they get weird when you notice that."

They were next. Bliss stepped to the side while Emory picked up their keys. During the elevator ride, Emory opened the maps app on her phone. "Okay, you're not far from the flower district, and you might like exploring Little Tokyo. Over here"—she scrolled quickly—"is the LA County Museum of Art, people call it *LACMA*—"

Bliss put her hand over the screen and smiled. "This is gonna be great." Her hand was saying *less phone more world*, her heart was saying *kiss her*, her head was saying *let it be*. Her ears were saying *move along*; the elevator doors opened to let them off with a soft chime. Emory exited first and found her room. She gave Bliss the key to the next door.

She put her bag in the corner and walked past the bed to look out her window at the city skyline before knocking on the door that joined her room to Emory's. The answer came quickly.

"Hi, neighbor," Emory said, beckoning her in. Emory's room was a mirror image of Bliss's: a king bed, an upholstered couch, a table, a desk. A closet and bathroom. All of it bigger than Bliss's apartment in New York. "Room okay?"

Bliss confirmed, and Emory suggested a late lunch combined with an early dinner, so they made their way to the hotel's rooftop restaurant and chose a table outside, near the pool. The table umbrella was perfectly positioned to keep them in the shade. Their view was amazing. A bird swooped past but left its droppings on the next table over. *I'm the luckiest. Good omens. Good vibes.*

Emory was still coming up with suggestions for Bliss, apologizing for not having a printed list. "Huntington Beach is great, and Redondo. You could go up to Griffith Park, maybe the zoo. And there are loads of amusement parks, if you're into that."

She slouched in her chair, warm and lazy. "Want to take the day off and go with? I wouldn't mind hearing you scream."

Emory choked on her water.

Oops. "I meant, uh, a rollercoaster ride is probably a good way to blow off steam." Bliss raised her arms to the sky and wiggled her fingers. "You know. *Aaaaah.*"

Coughing, Emory blotted a few stray droplets from her slacks. "I'm on the clock for most of the week." She straightened up as their order, two garlic-and-herb grilled cheeses with tomato and bacon, spicy fries, and watermelon, was brought to the table by a bored waiter. "But maybe Friday afternoon...." She took a bite of her sandwich. "Oh, this is really good."

Bliss dug in. After one mouthful, she knew she was eating the best grilled cheese of her life. On the top floor of a hotel with a view in Los Angeles. With a blisteringly hot, smart woman. Who defied her understanding of how people in business behaved. This was not where she'd expected to be a month ago. And she wouldn't have traded it for anything.

The sun was still up when they headed back to their rooms. Emory had an early meeting, and mentioned jet lag and time zones and other technical things that Bliss didn't feel at all. Her scalp was wide awake. Her legs could run a mile at a gym teacher–approved speed. She stood in front of the closed door connecting their rooms, thinking about knocking on it again.

If she understood Emory, if Emory was serious about nothing happening between them before their thirty-day contract expired...

One week left to go.

Bliss took a long, cool shower in the marble-and-chrome bathroom and wrapped herself in a fluffy robe that she was tempted to steal. She dried her hair. Unpacked her pajamas. Flipped through TV channels with nothing to watch. And she went back to the connecting doors and raised her knuckles, careful to keep from bumping her ring.

Then she crouched down to look under. The lights were off in Emory's room. She spun the engagement ring around her finger. Thinking.

Bliss went to bed. But it was a long, long time before she fell asleep.

seventeen

EMORY'S EYES WERE GRITTY. She'd spent half the night pacing in front of the door that connected her room with Bliss's, and the other half sprawled on the bed, staring at the ceiling. She never slept well the first night in a hotel, she tried to tell herself, but that wasn't true. She always got her best sleep after a westbound flight.

She showered, dressed, and made a sad cup of coffee in the room. Bliss was moving around next door, and Emory wished they had time for breakfast. Bliss might have had a few minutes to spare, but she did not. Her car was already waiting to take her to Glendale for her first meeting of the week.

Brunch with the founders of Authentiskate was followed by another ride to their headquarters in a nondescript office park, where they spent as much time pitching California's weather as they did their business authenticating, buying, and selling designer accessories.

Emory tamped down the urge to say this wasn't her bag—and maybe have the two serious young women who'd reached out to her miss the pun—so after telling them she didn't think they needed venture capital to succeed, and that their market might support a small enterprise competing with other services, but not grow to be one of the state's or even city's largest companies, she spent a few hours going over their business plans and aspirations with them.

Her generosity backfired; construction and an accident left her stuck in traffic for two hours. She should have taken the train.

Back at the hotel, she met Bliss for dinner in the restaurant. No grilled cheese on this menu. Emory decided on salmon and vegetables, and Bliss ordered French onion soup. "Won't you be hungry?" she asked, as she handed her menu back to the waiter.

"Nope," Bliss said. "I went to Union Station and Olvera Street, and I ate everything under the sun."

Under the sun was right; her nose and cheeks were a little pink, and not only from her enthusiasm about what she'd tried, things Emory had heard of but mostly couldn't call to mind in her weary state—horchata, mole, aguachile, chapulines, a freshly made tortilla that "changed her life." Emory listened to the day's adventures as long as she could before excusing herself, exhausted.

Tuesday began, a repeat of Monday, but worse. Emory was groggy and dehydrated, and had a long car ride to Irvine ahead, so no sad in-room coffee, just the realization that the lapel of her blazer was wrinkled, and she had to iron it hastily while her driver waited. There was an accident in Norwalk, and the delay was even longer than the one the night before; she had to call to reschedule for an hour later, ashamed and rueful. She wrote and deleted a half-dozen texts to Bliss. *Where did you go today? Having fun? Send pictures? Did I suggest things you liked? Are you eating delicious things? Am I too nosy?* She sighed and put the phone in her purse. Texting on the road would make her carsick, and she needed to use the drive time to think up things to say to Benjamin Thorston when she met him at the wedding.

And to think up what to say to Mari at all.

But Tuesday got better very quickly. Emory met with a young married couple, a nurse and a programmer, who Beatriz had given her a heads up about. They had designed a healthcare app that put the patient at its center, and that could integrate with small or large practices. Hospitals and doctors would pay a fee for use, but the patients never would, and they would have a comprehensive record to share with their providers.

It was ambitious. It was admirable. And they wouldn't settle for a minimum viable product. "My patients shouldn't have barriers to care," Juan told her, and his wife, Vivian, insisted she would be embarrassed putting out anything less than her best work.

After a quick demonstration on Vivian's phone, Emory decided to spend all of Wednesday with Juan and Vivian to go over their plans in more depth. It had been a while since she'd been pitched an idea that energized her so completely.

This could be her unicorn.

The trip back north went smoothly, and she found Bliss in the bar, sketching flower arrangements based on the glass collection she'd viewed at LACMA. Emory was wired and needed a trip to the hotel gym before she calmed down enough to reschedule her Wednesday meetings to Thursday to make time for Juan and Vivian. Bliss declined dinner, blistered and tired and full of bar snacks, and Emory suggested that she explore Little Tokyo tomorrow if she wanted to stay closer to home base. This time it was Bliss who went to bed early.

Emory, jittery with possibility, ordered a glass of wine for dinner and went to her room to prepare for the next day, wondering if she and Bliss would ever be moving in the same direction at the same time.

Wednesday was everything Emory hoped.

She was focused, exhilarated, at her very best. The only thing more she'd have liked to leave their daylong work session with was a name for the system. They decided that once Vivian had a revised mockup of the system backend, Emory would move things along at WW and Partners under the moniker Record Health until they came up with a name that was a hit with focus groups.

Thursday was the opposite: a string of mind-numbing introductions in the hotel lobby, with stupefyingly boring, underprepared drop shippers, all of whom had probably watched the same get-rich-quick video. Her thoughts kept sliding away, and she regretted not taking Bliss up on her offer to scream her way through a series of drops and barrel rolls. Without malice, she ushered her last appointment out the door mid-afternoon and went up to her room to change out of her suit.

When Emory had packed for the trip, she'd switched to autopilot once the dress for Mari's wedding was zipped into its garment bag. Her suitcase held her usual travel wardrobe: slacks and blouses, knit dresses, sweaters for air-conditioned restaurants, and blazers, but nothing truly comfy.

She felt a pang of regret that she hadn't tucked her yoga pants into her bag or remembered a swimsuit. Of course, on most business trips, there wasn't time for anything besides work and sleep. In the end, she showered and changed into her pinstriped button-down pajama set. She never left town without it; the top could work under a blazer in a pinch.

Emory spent a good hour flipping channels before giving up on television. She opened her laptop and wasted some time clicking around VenturePitchNews for a while, but she couldn't focus on any of the articles or keep her mind on any of the analyses of up-and-coming companies. She sighed and shut the whole thing down. Bliss wouldn't be back yet from whatever she had planned for the day. Emory hated to admit she'd lost track, caught up in the dizzying prospect of finding the project that would win William over, the one that would secure her the promotion at WW and Partners, so she could—

She wasn't sure.

Notch her belt.

Wear her title like a winner's medal.

Be junior partner.

Emory scribbled a note on the hotel stationery, old-school, asking Bliss to join her for dinner. She swung open the door to Bliss's room to slip it under, and came face to face with Bliss herself, one hand stretching to knock.

Her arms were overflowing with cut flowers. Bright gray eyes were visible over an explosion of leaf-green and white, yellow and orange, pink and red. She was carrying a store's worth of inventory. "Flower district?"

"*Taco trucks* and the flower district. I went in all these shops and got ideas, and then I thought I should buy a flower in each one, but the prices were so reasonable I ended up with bouquets, and I tried giving them away to people on the street, and mostly people were very suspicious, I don't blame them, I'd be suspicious too—"

Emory didn't remember deciding to move. Her arm went around Bliss, and she was trying not to squish the flowers, even as stems escaped and scattered around their feet. She parted a valley between them and leaned forward and—

Kissed Bliss on the forehead.

Bliss laughed. "What was that for?" Then she sneezed, twice.

Emory wanted to say: I can picture you walking down the street, handing out flowers, making the world beautiful. But all that came out was "You."

Bliss looked at her eyes, her mouth, her neck. The flowers started to slide from her arms.

And Emory broke the rules.

She kissed her. And kissed her. And kissed her.

Her mouth was so soft. *Slowly.* Emory wanted everything, all at once. But *slowly.* Gentle kiss. She tilted her head, searching for more, nipping Bliss's bottom lip.

Bliss tilted with her, opening her mouth, sucking in the tip of Emory's tongue. There was a gasp, a throaty approval—whose it was, Emory couldn't tell.

She explored. The cupid-bow top of Bliss's lips. The dark mole in front of her ear. A tender spot where the underside of her jaw met her neck. God, her neck, a little salty, sun-warm. She nuzzled her face into the curve of Bliss's shoulder and ran her palm from the knob at the top of Bliss's spine down over each vertebra, listening to her breathe out.

Emory was tightening. The small of her back. Her nipples. The tops of her thighs.

Dating hadn't been like this, in all these years. It had been forever since she'd *wanted* someone. So much that she was breaking all the rules she'd laid out for them both. She couldn't even remember the rules. "Can I—is this—okay?"

Bliss canted her cheek down to rest on Emory's head where it tucked into the collar of her shirt. "What do I keep telling you about how I'm very, very okay with this?"

Emory snorted against the cloth covering Bliss's shoulder. That was...not that sexy. *Oh my god. I am a complete tool.* "Um. Sorry about that. The snort part."

"The only thing you should be sorry about is that you stopped kissing me." Bliss ducked under Emory's chin and twisted them back up. The flowers that had been caught between them fell to the floor, encircling their feet. "And I'm sorry I'm not kissing you right now." Her fingers traced up one pinstripe, over Emory's elbow, and tugged at the lapel of her pajamas until they were face to face again.

Emory could have looked into her gray eyes forever. At the whorl of baby hairs that appeared when she tucked her hair back from her brow. At the thin, white scar on the ridge of her ear. And she closed her eyes and kissed Bliss again anyway.

She felt Bliss's mouth curl into a smile. "That's a start."

"Oh?" Emory placed her forehead against Bliss's. She wanted her closer. "You might have noticed I'm kind of a go-getter. I finish what I start."

Bliss twirled a loose blonde wave around her finger. "Go on."

That was what Emory needed to walk them toward the bed, her knees knocking against Bliss's thighs, until Bliss was right against it. "Let's see if this mattress is as bouncy as the one you have at home."

Laughing, Bliss spread her arms wide and launched herself backward onto the duvet. "Did it work?"

Emory shook her head and lay down beside her. "No pillows went flying." Bliss's short-sleeved aloha shirt, which she had paired with cargo pants and Converse, had ridden up. Emory caressed the creamy skin above her belt, and Bliss rolled toward her, grabbing Emory's hand in her soft one and twining their fingers together.

She hesitated. "Should I stop?"

Bliss's eyes widened. "No! I—I—" She climbed to her knees. "I think I wanted to hold on to you for a second. Make now last longer. That's all." She loosened her grip and tucked Emory's hand under the hem of her shirt. "I want you to touch me."

And Emory took over, inching her way up. Bliss's eyelids fluttered shut when she stroked the skin at the edge of her bra. She grew bolder, holding on gently but firmly, inscribing circles there with the heel of her hand.

Emory sat up, coming to her knees as well. Close again. She kissed the fluttering eyelids, the corner of Bliss's mouth, the hollow at the base of her throat that deepened each time a kiss landed. She kissed down from there, into the arrow of skin that pointed down from her collar toward the buttons of Bliss's shirt, and carefully thumbed them open, one by one, running her tongue behind, rewarded each time by the arch of her back, the tilt of her hips.

She was trembling. To hide her shaking hands, Emory balled Bliss's shirt in her fists and eased it off her shoulders. Her instinct was to hang it in the closet, but sometimes, her instincts were wrong, wrong, wrong. Emory dropped the shirt over the side of the bed.

Next order of business was Bliss's bra. It was blue and minimalist. She traced the thin strap from Bliss's chest over her shoulder, feeling each stitch. This was real. She ringed her arms around and carefully undid Bliss's bra. The tiny *snick* of the hook opening made satisfaction ring through her arms and a deep ache pulse between her legs.

Still shaking. Emory breathed in sharply through her nose. She teased the straps down over Bliss's shoulders, then off her arms. Bliss was everything. Skin lit from behind by afternoon sun. Peach fuzz limning her outline. Dark nipples puckering under her gaze. Under her fingertips.

Where had she left off?

She remembered. Emory bent forward to kiss the last places in the line toward Bliss's bellybutton. She could spend a lifetime exploring Bliss's body, inch by inch, discovering every shiver, every breath, every unashamed wriggle of delight.

And Bliss was having none of it. She coiled her hands into Emory's hair, pulling tight. "Goddamn it, Emory. *Fuck me.*"

Emory whipped her pajama top over her head and her own bra followed. She put one hand on Bliss's shoulder and guided them back down to the bed. They fumbled with Bliss's belt together. Stupid, stupid, stupid. The buckle wasn't the usual kind she wore with trousers, and Emory grew frustrated every second she could have been touching Bliss instead, but finally, it clicked free. Her fingers flew as she wrestled with the snap and zipper of Bliss's cargo pants before tugging them off, both legs at once.

Bliss's underwear matched her bra, azure blue, but in lace, a stark contrast to the utilitarian pants, making Emory's brain buzz with lust. The panties tied at the hips in little bows. How was she supposed to *hurry* when she could tug the ribbons and watch the slow unraveling of the knots against the plane of Bliss's hipbone? How, when she could brush her thumb against the ridge that elicited a whimper, then down the seam at the top of her thigh to where heat radiated?

Bliss was wet, and Emory was throbbing in so many places she wasn't sure she could have named them all if she tried.

She had forgotten how good this could feel. How desperately she wanted to *feel*. How words fell away. Emory dragged Bliss's underwear down her legs and kicked it aside.

She had *almost* forgotten.

But her body remembered.

Bliss groaned. "*Emory.*"

Emory gathered them close. She pressed her nose to the top of Bliss's head and inhaled the lemon of the hotel's shampoo, the salt grit of the day, the faint scent of crushed flower petals. She let out a quiet snicker, no more than a huff of breath. "Okay, okay." And she waited a moment more, reveling in the way their skin felt, in how their breasts touched, and whispered to herself. "I give thanks to the boob, the holy boob."

Bliss had a freckle on the top of one, and she couldn't help herself. Her mouth was there, worshipping and sucking, while Bliss ground forward in search of what she craved.

"Emory. *Please.*"

No more delay when Bliss was begging. Emory slipped her hand down between them and teased into the damp curls at the apex of her thighs. Bliss bent her leg over them both, hissing as Emory caressed the slash of her lips, slid between. She circled Bliss's clit with her thumb, slow at first, then firmer and faster to match the pace of Bliss's rhythmic gasps.

"More." Bliss's ankle urged her on, bearing down against the back of her knee.

More.

Emory obeyed, mirroring the swirls above with a finger at her opening. Bliss was slick, hot, impatient.

"Nnnnnnh—"

Emory froze, waiting for the *n* to become *no*. She would do nothing that Bliss did not deeply desire. But Bliss tilted her hips to fit her silken core over Emory's questing finger. Emory thrust into her, stroking, beckoning her closer and closer to the edge. They rocked together, Emory cradling Bliss in one arm and plunging into her with the other.

She sensed the first fluttering against her fingers and urged Bliss on, though Bliss, moaning, was past the point of hearing encouragement. Tingles washed over her body. She deepened her strokes. "Yes. Bliss, yes."

And Bliss, bathed in the pink evening light, shuddered and cried out wordlessly. Her taut lines collapsed into Emory, and Emory guided Bliss's head to her shoulder and flipped the duvet over them both so she would be cocooned on the way down from the heights.

Bliss's fast breaths eventually came slower, and she snuggled into Emory's collarbone, eyes squeezed shut. Emory smoothed Bliss's hair away from her sweaty forehead and placed a kiss there. "Thank you."

This made Bliss laugh, startled, and look up at her. "For what?"

"For—for showing me. For trusting me." It wasn't nothing to let someone be with you. To be with someone so openly. Not for Emory, anyway. "So—thank you."

Bliss stretched her arms over her head, then let out a long sigh of satisfaction. "That sounds so final. But that's wrong." She took advantage of her position on Emory's chest to flick her tongue over Emory's nipple until it stiffened against her mouth. Then she tugged at the drawstring of Emory's pajama pants, stealing one of Emory's best tricks. "Like I said, that was a start. We're not done."

They were not. Not by seconds. Not by minutes.

Soon Emory was clutching the headboard with one hand and cupping the back of Bliss's head with the other, spread wide, begging even harder than Bliss had. Bliss was everything, every sensation, every emotion.

Bliss. Bliss.

Bliss.

And Emory didn't know if *Bliss* was a name or a feeling or a prayer.

eighteen

BLISS WOKE UP ALONE IN a tangle of sheets, still naked. Her stomach growled. No surprises there; she hadn't had dinner two nights in a row. Emory had found a sawdust-flavored protein bar in her bag when Bliss was hungry in the overnight stretch when room service wasn't delivering. It had been completely gross, but she'd been grateful for the fuel when, in the wee hours, she and Emory found themselves awake and aroused, and they'd had the sleepy, slow sex that Bliss had been too frenzied to wait for the first time around.

She grabbed her phone and flipped the camera for a selfie. That was real, wasn't it? They'd had sex? That *Emory* had initiated? That felt—right? Bliss touched her face, her kiss-swollen lips.

No.

You didn't touch somebody like that and limit the description to *sex*. She was different now. All of her body was different now.

Yes, what they'd done was sex. And what they'd done was making love, too.

Bliss rolled to her side, contemplating this. In the hours before dawn, while she slept, it must have rained, washing away the haze over the mountains. The sky was clear and beautiful. Her kind of vibe.

She was supposed to get up. This was her last free time in Los Angeles. Instead, she wanted to spend the whole day in bed with Emory, pretending they were really engaged, that they didn't have to spend tomorrow at Mari's wedding and fly home the morning after. She stretched, arms and legs reaching for the corners of the bed, nothing covering her except a corner of the sheet that draped across her hips.

Emory came through from the adjoining room, dressed in her pajamas again and pushing a cart with covered plates. Her hair was sleek and wavy on one side, and the other was a tangled nest that stuck out from her head, and Bliss was certain she hadn't looked in a mirror at all. She smiled, and Emory smiled back, and suddenly, Bliss felt naked in a metaphor kind of way instead of a literal one. She pulled the loose sheet into a makeshift toga.

The room service cart had a sticky wheel, and after a couple of tries at parallel parking it next to the bed, Emory lifted the trays onto a clear space next to a pile of duvet and whipped off the silver

214

plate covers. "Voilà! Breakfast. Let's see if their French toast is half as good as yours."

Breakfast in bed was completely agreeable. They sat cross-legged, sharing the French toast and a cheese-filled omelet. Bliss chewed, and swallowed, and stabbed her fork into a sliced strawberry garnish, and tried to figure out how to ask for what she wanted in the light of day.

Emory beat her to asking questions. "What's on the agenda?"

She sipped her coffee, contemplating. "I made it to everything nearby on my must-see list. I need to pack—" Bliss startled at the numbers on the alarm clock's display. "Check out is in an hour."

"We get an extra hour because I have a lot of frequent stay points with the chain." Emory leaned to look over the side of the bed where the floor was scattered with yesterday's flowers. "And that's lucky for me," she added ruefully. "I have chores."

Bliss considered the flowers a happy sacrifice to everything that had happened afterward. Before she could bring the conversation back around, Emory changed the subject. "Are you a mountains person or a beach person?"

Bliss shook her head. "I don't have my questions paper! You go first."

"Everywhere, but I'd rather the mountains." Emory waited for Bliss's answer. "I'll remember even if it's not written down."

Surely geographical preferences weren't make or break. She answered truthfully, "Everywhere, but I'd rather the beach."

"Then let's go to Santa Monica?" Emory raised her eyebrow and pointed her fork at the last bite of omelet.

Bliss wasn't sure which question she was supposed to answer. She wanted both. And Emory's suggestion didn't make sense. "Don't you have meetings?"

Emory's lips curled up in a pleased, catlike smile. She looked both ways dramatically and then held a cupped hand up to emphasize her whisper. "I canceled."

Maybe—maybe they could— Bliss flopped backward and crossed her arms behind her head. "Jealous of my vacay, huh?"

The joke hung in the air. Emory folded her hands into her lap. "I thought we could spend the day together." She reached into her pocket for her phone and started swiping and tapping, all business.

"All right. That gives us a chance to finish up our questionnaire," Bliss said, retreating to the land governed by their contract.

The world didn't change in one night.

Then Emory tilted her phone toward Bliss, showing her the logo of a rental agency. "We can get the car in an hour."

Bliss's heart leaped. "Better not shower together or we'll be late."

Emory blushed and rolled her eyes, and Bliss loved it. She leaned in for a kiss and got the tiniest brush of one in return against her cheek. "You're right." Emory stole the last bite of eggs and sashayed to her room, calling over her shoulder, "Better hustle!"

———❧———

At a quarter to noon, Bliss tucked a blossom into the front of her sundress and another into the knot of Emory's ponytail. They checked out of the hotel and rolled their suitcases to the portico, where a driver from the car rental agency waited with a cherry-red convertible.

"*Em-o-ry.*" Bliss couldn't say her name without drawing out every syllable. This was all too much.

"What?" She signed the paperwork and popped the trunk. Their bags fit inside, barely. "I can use it for the weekend and drop it at the airport on Sunday. It's practical," Emory said, so nonchalantly that as Bliss buckled herself into the passenger seat, she wondered if Emory was enjoying herself or if the car was to impress Mari. But when Emory pushed a button, grinning with delight as the top rolled down, Bliss's suspicions dissolved.

Twenty minutes later, they were sitting on the freeway westbound, but some of the fun had worn off. Traffic was at a standstill and no wind whipped through their hair. Bliss fiddled with the radio. Every station played ads. The Bluetooth didn't work right, and all of their useful cords were packed away in the trunk. The sun beat down. Exhaust fumes filled the air.

It was a bad vibe. Bliss tried to remember that bad vibes weren't bad omens. She leaned her arm on the car door and a motorcycle zoomed past, inches away. Bliss tucked herself back into her seat.

The best way to get rid of bad vibes was to sweep them away. But instead of asking her questions—are you nervous about the wedding, what did last night mean to you, what happens to us when this contract is over—Bliss decided to live in their sunshine bubble a little longer. She pointed to the nearest exit. "Get off here."

Emory frowned. "We're not even close!"

Bliss waved her on and directed her to Santa Monica Boulevard, which her maps app said would take them all the way to the beach, and, bonus, was part of Route 66. They passed salons and cell phone stores. Dentists and laundromats. A movie prop shop. A car wash.

Empty industrial buildings gave way to the polished backdrop of West Hollywood and banners for upcoming Pride events. A siren blared and they came to a halt while fire engines exited the station ahead.

"Road trip. Where would you go?"

Bliss considered. "I want to go to Maine, but that's only about a day's drive from Brooklyn. Maybe across Canada, one end to the other. Touch both oceans. You?"

"North to south along the coast here. I like the idea of being on the edge, land on one side, water on the other. Seeing the moon while the road spools out ahead of me." Emory was quiet for a few blocks. "Karaoke song."

Easy. "Moves Like Jagger."

"That was not what I expected." Emory checked the mirror and went around a truck blocking the lane. A crane extended from the back and a huddle of workers watched as a sign was hoisted onto a building—more pedestrians than Bliss had seen in blocks.

"I picked it out when I was a teenager. Luckily, nobody can resist the chance to sing along with the *oohs*, so it's a good one for crowd participation." Bliss wished she had thought to tuck her questions paper in her purse. "Okay, I am having a really hard time imagining you at karaoke."

Emory laughed. "You would be right. I've never been. I can't carry a tune, so it's for the best."

Bliss's turn. "What would you change about how you grew up?"

The question made Emory fall silent for so long that Bliss wondered if she'd heard her ask it. Finally, she said, "I wish my parents had asked me questions like this." She didn't say more.

Bliss had already told Emory her worst memory of growing up, over and unchangeable, so she asked another question. "Forgive or forget?"

"Forget," Emory answered immediately. "Actually, I don't know. But I suppose I would want to move on, and that doesn't require forgiveness, does it? If you can put something or someone out of your mind, they can't take up space in your brain. Or— maybe I don't know how forgiveness works. Or maybe it's a different kind of letting go, but it seems like a very big word, for very big problems."

A stray dog, mangy and growling, ran into the street from between two parked cars. Emory slammed on the brakes, and her right hand flew up, pressing Bliss against her seat like she was a precious package. The dog snapped at the front fender and disappeared across the road. "That was close," Emory said.

Bliss clasped her hand over Emory's. Emory was a careful driver. She'd kept them safe. Whatever she wanted to forget instead of forgive, Bliss would support. "Forgive. I would prefer to be asked for forgiveness, but I'm not going to go find that dog. I forgive it for running out into the street and I hope it never does that again."

A car came up behind them and honked, gesturing. Emory glared into the rearview mirror at the offending driver. "And I'm going to fight the urge to flip that guy off and forget all of this."

Bliss squeezed Emory's hand again and set it back on the steering wheel. "Pedal to the metal. But, like, speed limits pedal and safety metal."

Emory complied. The street soon widened, with a divider of palm trees in the middle, taking them through Beverly Hills, which Bliss hated on sight, but in a hot, bored sort of way instead of her usual rancor at anything that smelled too much like money, too much like a giant sign reading KEEP OUT. The second she realized they'd crossed over to what the map said was Century City, she felt her shoulders relax. This place had the tiniest bit of scruff around the edges—weeds growing in among the landscaping—and a shopping mall with stores she could probably go into without feeling small. *Much better.*

Eventually, they got to Santa Monica proper. A soft haze filled the sky and the air changed. Bliss couldn't have said how she knew, exactly, but they were near the ocean. They found a parking garage, and after a ten-minute struggle—the top on the car didn't close up with the same button that folded it down—they were on the promenade.

Bliss couldn't have cared less about the mall or the chain stores. She dutifully followed Emory in and out of a few places, and Emory noticed her—well, she hoped her attitude came across as *politeness*. After that, they window-shopped, Emory gravitating to soft, neutral-toned workwear and Bliss to bright patterns and geometric shapes. A design-job nightmare, but it wasn't a problem for her off-duty brain to combine the two aesthetics into a mental inspiration board.

What stopped Bliss in her tracks were the street performers. There was a troupe of kids jumping rope and doing tricks. A man impersonating a famous singer with a shiny sequined glove. A pair playing a zither and a flute, but not harmoniously. A woman holding so still that Bliss wasn't sure if she was a mannequin or not (until she sneezed). "Just like in New York. But our buskers are different."

Later, they walked along the waterfront. Bliss slipped her hand beneath Emory's, and Emory's fingers tangled in hers. There was nothing else Bliss needed today, not with Emory at her side and the red sun sinking toward the sea.

They went down to the beach, not really dressed for the sand, but Bliss stood in the water barefoot, lacy waves wrapping around her ankles. "I've never touched the Pacific before," she said, and Emory put her arm around Bliss's waist like she was better than any ocean.

They climbed back up from the sand to the pier and walked to the end, where a massive, glowing Ferris wheel rotated. Bliss was sure her eyes were emoji hearts. "It's solar powered," she said, making her case. Emory looked up at the wheel, dubious, but she lived in a nest in the sky. She could handle it. Bliss dragged her into the line.

By unspoken agreement, they sat facing the water. The sun was a half-circle, waiting, Bliss thought, for them to go up before it went down. A breeze picked up as they were carried around the wheel. Emory rubbed her arms. "I didn't think it would be this chilly."

"We'd better snuggle for warmth or we'll die of hypothermia," Bliss added. She made good on her hyperbole, ducking under Emory's elbow. Her head fit nicely against Emory's shoulder, and Emory's chin grazed her forehead. They swung with the movement of the wheel, each sway tightening Emory's arm around her. Bliss felt a little guilty for causing Emory's stress, but only a little. She liked the squeeze.

The wheel boarded its load of passengers and they sped up, floating over the top and down again. The sun slipped away, and they were bathed in the surreal glow of neon lights. Bliss burrowed her face into Emory's shoulder and pretended the ride would last for hours. Days.

Days like this, long and hot and simple. Nothing to do besides wake up together and wander a neighborhood and see new things, ask new questions. Like the one on the tip of her tongue. "What's your perfect day?"

Emory took a slow breath in that Bliss could feel against her side. "Perfect? Hmm. It's not sitting in traffic, or almost hitting a dog, or..." A flock of gulls passed between them and the last sliver of sunshine, too far away for their cries to be heard over the waves and the soundtrack of the pier. "I haven't had a perfect day yet. But when I do, I think it ends something like this."

They made the drive to Malibu in the dark, Emory at the wheel, with the top raised against the cooling night air. The trip was less than an hour in total, but it was long enough for Emory to contemplate tomorrow's wedding and to notice the tension in her biceps. It was all the driving, she decided. She didn't have to drive except on work trips when it wasn't practical to get a car or take public transport, so her muscles weren't used to paying attention for so long. That had to be it.

"Turn right in four hundred feet," her phone commanded, and she did, following a steep, winding road.

She thought Bliss was sleeping, but on the first curve, Bliss clutched the door handle tightly. Emory eased off the gas. The last thing Bliss deserved was feeling unsafe. Unsafe around *her*. The person who broke her own rules. The person who couldn't even think about that right now. "Sorry."

"S'okay," Bliss replied. She did sound sleepy, which comforted Emory a little. Emory wasn't taking the curves too fast for them both. Hopefully.

But they were both brought alert as the resort entrance came into view. A blockade was set up and cars waited in line to pass. Emory inched forward. A swarm of security surrounded the car and she rolled down her window.

A burly man in a dark suit approached. "Identification, please. Both of you."

Their IDs were checked, flashlights were shone in their faces, and their names were spoken into a radio before they were signaled to move along. Emory steered them into a sweeping driveway and parked in front of the resort entrance.

The Spanish colonial–style building loomed over them, more imposing than the photos online had prepared her for. It was lovely—softly lit, landscaped to perfection—though what she could see was blocked by a cadre of staff. Several loaded a family and luggage onto golf carts, headed toward villas that Emory had noticed on the resort map; others huddled together or directed cars to the curb. A valet took Emory's keys and a bellhop whisked their luggage away.

Emory looked at Bliss, who was taking a discreet selfie next to a bougainvillea in vibrant pink bloom. "Do you mind if we go right up? I'm feeling a little off." She touched a hand to her stomach. Maybe she'd had too much Ferris wheel.

"Emory? Bliss? I'm Jessica." A young woman with shiny dark hair and a sleek black dress offered her hand, then took quick photos with her iPad. "I can take you to your room."

"We need to check in—" Emory began, but Jessica held her off.

"Marilee and Benjamin have handled all of the check-in details for guests, so we can skip going to the desk." Jessica led them through the lobby to a bank of elevators—incredibly slow ones, it seemed—and escorted them to a double-doored room on the fourth floor, where the bellhop was already waiting with their bags. After confirming that the key cards she held worked, Jessica bid them goodnight.

They followed the bellhop into the room, and Emory dug in her purse for a few dollar bills. "No need," the bellhop said, holding up a hand as he backed out of the room. "Marilee and Benjamin have taken care of everything. Have a pleasant evening."

Everything, including providing the staff with a script, it seemed.

Emory wasn't sure she liked having all her expenses paid. The irony. She hoped Bliss found their contract amusing instead of patronizing.

Bliss was laughing and flinging wide a set of French doors that led onto a balcony. Beyond her silhouette, the full moon inscribed a path across the ocean and onto a wide lawn where an army of workers was setting up chairs in neat rows. "This is great, future wife!" she exclaimed, and went outside.

"I made a reservation for two queen beds," Emory said, to be clear. This one was big—maybe the largest she'd stayed in—dominated by a four-poster bed hung with gauzy white curtains. There was more than enough room for a sitting area, a dining table for ten, a wide-open space with tastefully arranged yoga mats, and a wet bar. Through a half-open door, she glimpsed a spa bathroom that also appeared to be bigger than was truly necessary.

Emory dumped her purse on the dining table. In the center was champagne in a bucket of ice and a platter of fruit and cheese with a note tucked underneath. It read, in script handwriting that was definitely not Mari's:

Eat. Drink. Be merry, baby.
Wanted you to have the best because you were
always the best. —M

She put the note in her purse. Bliss called over her shoulder, "Come out here! It's so nice." And Emory plastered on a smile and went out to the balcony.

Out to pretend they were engaged for a little while longer.

nineteen

A LITTLE TIPSY, A LITTLE sun-spent, and sated with cheese and bites of fruit, Bliss collapsed face-first into the bed. Emory stood at the open balcony doors a little longer, listening to the breaking waves, watching the staff finish lining up rows of chairs before they disappeared and turned out the lights. Eventually, she slipped under the duvet with Bliss, who curled against her side in the darkness and kissed her neck before going motionless with slumber.

Emory wished she could sleep like that. Her mind was busy and blank at once.

So awake.

She shouldn't have slept with Bliss. No matter how satisfying it had been. It wasn't ethical.

But it *felt* right.

Nevertheless, there were supposed to be rules. Rules that Emory had set to keep everyone clear about their arrangement, even if Bliss said she didn't feel pressured. Her consolation was that there was only tomorrow to get through, and the flight home, and then their engagement would be over. Paid. Done.

Bliss would be gone.

That was a bleak thought. And inaccurate. Bliss would still come by the office to water the plants. They could stay friends.

At least the memory of Bliss moaning her release kept her mind off the wedding.

The wee hours passed, and Emory must have slept, because she was startled by the sound of cardstock being slipped under the door. Bliss rubbed her arm and got up to report that it was a list of activities, and her enthusiasm was so genuine that Emory sent her off for yoga and horseback riding with the excuse of having to work for a while since she'd taken Friday off.

Bliss, dubious, let her be. And she *did* have to work. Emory washed, dried, and curled her hair, which was a lot of annoying work. She practiced her introduction. "Hello, Benjamin. Nice to meet you. I'm Emory, an old friend of—"

She rubbed salve into her lips. "Hi, it's Emory Jordan. Congratulations."

Emory really didn't care if she met Benjamin Thorston or not. If she managed to connect him to WW and Partners, he'd be another one of her business associates. Maybe he'd be memorable. Maybe he'd be boring. It didn't matter what she said to him as long as it was pat and easy. "I understand we have something in common besides Mari."

Seeing Mari again would be harder. She leaned close to the mirror and poked the pores on her cheeks. The tiny lines near her eyes and mouth. Emory dug through her makeup bag for face cream and dabbed it on. "It's been years."

Little pats of moisturizer under her eyes. "Hi, how are you? This is Bliss...."

A dab more around her nostrils. "It's been a while. Looking good!"

Everything she said sounded stupid. Every expression in the mirror looked stupid. Profoundly, inescapably stupid.

Emory wrapped herself in a fluffy bathrobe and forced down a protein bar, because hell if she was going to order a club sandwich from room service and have it charged to Mari. A double-decker club sandwich and fries. And cheesecake. She shoved the menu deep into a drawer so she wouldn't be tempted and promised herself that she could have whatever she wanted as soon as she left this irritatingly perfect hotel.

In the afternoon, Bliss returned, hot and dusty, and Emory finished her makeup while Bliss showered and dressed in the long, gold dress she'd chosen. Emory admired her combination of vintage style and edgy hair. She'd never pull it off herself. It was enough trouble to worm into her shoes and shapewear.

The one thing she couldn't quite do was get into her dress alone, so Bliss zipped her up and put a warm hand on her back.

God, she was probably clammy. "I still think nobody's going to be looking at the bride when they could be looking at you," Bliss said, an echo of their shopping trip weeks ago.

Emory squeezed Bliss's shoulder. Awkward. Arm's length. "Thank you."

She didn't know what else to say. She had practiced all of her formal introductions, but had never practiced *I don't deserve you, I know this is ending, I don't even know what to wish for.* So she tucked the rhinestone-trimmed clutch that Dana had picked out under her arm, shook her hair over her shoulder, and checked for loose threads in the full-length mirror near the closet.

Then she took Bliss by the hand and headed out for the wedding, determined to be that woman who was indeed living her best life.

Her best life began with waiting for the elevator. Bliss hummed softly and swung their joined hands, but Emory craned her neck, looking for the stairs. Just as she spotted the exit sign, well down the corridor, a *ding* announced the elevator's arrival. The doors opened, revealing a car stuffed to the max with giant men in tuxedos along with a petite blonde woman in head-to-toe silver sequins.

"Bliss!" the woman exclaimed, and stuck her arm out to block the doors from closing. "We can fit you! Squish over, everybody. Let's go, let's go!"

"Katie, hi!" Bliss wedged herself roughly into the car like she was going to be left behind by a subway at rush hour, and Emory sucked in her everything and made it into the elevator as the doors shut, scraping across her backside. She was touching *way* too many people she didn't know, especially a man even taller than she was, and she kept her eyes carefully trained on his bow tie and tried not to think about how his thigh aligned uncomfortably with hers. It was better to hold still than risk getting closer.

Katie continued chattering, loudest in the overfull car. "This is Bliss. We went horse riding this morning. Bliss's first time and she was a natural."

"And this is my fiancée, Emory,"

This shut the petite woman up completely for about five seconds. "Emory—"

She was interrupted by a deeper voice. "Are you Emory Jordan?"

Emory looked up at the man against whom she was pressed so intimately.

Benjamin Thorston.

Bliss carried on cheerfully in an echo chamber a million miles away. Emory heard her say, distantly, "Emory works in venture capital."

"Oh, interesting. I mean, I know. I know..." He trailed off in the way that told Emory he knew her name already. "I've been thinking about getting into investing in other people's companies," Benjamin said. Up close, he had unnaturally white teeth, perfectly swept-back blond hair, chiseled features, flawless skin. Mari was the movie star, but Benjamin would have turned Emory's head if her head turned that way. "Yes. That's what I'm considering."

"Let me give you my card. I'm happy to have a chat—" Emory instinctively raised her handbag arm to dig through her clutch and managed to smack Benjamin in the crotch. A grimace of pain flickered across his face. "Or maybe later." Emory rested the clutch against her bodice. Dear god. "Busy day for you and Mari."

The elevator doors opened and they spilled out into the lobby. Benjamin stood back to let the rest of the group exit first. She waited to say what she was supposed to say. "Congratulations. My best wishes to you and Mari."

Benjamin nodded. He opened his mouth like he wanted to say something, and nodded again at the ceiling instead of at her.

The petite blonde, face full of concern, gave her a tight smile and a wave while she steered him away. "Nice to meet you, Emory. Maybe see you later, Bliss. C'mon, bro. Photographer's waiting."

"I can take your card," said one of the men from the elevator, who introduced himself as Benjamin's assistant. Emory traded cards with him quickly and as soon as the assistant was out of sight, she looked around for somewhere to collapse.

Bliss steered Emory to a velvet settee and disappeared while Emory contemplated the wave pattern in the carpet. After Emory counted six pairs of open-toed sandals, four pairs of shiny dress shoes, and three boring black pairs that likely belonged to hotel staff pass through her field of vision, Bliss returned with a plastic cup of liquid that tasted like it had been steeping cucumber peels in a swamp.

The fanciest lobby water invariably tasted the worst. Emory drank it anyway, listening to the pulse in her ears fade into the background.

"I guess Katie from my horse ride this morning is Katie, Benjamin Thorston's—sister, probably. Relative for sure. I would have warned you if I'd figured that out in advance," Bliss said, in soft tones barely audible over the bustle of wedding guests pouring out of the elevators.

"It was always going to be weird," Emory said. And now the part where she met Benjamin was over. She was supposed to feel better. Did she feel better? She could hear. She could breathe. "I don't have to do that again."

She could stand on her own two feet. She could hold Bliss's hand. They joined the flow of guests to a lavish garden of trimmed hedges and water features. Waiters circulated through the crowd offering canapés Emory couldn't identify and trays of sparkling drinks. Bliss snagged them two glasses of seltzer with lime. "For something non-alcoholic to hold," she explained.

Emory was grateful. They strolled through the garden, which thronged with guests enjoying the cocktail hour in the hazy light that drew a line between afternoon and evening. Bliss nudged her. "Let's play a game. Spot the celebrity."

"I hardly know any celebrities!"

"Same," Bliss confessed. "But I think that guy over there has a talk show." She pointed the rim of her glass discreetly at a balding man with a round head who Emory was certain worked in accounting somewhere.

Ah. She got it. A game. "The guy next to him, tweed jacket. Serial killer."

"Wow, *gasp*." Bliss put the tips of her fingers over her smile. "And the white woman in the, uh, appropriative outfit. Famous actress with her own line of sketchy wellness products. Also a serial killer, but not on purpose."

Emory chuckled and searched for her next story. "That woman, over by the square arch without any vines. The one with dark brown skin and the froofy yellow dress. She's a pop star whose latest single is at the top of the charts and she's mad she wasn't asked to perform at the reception."

Bliss squinted. "I think she actually *is* a pop star."

"Oh." Emory drained her seltzer.

A low bass thump started up, blasting from speakers they couldn't see. Curious, they followed the sound and the gaggle of guests to the main garden, where ushers beckoned them to take their places for the ceremony. Wrangling the crowd was no small job, and Emory and Bliss both were more than a little tired of their folding seats before the modern party music switched to more traditional pieces. Bliss leaned back on two chair legs and Emory resisted the impulse to right her. "What do you think, flower expert?"

"It's nice enough. Impressive in scope." Bliss tipped forward to the correct and safe position in her chair, which brought Emory relief, but not enough—her stomach was jumping. "The pink flowers look washed out next to the orange and yellow. They'd look better if they were equally saturated, for this palette. The setup's not my style, but it's also not my wedding." She wriggled in her chair, folding her skirt around her legs. "If it were, I'd pick different chairs. What do you think? Everything you expected?"

It was, she had to admit. Sort of. So far, the experience was a lot more restrained than Mari's imagined wedding had been back in the day. "Mari wanted to get married at sunset. And I think—"

What she thought was cut off by the strident notes of a not-so-serious current hit about getting married, and when Emory turned to see the wedding party, she glimpsed the current hit's suave singer performing live on a raised stage. Her thoughts about restraint had been premature.

First down the white carpet came the parents and grand-parents, then a string of bridesmaids and groomsmen, a poodle ringbearer, and neither last nor least, two girls—Emory recognized them as child actresses on some sitcom with a title she couldn't remember—strewing deep red rose petals.

The music changed. They stood for the bride, who wore a veil that shadowed her face and trailed behind her. Emory couldn't see beneath it, maybe because of the layers of tulle or maybe because her eyes were weirdly wet. Helicopters flew overhead, muting the sound of whatever the bride and groom vowed to each other as the sun slipped into the ocean beyond. Bliss held Emory's hand. Her palm sweated. A tear got in her mouth.

There was applause. The officiant made an announcement that Emory tuned out as she watched the groom kiss the bride. Suave recording star started up again. Bliss bent down and found small boxes under their seats, and they opened them, releasing dozens of butterflies as the wedding party retreated.

The ushers worked their magic, herding the crowd around the far side of the main hotel to an alley of booths. Some offered old-fashioned carnival games, others were set up with props for selfies, and still others offered miniature hot dogs and cotton candy. A carousel rotated idly in the distance. The whole thing was as extravagant as Mari had always wanted—and as Emory hadn't.

She marched up to the nearest booth and whipped a softball at a pyramid of milk bottles. Two strikes, and the third ball hit the stack. The top bottle clattered to the floor.

Bliss came up next to her and put a hand to the small of her back. "You okay?"

"Trying to win the prize," she said, through gritted teeth. She was at a beautiful wedding. She wasn't stressed.

Bliss looked at the plush toys hanging from the top of the booth with her wide gray eyes. The nearest one, a snake, was coming apart at the side seam. A wad of polyester peeked out. "You could buy something better than these stuffies, you know."

"That's not the point." Emory stepped aside for another guest, calculating her wait for a second turn, but a group of people Emory was starting to think of as "wedding logistics" infiltrated the carnival to check people's faces against photos on their tablets. A worker with a name tag reading MALIBU ELITE WEDDINGS had Emory and Bliss pose for a picture while another worker consulted a list and led them directly to seats in what Emory assumed was the hotel's largest ballroom.

The banquet was another level up from the carnival. Emory and Bliss were seated in plush chairs where their names were embroidered on cards with rose-gold thread, handed menus for a multi-course meal, and treated to the mumbling tones of a speech from the best man, who was apparently using a microphone for the very first time.

Glittering, silk-bedecked stilt walkers traversed the room, unfurling wings and breathing fire (which made Emory nervous, given all the people and all the drapery) while servers laid bowls of soup adorned with gold leaf underneath the enormous bouquets that doubled as lamps at each table. Aerialists uncurled from the ceiling with bottles of water and wine. Emory realized that the mirrored accents on the vases were positioned to let you see yourself and also check out the people behind you.

Mari and her groom, and their wedding party, reigned from a dais where wine flowed freely and the laughter was audible. Emory thought, for a brief moment, that Mari's eyes locked with hers, but Mari turned to Benjamin and clinked their glasses together. She shook her head at herself; there was no way Mari would find her in this crowd, in this overstuffed, overdramatic room.

They tasted a multitude of small plates and were eventually served the fish course, Pacific salmon wrapped in pastry with farm-fresh organic vegetables. The suave recording star crooned the happy couple through their first dance, a swirling waltz in a circle of performers that ended with one of the aerialists shooting a flame-tipped arrow through a hoop and igniting a heart-shaped display, sending the crowd into cheers.

It was a lot. Emory traded the fish for a plate of lamb and pushed its accompanying couscous into a square with her spoon while the bride and groom cut their wedding cake—a monstrosity of a cake, layers upon layers, flowers and jewels and fondant—with a sword.

Emory wasn't a big fan of cake.

Cutting pieces for hundreds of guests wasn't a quick task for the catering staff, and after a while, the bravest guests found their way to the dance floor and others started slipping out the side doors for a smoke or yet another chance at the carnival. "I'm going to the bathroom. Right back," she shouted over the din.

Bliss was halfway through her lamb. She reached out a hand to Emory's elbow. "We can leave. I'm just eating things because people keep putting food in front of me. And because it's delicious," she added, stabbing another bite of lamb with her fork.

"No, really, right back. Stay." Emory tucked her napkin next to her plate and her clutch behind the cushion of her chair. She winked exaggeratedly, which probably made her look like she had something in her eye. "I'm sure the real fun is yet to come. As is dessert."

Bliss didn't laugh, but she let Emory walk away without argument.

Going to the restroom took her a good ten minutes because of the shapewear, and when she was done, she washed her hands twice, listening to the drunken gossip of some women who Emory eventually surmised were wives of Benjamin's associates. Thankfully, the gossip was about their own lives and not Mari's, but Emory was curious nonetheless. How did Mari and Benjamin meet? What was he like after hours?

What did he have that Emory didn't, besides an extra couple dozen boatloads of money?

Emory walked past the ballroom and farther down the corridor to where signage announced executive boardrooms. One had its doors open, and Emory stepped inside, thinking to adjust the right leg of her shapewear, which was hitched up and twisted. Weak perimeter lighting illuminated a stack of boxes in the corner, a few rose petals on the floor, and scraps of ribbon and tissue on the table. All the chairs had been shoved into another corner of the room. Whatever project was being staged in here had recently made a hasty exit through the open French doors at the other end of the room. In fact, someone was lingering in the shadows beyond, and Emory was suddenly glad she hadn't rucked her skirt up to fix things. "Hello. Sorry, just wandering around," she called out.

Mari stumbled over the threshold in her wedding dress, trailing her train in a knot behind herself. She had a goblet of wine in one hand and a flowery hair comb in another. "Oh." Mari laughed. "Went out for some air and got lost."

Emory said, "Congratulations," before realizing that Mari was beyond *tipsy* and living in the realm of *solidly inebriated*.

Mari took three meandering steps forward and reached for Emory's left hand. She contemplated the engagement ring there, and Emory looked at Mari's red-rimmed green eyes, at her carefully arranged blonde hair, at the bare shoulders she'd massaged for her so many nights. Mari was thinner now, sharper. Her forehead was smooth and unlined in a way that Emory perceived as unnatural. The price of celebrity. But she was still Mari. And Emory didn't know what to say.

"I wasn't sure you'd come, Em." Mari rubbed her thumb over Emory's knuckles clumsily, knocking the gemstone of the ring to one side. "Since you're getting married yourself, these days."

Emory nodded. She was getting married until midnight, then she was flying home in the morning and taking her rented engagement ring back to the jeweler for a refund on the deposit. Even though it was a perfect fit without any adjustment needed. Emory wondered if she'd miss seeing the glint when she moved her hand. "These days. Mari, I—"

Mari swayed forward and put a finger to Emory's lips. "Shhh. I am *sooooooo* glad you came. I wanted to tell you." She gulped her wine, and Emory wanted to take the glass away from her. No good would come of drinking more, and whatever performance Mari wanted to put on, she didn't need the booze. Emory could tell when Mari was acting, wasted or not.

"I wanted to invite you, tell you, because I wanted to apologize to you, all this time." Mari paused to stifle a hiccup. "Well, maybe not all this time. We both know that. But I want to apologize to you now. I shouldn't have put it off."

Emory wanted to believe that Mari had been thinking for years about how they'd ended things. She'd known her so well, and now, the idea that she didn't know Mari anymore—Mari never wanted to *say* she was sorry—brought her brain to a halt. "You're apologizing for the way you broke up with me."

Mari's mouth fell open, revealing more even, white teeth than she'd had during their college years. Emory tried to focus. The outside was not the inside. Erasing imperfections was part of the job for an international superstar. The Mari she knew would have been all in on cosmetic work. But Emory couldn't help remembering that she'd suffered the fallout of Mari's ambitions.

"No, no." Mari tried to set her wineglass on the table but missed. On her second try, she set it on its side, slowly, and it wobbled in a half-circle. "I mean. I mean actually." She put her hands on her cheeks, then put them, overwarm and sweaty, on Emory's, holding her in place. "Actually, I'm sorry for saying yes to you." Her eyes welled with tears.

241

Emory reached up and put her hands over Mari's. She hated it when Mari cried. Real tears or fake ones, it didn't matter. Tears of her own threatened to spill over.

"I didn't want to marry you," Mari sobbed. "I didn't know what it meant to be married back then. But we'd been unhappy, Em, you were so unhappy. I wanted to say yes so you'd be happy, at least one of us would be happy. And then it got harder and harder. I kept thinking you'd figure it out when I left."

Creeping cold spread through Emory's chest, like she'd taken some cheap, minty heartburn relief medicine. She couldn't hold it in any longer. Emory cried, gasping, wet. "You never loved me. You let me *think* you loved me."

"*Nooooo,*" Mari moaned. "I loved you. I just didn't love you in the way I needed, the way *you* needed, to marry you." She turned her face up to the ceiling and squeezed her eyes shut, sending a waterfall of tears over her cheeks. "I wasn't ready to love anybody like that back then. Not even you."

"All these years, you let me think—" Resentment, mean and long-held, sent splinters out from the iceberg in Emory's heart. "You should have told me the truth when you left so that I could move on. And you are perfectly ready to love rich, handsome, famous Benjamin Thorston, who conveniently doesn't get in the way of your aspirations to fame."

Mari didn't take the bait. Didn't mention what Emory already knew from a guilty late-night session searching online gossip sites—that Mari had been famous before she and Benjamin ever met. Mari didn't bite back.

Instead, she did the one thing that mattered to Emory most. She gathered herself. She let go of the drama. She told the truth.

"Yeah," she said. She trailed her hands down, wiping away Emory's tears, clasping her shoulders. "Despite our pre-nup. Despite my management telling me off for ruining the fantasy that I'm an attainable and available bachelorette. Despite us not getting what the other one does at work. At all." Her voice softened. Her words were simple. "I love him."

Emory inhaled a shaky breath. There it was. Undeniable. And she knew, deep down, what she'd come to Malibu to do. She braced herself for the pain of a hollowed-out heart, for letting Mari go—

And it didn't hurt.

She examined that feeling, like pushing on a fading bruise.

Old habits died hard, and Mari had turned into a habit. There was nothing left in Emory's heart to let go of. There hadn't been for a while. Only a shadow to haunt her. To make her think that she was supposed to hold the wound together when the scar had faded. While she hadn't been paying attention, her heart had filled up again. And her heart felt the opposite of pain. It was big, and whole, and *wonderful*.

"There's someone else for me now," she heard herself say, "so I understand. I wish you all the happiness. I'll forever be glad that you showed up at my dorm room and asked me to come out of myself." That was real and true. There wasn't anything for Emory to regret.

Mari came in for a hug. They teetered over, half onto the table, all arms and sniffles. "That's good." She pressed her lips to Emory's cheek, then slid them to the corner of her mouth. "One last kiss for the bride, for luck?" she mumbled.

Emory stretched her neck to one side, Mari following. She couldn't be mad. "Babe, you're really lovey when you're drunk. You always have been. So no." Hopefully Mari would leave that habit behind, Emory thought, in the marriage to come. But that was a problem for Mari to figure out, not for Emory to stay awake nights fretting over.

She rubbed Mari's back. Not much longer before it was going to be puke time. And there were guests coming down the hall. She could hear laughing and Mari's name. "Come on, you'll regret this later. If you remember it."

"That's why I don't drink anymore," Mari slurred, sliding face-first into Emory's cleavage, one hand grabbing Emory's tit to arrest her fall.

Later, it seemed strange to Emory that she was distracted from an accidental and slightly painful boob grab by silence. She turned her head toward the hallway and saw Bliss standing in the door-frame, utterly calm, utterly still. Her eyes took in everything, but her expression was unfathomable.

Mari let out a wild groan. Anyone who didn't know Mari would think that the sound was an expression of pleasure and not a groan of impending vomit. And Bliss didn't know her.

She backed away and disappeared.

"Wait!" Emory cried. Mari wrapped her arms tighter around Emory, making an awful gurgling sound. Emory levered them up and, penguin-style, walked Mari toward one of the leather executive chairs.

Mari clung to her arm. "Em, I don't feel so good."

Emory cast about and found a wastebasket, which she shoved into Mari's hands. "Sorry, hon. Someone else is going to have to hold your hair back now."

One last kiss on the forehead.

Then she ran.

There wasn't any point in shouting for Bliss. The hallway was empty, as were the places where it branched off. She tried all the nearby doors, but the other meeting rooms were locked. Emory slowed from a jog to a fast walk at the ballroom, afraid to trip over a chair leg or a stray purse. Bliss wasn't at their table. Their places were cleared and the staff was discreetly pulling some of the tables off the floor, but Emory found her clutch behind the cushion of her chair. One single thing was where it was supposed to be, at least.

The reception had moved into a new phase while she had been with Mari. The best man was swearing into the microphone, creating feedback that made Emory cover her ears. She kept moving, pushing through the dance floor, squinting against the now-flashing lights from the DJ booth. *Where is she?*

A loud *pop* startled the person who shimmied in front of her, causing them to scream, but Emory couldn't hear their yell over the noise. She elbowed her way to the doors that led out onto the gardens. A crowd had stopped in their tracks to watch the finale of a fireworks display. She could see over their heads, past the lights of the carnival booths, and with every flare of blue and red, every burst of white and purple, she looked for Bliss. When the group moved, she stepped over a girl who plopped herself down on the ground and refused her date's pleas to *get up, you're embarrassing me.* There was no one she recognized in the garden, and she ducked through a set of sliding doors into the main lobby.

In the bathroom, a starlet Emory almost recognized was snorting a line of white powder off the sink. She slammed open the door of each stall. Empty. Emory went back to the lobby, where two Malibu Elite Weddings personnel swarmed every one person, passing out gift bags to wedding guests.

Emory searched her clutch for her phone. No texts. No service. A narrow rift opened in the crush, and Emory was through the front doors and into an absolute disaster of people shouting for the valet. A line of cars stretched back toward the resort entrance. Everyone was departing at once. She didn't blame them.

Bliss wouldn't have been able to leave in this, would she? Emory checked the time. How long had it been since Bliss disappeared? She'd spent precious minutes getting out of the ballroom, and searching the bathroom, and then trying to get through the lobby—

Emory ran around the side of the hotel. The doors of the boardroom remained open, but Mari and her vomit wastebasket were gone. She hurried down the hallway to find a line for the elevator, and passed it by, slamming through the door to the first stairwell she found. Up one flight, two, a stop on the third to shuck off her heels. Four. This way, then she saw that the room numbers were getting bigger instead of smaller. Back the other way. Room key out.

Their room was quiet and empty, with only a single lamp switched on. Emory checked the closet, and the bathroom, and beside the bed, and out on the balcony.

Bliss was gone.

There was no note. But in the center of the dining table was Bliss's copy of their engagement contract, ripped into four neat, square pieces, and the engagement ring, displayed in its box.

"You still owe me"—she checked her phone—"two and a half hours." She laughed hysterically, without mirth, at *herself.* This was *her* fault. She knew what she'd looked like, tangled up with Mari: like every relationship in her life was some kind of transaction, a deal to be made at the right time. She tossed the scraps of paper into the air.

Fuck. Fuck everything.

247

She'd fucked up everything without doing anything at all. "You can't rip that up until midnight. It says so in article eight, section three."

The contract said one thing, but Emory knew there was an invisible clause holding them to a high standard. To being the women they wanted to be, worthy of loving and being loved. Loyal and honest. And Bliss thought Emory had been in breach.

She sent off a string of texts, hoping that they would go through with one bar, holding her breath while they stayed on *sending* and sighing in relief when they changed over to *sent*.

It's not what you think. Nothing happened. Please let me explain. If we could talk, that would be better.

The answering *ding* came immediately.

But it wasn't a text. It was an app notification. Her flight was boarding. She tapped it.

Bliss had changed her ticket home, and there was no way Emory could catch her. There was no car fast enough. No way to leap over Los Angeles traffic and fly through airport security to find Bliss at the gate and beg her to understand.

Emory's thumb trembled over the button that offered the chance to CANCEL.

She was not that person. No matter what Bliss thought of her.

Emory turned off the ringer. She set her phone on the nightstand and crawled between the sheets of the ridiculous four-poster bed. For the second time that night, she cried.

For the life she'd thought she wanted.

For the grief that had disappeared when she wasn't looking.

For the years lost.

For the pain of everything now.

For Bliss. For Bliss.

For Bliss.

july

twenty

ON A HOT MID-JULY day, Bliss leaned on the counter at Park Slope Express Floral, reviewing the payment from WW and Partners and transferring it to the gig worker who had taken her place as plant-lover and pot-waterer. The confirming email didn't come from Beatriz Reyes this time. Maybe Beatriz had moved on from being underappreciated at the front desk and taken on more interesting work.

Bliss had taken on more interesting work herself, accidentally. She'd come back to Brooklyn, asked Selma if she knew someone who'd take over her Bliss Foliage appointments because Emory was going to be with Mari and it was weird, and Selma had put her to work full time at the shop. As Bliss mastered new sections of the business, Selma had given her a raise, over Bliss's protests. She'd slowly stopped protesting as her checking account dwindled again. Her thirty-day engagement had only paid three months' rent.

The shop was quiet, but Bliss ignored the group chat messages coming through anyway.

> Erika: Let's get our plan together for Labor Day. Boston, or, like, Maine?
>
> meowsville: haven't rehomed 5 of 7 rescue cats, so y if Boston, n if Maine, don't worry about meow
>
> meowsville: *me
>
> goofbot2000: Bliss you coming, my roommate moved out, ensuite all yours, don't wait for September
>
> Charlize Horse: What has Brooklyn got that Boston doesn't
>
> Erika: Two more letters.

For most of the day, Bliss had been trying to draw some new floral designs for autumn in her journal, but the summer temperature was distracting her. It was so hot and humid that the air conditioning in the shop couldn't keep up.

Bliss raised her elbows and flapped her arms, chicken-style, trying to do for her armpits what her antiperspirant couldn't. All she had to concentrate on for the moment was watching the door, but later, she had three funeral wreaths to make up, and that was always hot work. And, in fairness, not all of her work was for Selma; some of the pages of Bliss's journal had turned into illustrations of the questions she and Emory had asked each other, and drawing her latest, a Ferris wheel, had made her especially sweaty.

She slammed her elbows against her sides to hide the pit stains, if any showed up against the black t-shirt she had on, when the door opened, but it was just Selma, back from lunch. "Brought you something," she said, and set a white box from Two Sunshines in front of Bliss with a flourish.

Inside, there was a cupcake bedecked in buttercream with the message HAPPY BIRTH across the top—the DAY had slithered off the side in the heat, and the icing was threatening to dissolve next. They scrutinized the mess together. "Well, I tried."

Bliss swiped a fingerful of frosting and licked it off. Lemon. Her favorite. "It still tastes good. I like my cake warm anyway."

Selma shook her head. "Don't thank me yet. I'm sweetening you up—" She considered Bliss, and her sweaty shirt, and—Bliss guessed—the smudged eyeliner collecting under her eyes, as she hadn't washed her face after leaving work yesterday. "You don't look so good, and I thought you'd been looking better."

She held up her palms. Who knew anymore? She came to work, she went home. Sometimes she even washed her face. Just not yesterday.

Her shrug wasn't enough for Selma to let it go. "Are you ever going to tell me what happened?" Selma picked up Bliss's abandoned sketchpad and pointed to a wreath that spelled out BOO HOO HOO HOO in purple, orange, and red. "What has you drawing some of the ugliest arrangements I have ever seen in my whole ding-dang life?"

Bliss stripped the page from the notebook and feathered it to shreds between her fingers. She felt her mouth turn downward, her brow lower, her shoulders sink. "I...well. I'm not great." Selma came in for a big hug, squashy and comforting. And, frankly, warmer than Bliss could handle, given the malfunctioning aircon, but she stuck it out. "Sorry. I'll try to get back on the good vibes train."

"Honey, it's your right to be sad if you need to be sad. You don't have to make the world beautiful every second of every day. You've gotta feel all your feelings." Selma let go and handed back the sketchpad. "And if you've gotta feel them on paper, feel them on paper and rip them up. I'm not judging that part."

There was more. She could see it on Selma's face. Bliss braced herself for the part she *was* judging.

"I saw that movie star, the one from that wedding you went to, on TV last night."

Bliss put her face down right on the sketchpad and tuned out. The top page soaked up the oil on her nose and forehead. Maybe the stain would look like one of those Rorschach blots. Inspirational. Design-worthy.

"...a new film role and pictures of her canoodling with her husband." Selma paused for breath and changed course. "Maybe you should talk to Emory. Don't you think if she and that starlet were—I don't know. When you're famous, everything's on the news, right? They're always in people's business. Especially if you're gay."

That wasn't a given. Emory had texted that *it's not what you think*, but Bliss was sure of what she'd seen. She didn't need to think at all.

She didn't want to be the woman you slept with while you waited for the woman you wanted. The woman you had fallen in love with.

"Emory's not going to come back for me." *It was all a lie.* "We had a contract, not a promise." *And fucking is not a promise.* "I don't have lengthy relationships. It's a gift. And as soon as she had the chance, she got back together with Mari. I caught them kissing. That's probably who she was thinking of the whole time we—"

You were supposed to believe people when they told you who they were. Was Emory Ferris wheels and kisses at sunset, or was she a lying-liar-who-lies businessperson, just like Bliss's father had been?

If Bliss could see her again, look her in the eye, she'd know for sure.

But if she stood in front of Emory and saw a cold-hearted corporate drone who'd used her, her heart would unravel.

That's why she was afraid to text her. To call her. To find out why Emory hadn't turned up on her doorstep. Even if a place in Bliss's heart kept insisting that maybe she had jumped to conclusions, that maybe Emory was telling the truth and Bliss had been mistaken. But—

Better not to know. Better not to get hurt again.

Bliss straightened up and rubbed her face. "I got carried away and now I have to move on. How do I move on?"

She looked to Selma for answers, but Selma was focused on a picture on the wall, one of her and Rosie squinting into the sun, laughing and holding hands. "You think about it. And you think about it again. Until you don't think about it anymore, I guess." Selma stuffed her hands into the back pockets of her jeans. "Or you think about what's next instead."

Bliss leaned her shoulder against the brick and peered at the picture of Selma and her wife. "So what's next?" Anything for a distraction from the same thoughts swirling around her brain all day, every day.

"Well, that's actually what I was sweetening you up about." Selma beckoned her outside and locked the door behind them. It was even hotter on the pavement with the overcast sky threatening rain. In the gloom, even the rainbow flags on the neighborhood storefronts seemed faded and droopy.

She waited, sweating profusely, while Selma sorted through her extensive ring of keys and unlocked the other door at the front of Park Slope Express Floral. This second door was sturdy, metal, and completely boring, and painted like the rest of the building, so Bliss hadn't really thought about what was behind it.

The door opened onto a long hallway that Bliss realized ran around the back of the store to where they stored their trash. She'd never gone past the bins because they had to take the bags out to the curb in front, and from this angle, she saw that it was easier to take them through the shop instead of down the narrow corridor.

A staircase stretched above them. Selma had to grip the railing and pull herself up each step, which apparently tired her out, as she took a break halfway. "Arthritis," she said, between big breaths. "Still strong and kicking, but stairs are my nemesis."

She patted the railing and levered herself up a couple more stairs. "Me and Rosie talked about an elevator, but we didn't need it, and I keep putting it off. You can do it in the back corner. Had an architect come out to take a look already."

They reached the landing and Selma searched through her keys again. She opened the door to a living room that stretched across the width of the building. Beyond, Bliss spotted a dining area. Selma beckoned her through and gave her the tour: a compact, updated kitchen, then back around to the front door, where a hall led to a bedroom and a well-appointed bath. "The rest of this floor is unfinished," Selma said. She lifted aside a plastic sheet to show Bliss the space, which was a warren of half-framed walls and exposed studs. "Couldn't figure out what to do with it. The third floor is empty. We never started any work up there."

Bliss followed Selma back to the kitchen, where Selma searched the cupboards for a packet of cookies. She poured two glasses of lemonade from a pitcher and they sat down at the table. Selma took a bite of cookie. "Look. This apartment—you could turn this into something. Turn this whole building into a home. I see how you are with the shop—"

This was confusing. Bliss took a drink of lemonade, trying to get her bearings and figure out what Selma wanted. There was no way Selma wanted her to move in or something weird. Right?

"—and me and Rosie thought we'd pass it down to somebody, some day. You know, it's profitable. The neighborhood is great. People always need plants. You've got a real knack for bridal too. And then there's for sure gonna be another funeral any minute." Selma took another cookie. "Not saying that to be funny, it's just how things are."

Bliss wasn't fazed by the bleak humor, but she also wasn't any less confused. "I like working for you, Selma. You're probably the best boss I've ever had. I never dread coming in, and I don't feel miserable when I leave. So whatever I can help you with, I will. What do you need?"

Selma got up for more lemonade and brought back the whole pitcher. "I have to confess it's less about what I need and more about what I *want*. I want to move in with my sister in Vermont. She's got grandkids and extra space and no stairs, and we're both pretty set in our ways, but we also want to spend time with family while we can. What I *don't* want is for Park Slope Express Floral to fade away and the building become another pharmacy or bank."

She clutched the pitcher against her chest and Bliss realized that Selma was nervous—scared, even. Then she sighed and set it on the table between them. "I know, I know. It's business and you don't like business. But what if I stay here for the rest of the summer and I train you, and then you buy the shop from me?"

Bliss couldn't wrap her head around the idea. Selma talked faster and faster. "We'll set something up for payment in installments out of monthly profits. I've got it figured out, and you wouldn't feel strapped for cash at all. I'll introduce you to my suppliers, to the people I know who've got the goods on who's having a bar or bat mitzvah, or a party, or a wedding coming up. Years of resources at your fingertips."

In all her job searching, in all her casting about for a place to land, even in coming up with Bliss Foliage, Bliss hadn't seriously considered that plants could be more than a hobby or a part-time job. She spoke aloud, entirely by accident, the first thing that coalesced in her brain. "I'd work there every day."

Selma rushed to reassure her. "You can hire someone, and maybe another part-timer, for the store right now. I didn't keep on a lot of staff because I didn't have anything else to do but work anyway. Your internet"—Selma wiggled her fingers to cover all the things she didn't know and often stated she didn't want to know about social media—"*magic* has increased profits quite a bit."

"Who would sell their entire business to *me*?" Bliss said, this time not so much by accident. She wasn't in dire straits anymore, not with her regular shifts at the shop, but neither was she rolling in dough. Her friends in Boston would take her in while she got on her feet if she wanted to start over in Massachusetts. It wasn't a bad idea. Boston suited her.

But so did Brooklyn.

"Theoretically, nobody. But I own this building outright and I don't need a million dollars from it. Like I said, I don't want it to turn into one more pharmacy-slash-convenience store." Selma swiped away a ring of condensation from her glass with the back of her hand, clearly agitated. Then she slumped back in her seat. "I'll be honest. Working at the shop full time can be a tiring job. I know that better than anybody, and I know my love for it doesn't have to be anybody else's love."

Selma stood and went to one of the paned windows that brought in light from the front of the building. A few potted plants were tucked into the corners of the windowsills, and a crystal suncatcher hung from a wire stand. The whole room was bathed in afternoon light, and Bliss thought that for such a big space, it was a cozy one—and, blessedly, it had a working HVAC system.

"There's a lot of space here. Put in that elevator and the third floor could be a restaurant or a wedding showroom for the shop. Apartments. A queer community organization. I don't know. A lot of possibilities. I started working in a flower shop in high school and I decided that's what I wanted to keep doing. But you could do something else. The point is, for now, the shop is sustainable."

Despite looking out at the street, Selma seemed like she was seeing something far away, or maybe long ago. "Money won't buy you love. It won't buy you happiness. You know that already. But it gives you the freedom to take care of the people you care about. Family. Your mom. Your community, the people in it who need beauty. Yourself."

Family. Bliss couldn't come into the middle of one and take what was theirs for her own. "What about Ken? And Ethan? And—"

Selma turned and raised her hand in that way only women of a certain age and grace can get away with. "We already talked. Some of us do that, you know. Talk to people." She gave Bliss a raised eyebrow that immediately twisted Bliss's lips wryly to the side in shame. Called out. "You're right, I did think of my family to take over running Park Slope Express Floral. Ken's not interested in anything more than some shifts to keep active in retirement. You know he was an engineer? Big change!" She shook her head. "His kids don't want to take over the shop. They work in fancy offices and have what they need. So it's up to me. And for me, it's not about the money. It's about the legacy. Plus, look at that great kitchen! Refurbished five years ago. Can't let that go to waste!"

Bliss laughed. That was very Selma. And it *was* a nice kitchen. The kind of kitchen you made French toast and coffee in on the weekends, but not so big you felt bad filling the fridge with takeout. She'd paint the wall next to it a grayish teal, and she'd pick out terra cotta dishtowels. An herb garden for the island. Add a magnetic strip for knives. Lemons in a bowl.

There was a thick manila envelope on the kitchen island right where Bliss would have put her bowl of lemons. Selma brought it to the table and set it carefully in front of Bliss. "I put this together with my lawyer. I know you might not have great feelings about contracts lately, but think about it a little. Maybe this is your moving on."

Restless, Selma took her empty cup and filled it with water from the sink. She moved back to the window and started watering the plants there. "This place has known a lot of love." Her knuckles bumped one of the crystal suncatchers. It caught the light and the prism refracted a rainbow onto Bliss's shirt.

Right over her heart.

"It could know more love, if you let it."

Over her heart that needed more love. Her heart that had to make an enormous decision when she had no one to discuss it with. A decision to let go of the past, to stop pushing away safety and comfort because she didn't deserve to have those things.

Emory would have known what to do. She'd know how to look at the numbers and decipher their secrets. Bliss missed her counsel. Her kisses.

But Emory was gone. And deep down, where the ghosts held on, Bliss knew that whatever she decided in this moment was about even older wounds—and whether this opportunity was what she needed to heal them.

Her phone buzzed.

> goofbot2000: Bliss for real, im looking for a new roommate
>
> Charlize Horse: Boston has six letters, superior to seven
>
> Erika: Eight. I'm starting a spreadsheet for everyone to put in their Labor Day potluck claims.
>
> meowsville: im bringing kittens

Charlize Horse: We'll drive down and help you pack
slash move

Selma emptied her glass and came back to the table. She was never one to let things hang. "So what's it going to be, Bliss? I can give you a little time, but you're the only one who knows if you're ready to move on."

She already knew what she wanted.

Deep breath.

Let go.

september

twenty-one

LABOR DAY WEEKEND MARKED THE official end of a summer that Emory didn't at all enjoy. She went to work in the steaming hot mornings—like so many other women, with the back of her sheath dress halfway unzipped and her heels in a tote bag, and even that wasn't much relief from the roaring heat of the subway. The phone rang and the meetings happened and she kept her eyes on her own screen, once she broke the habit of looking to see if Bliss had texted her back. In the evenings, late, she packed her shoes back into her tote, shivering from the bleak, artificial cold of the office, and went home again.

When Beatriz asked why Bliss was sending other people to the office instead of coming in herself, Emory had to tell her half of the truth. She hit the button on the coffeemaker in the kitchen and lowered her voice, but Adam Carrington came through the doorway on the words *broke up*, and she'd been dodging the whispers that she'd been dumped by her fiancée *twice* ever since. The rumor became the truth. What was she supposed to say? The truth was worse than the rumor.

Beatriz was the one bright spot in the empty weeks that stretched out through the hottest days of the year. When the opening was posted for a replacement analyst, and Emory and Jeff were tasked with hiring, they'd given Beatriz the green light. So far, Beatriz was absolutely killing it—she always saw the story behind the numbers—just like Emory had known she would.

Over Independence Day, while the office was empty and she was elbows deep in the Mackenzie Aeronautics embezzlement mess, Emory had the idea to remove the plants from her office so she wouldn't be reminded every day of her worst screwup ever. She'd managed to stab herself with the cactus—apparently, the cactus had a talent—and she'd had to pluck out the spines herself, thinking of Bliss's soft hands the whole time. After a good cry, and another go at gifting her greenery to the interns, she gave up. The arrival of the cactus had been coincidence, but the fern had been picked out especially for her, and who was Emory to remove it?

At least, that's what she kept telling herself.

But on a blisteringly hot Friday afternoon in early September, she was wondering again whether she should clear off the windowsill. Clear her mind. It wasn't healthy to obsess.

There were footsteps in the hall. Most of the executive end of the office was empty, so it was probably Beatriz, or another analyst, coming by for a chat. She kept picking at the sandwich she'd been trying to eat for the last half hour. Her blazer was slung over the back of her chair, and her shoes were off under her desk, and that all felt fine. TGIF.

To her great surprise, it was William who poked his head in her door. She hadn't realized he was in the office. "Have a good weekend. Spending time with family?" he asked.

Emory quickly chewed and swallowed a mouthful of spicy Italian meats and cheeses and folded the Subway wrapper into a drawer, which she immediately slammed shut. "Nothing on the agenda. Sticking around here." She doubted William knew where her family resided. A smile for his attention would have been nice to offer, and expected, but Emory was pretty sure she had lettuce caught in her teeth.

"Well, then, see you next week." He disappeared beyond the doorway. Before Emory could force her shoulders down where they belonged, he returned. "I was sorry to hear that your plans have changed. Beatriz let Ellen know."

Emory had forgotten about Ellen's celebration dinner, and of course Ellen would have called Beatriz to help arrange the date, and it wasn't a secret that her engagement was over. Which meant that, even if William had been silent for the conversation, Ellen would have analyzed her breakup from all angles.

Awkward.

"Thank you," she said, at last.

William opened his mouth as if to say something else, but instead raised his arm in a stiff wave and backed out of the room.

Emory took out her sandwich and gnawed on the rapidly hardening crust. She should have bought a cookie. No, two cookies. Three. Three was the right number of embarrassment cookies to eat after a conversation with your boss about your failed love life.

Another half hour of trying to choke down her sandwich and a trip to the kitchen for more coffee later, Emory settled back at her desk. Her email was no longer the inbox zero she'd accomplished before lunch. At the top of the list was a message from Juan and Vivian. RE: LET'S COALESCE TO HELP PEOPLE CONVALESCE. They wanted to accept the investment Emory had extended on behalf of WW and Partners.

"Fuck yeah, my unicorns," she said out loud. It was perfectly safe to shout her glee when William was already gone. Emory composed a two-line, more-to-come email to the partners. Then she shoved back her chair and ran down the hall, barefoot, to tell Beatriz. Beatriz was getting credit for finding them in the first place, and a raise, and then she'd be able to take the night classes toward the MBA that she'd been considering. They were going to open the bottle of bourbon Emory kept in the bottom drawer of her desk. The one she'd been saving for her Big Big Big Deal, for that someday when she achieved more than middle-of-the-road success at WW and Partners.

The cubicles where the interns and analysts sat were empty, as were the shared offices for the more junior staff. Most of the lights were off, and a man in the building's housekeeping uniform went from row to row, emptying trash cans and dusting desks. Everyone else had taken advantage of the long weekend.

She was the sad sack who didn't have anywhere to be.

Emory walked back toward her office, feeling the weight of loneliness on her shoulders. But she pushed them back, lifted her chin, and forced herself into a brisker pace. She had a call to make. Juan and Vivian should hear from her.

There was no answer. They were probably off on their own weekend adventure. Off making a toast of their own. She left a message. *So pleased. Hope you get a chance to celebrate tonight! Talk next week.*

One good thing. Even with no one to share her accomplishment with, she had one good thing.

Investments like the one WW and Partners had made in Vivian and Juan wouldn't pay off for years. Even with all of Emory's confidence in them, her rational side knew that their company might never take off. But it *would*. She could feel it in her bones.

Emory queued up a playlist: Success Dance. Still barefoot, she twisted and shimmied in the limited space in front of her desk. Volume up, she climbed onto one of the guest chairs, raised her phone in the air, and shook her backside like she actually did not care. She *kind of* did care, but the absence of her colleagues and the knowledge that the office towers within sight were probably also empty gave her the confidence to go like it was her birthday. Who would look in her window on a Friday afternoon when they could be at street level, sipping cocktails at the bar in Bryant Park?

With the volume at 100%, the alert ping was so loud through the speaker that Emory startled. She had new email. Hips to the left. Hips to the right. From William. Adjust feet so that she didn't tip the chair over. *Thank you for all your hard work in landing us the new deal...for resolving the problems at Mackenzie Aeronautics for the best possible outcome...pleased to give you a one-time bonus....*

Shimmy from her shoulders down to her toes. A very nice number. With what she'd been socking away in savings and investments, if she wanted to run away from it all and be a—be a goat farmer, or sell artisanal homemade pickles, or spend ten years writing the Next Great American Novel—she could do that tomorrow. *If* she was smart about it. *If* that was what she wanted. But she was committed to venture capital. To securing the promotion to junior partner. To making all the crap that had happened this year worth the heartbreak.

The beat was interrupted by another *ding*. Another email. Also from William.

RE: NEW LEADERSHIP.

William was pleased to inform everyone that he would be stepping away from his role leading WW and Partners at the end of December, and his son, Weston, would be filling his shoes.

The same Weston who spent most of his days filling a pair of golf shoes.

For the rest of the year, William would be gradually handing over the day-to-day management of the company to Weston. And that, thought Emory, would be interesting. She tried very hard to reserve judgment.

Ding. RE: PERSONNEL.

Adam Carrington was promoted to junior partner. Emory skimmed the email. His promotion was *so* well deserved. *His hard work and long hours secured a host of important pharmaceutical investments. Next year, he'll become a family man, marrying a lovely young woman who is involved with some of New York's most venerated charities and arts institutions. Adam, a solid golf partner and friend to many, will be moving up.*

Emory almost threw her phone through the window. But she kept scrolling, and as it turned out, William had buried the lede.

Benjamin Thorston was joining the firm as partner. He and Weston had been paired at a charity golf tournament and hit it off, wrote William. And there was more, but Emory closed her email. She listened to the cheery pop tune roaring through the speakers, something about women shaking it to make it, and then she swiped the volume to zero, turned her phone off, and climbed down from her chair.

William got his exit. Weston got his inheritance. Benjamin got—to be fair, she didn't care what he got. She was relieved that as a partner, he likely wouldn't be involved in the day-to-day of the office.

And Adam Carrington got his kiss-ass payoff.

She was furious. She'd wanted that promotion with her whole heart.

Hadn't she?

Emory squeezed her eyes shut and deliberately crumpled her face into a frown. She held her hand to her mouth, waiting for the tears to come. And waited.

And waited.

What if she kept doing what she was doing, what she loved, right where she belonged?

One half-tear bloomed in her right eye. Emory blinked, twice, but it didn't fall. She looked down to see if she'd missed any drips falling to her blouse. It was pristine—not even a drop of Italian dressing or a crumb of multigrain roll—except for a rainbow dot over her bellybutton like she was some kind of goddamn cheap teddy bear.

That was her breaking point. Emory reached out for the crystal that decorated the cactus Bliss had left on her windowsill all those weeks ago, and when she pulled, the pot tipped to the floor and shattered, but not before gifting her with a spine in her wrist on the way down.

The fight went out of her. All she could do was stare out the window at the glass palaces of midtown Manhattan, wondering if she was reflected back in their nothingness.

———∞———

Emory didn't set foot outside all through the long weekend. Belatedly, she wished she'd made plans to get out of town. She had no idea where she would have gone. North, along the coast, maybe. Instead, she sat on the couch, trying to lose herself in a novel, but the wartime drama and intrigue within its pages was no match for the questions running laps in her brain. What was she doing? What did she want to do?

How the hell was she a mystery to herself?

She needed a career plan. Which would have been easy to make if she had any idea what she wanted to do next. Or when she wanted to do it. Or where.

Never mind that she knew she was missing a certain *who*. She couldn't think about that person. This wasn't the time.

On Monday morning, Emory uncorked a bottle of red wine and cracked open a window. Late-summer heat rushed inside as she stared at the white sails of boats gathering in the blue of New York Harbor. Nothing was stressing her. The junior partner role was filled, and she didn't have to worry about competing for a promotion anymore. She slumped into the couch cushions and put her feet up on the windowsill.

Maybe that was the wine talking. Emory rarely drank more than a glass when she was alone, but she was having a mug with a side of lukewarm oatmeal. Since it was a holiday, the wine was a legitimate part of bottomless brunch, she reasoned. A very hot brunch even if her oatmeal was going colder by the minute. She

277

wiped the sweat gathering in her hairline. Then she sat up and slammed the window shut.

The best way to take her mind off things would be to get back to work. Emory found her work bag and spread her tools out on the coffee table. Laptop. Phone. Folders. Her laptop needed to install an update, so while she waited, Emory refilled her mug and checked her phone.

No response from Bliss to the frantic texts she'd sent after Bliss saw her with Mari at the wedding. Not even a confirmation that Bliss had received the final payment for services that Emory authorized through the transfer app first thing when she woke up the morning after. But she knew that already.

Bliss didn't owe her anything. Their contract was long over. She didn't have to pretend she liked Emory anymore.

That didn't stop Emory from rereading the texts they'd sent each other. She lingered on one, a picture of Bliss holding a bouquet of flowers and looking up at the camera with her big grey eyes. Emory had responded with a heart so casually that it was hard to believe in the present. How had she not known that heart was growing from an emoji into something real?

Emory sighed and put her phone aside. The laptop hadn't finished updating, so she pulled the stack of file folders closer. Inside the one on top was her copy of the contract—which stated in no uncertain terms that both copies were to be destroyed at the end of the thirty-day engagement.

And Emory hadn't followed through.

She gripped the papers and tore them in half, and in half again. Then she went to her bedroom closet and took a shoebox from the highest shelf, and she placed her part of the contract with the shreds of Bliss's copy. Her copy of the questions they'd asked each other was at the bottom of the box, folded small and secured with a binder clip.

Emory got dressed in a pair of ratty black shorts she'd had for a decade, the kind she said she kept around for messy projects like painting but really kept around because they were comfortable, and pulled out a t-shirt from the bottom of the same drawer she set aside for old clothes. It was orange with white stripes, so once she was dressed, she looked like an escapee from a Halloween store. Emory shoved the little bundle of questions into her pocket and returned the box to its hiding place, trying not to think about how that was sort of like forcing what had happened into the closet.

Wait, no. That metaphor was a bridge too far. Or something. Wine made her love idioms a little too much.

Back on the couch, Emory recommitted to work. She paged through a legal pad where she wrote down new ideas, and not two weeks ago, she'd had a conversation with a flight attendant where they'd joked that someone should expand those tablet-enabled terminal diners into a forgetful traveler delivery service, so you could have goods like a pillow or the eye cream you hadn't packed delivered to your seat during boarding. *Okay, great. Both sides of the relationship have a problem. Flyers want comfort and convenience. Airlines don't want to carry extra stuff around and waste*

279

fuel. Infrequent flyers might not know about the service, the delivery window will have to be managed carefully...

She was getting into the groove. Emory sketched out figures on her legal pad and added them up on a calculator.

One of the columns added up to 81155.

Bliss.

Every time Emory thought she had her brain cleared out, her train of thought got derailed by Bliss. Metaphor. That wasn't a great one. But her world was repeating. She'd untangled herself from Mari, after long years, and didn't want to spend her next ones hung up on Bliss. Hung up like a phone. Also a bad metaphor. Actually, that was a simile.

Emory poured herself more wine. Then she pulled out the lump of getting-to-know-you questions from her pocket where it poked her in the hip. Once it was in her hands, she took off the binder clip and unfolded the paper, smoothing it flat on her lap.

There were too many blanks. Emory crumpled the paper back into her pocket.

She sent a text to Francis, who was spending the weekend in San Jose. *Hows parents?* When she drank wine, her typing got tipsy. Francis claimed that texts weren't supposed to be perfect. They agreed to disagree in all sober situations.

Good. Funny story, mom's sisters paying a surprise visit from Busan, Francis sent back after a few minutes.

Oh wow, you OK, Emory replied. Baby Sophie must have been a big surprise to Francis's aunts.

Way better than xpected, bc Sophie is so cute i think. Will see.

Emory knew it was more complicated than that, but Francis would tell her all about it when she got back, if she wanted to. Selfishly, she wished that Francis was already home. Francis could always tell when it was time to wait and when it was time to push—

But ur worse than xpected. U tipsy?

Y, Emory texted back.

Knew it. Wallowing in Bliss again, have you had wine? Should you stop?

Well, not in *bliss*, small b, but Francis was right. Emory had told her that they'd broken up, and the circumstances of why, leaving out the contract. That was a confession she didn't know how to make. She and Francis were long overdue for a talk that didn't focus on her juggling work and Sophie, and it was Emory's fault for avoiding the hard parts, like the truth. *I missher.*

Lose your autocorrect?

Guesso.

You text me this every weekend, Francis replied. *For three months. And ilu but family calls now.*

Is too late?

How would I know. Either let go or stop wallowing and go get her tiger.

Emory snorted. She almost texted back that Bliss didn't have a tiger. That was avoidance. Emory could see the invisible comma in the last sentence. *She* was supposed to be the tiger.

She grabbed her keys and her wallet and picked through her shoe rack for a pair of open-toed sandals. They still had the tags on them. Emory buckled them on anyway and left her apartment. Her knees were wobbly, but that was wearing off.

The elevator took a very long time, and when it came, she leaned against the wall, towering over a kid in a stroller who was clutching a stuffed tiger.

"Tiger," she said out loud, pointing and making her best *I have interacted with a child before!* face. This got her a blank stare. She curled her hands into claws and whispered, "Raaaah!"

The guy pushing the stroller glared at her. He was a definite no on the interactive tigers.

Fine. *She* was the tiger, after all.

Outside, Emory turned toward Kensington. After a few blocks, her feet started to hurt, and she regretted not bringing any water. She soldiered on all the way to Bliss's place because even though she had left her phone behind, and she was going to do this on her own two legs. All the way down past Prospect Park. All the way down the tree-lined street where Bliss lived. All the way up the back stairs to her apartment.

Where a man with a strong resemblance to a famous grunge rock star answered the door, accompanied by a cloud of pungent smoke and the sound of a metal album raging in the background.

"Bliss," she blurted out before she could stop herself. Of course Bliss had moved on. Of course she'd moved on to someone who was chill. Chiller than Emory. Not even remotely corporate.

"Ah, dude, she moved out." The man shrugged his shoulders. "Sorry, don't know where she went. The property owners could tell you, maybe, but they're not home."

Her chest seized. Not from the smoke, but because she was starting to panic. "Did she move in with her mom?" Emory shouted over the music, not that it mattered. This guy didn't know.

He shook his head. "I don't know her mom."

"Boston!" she exclaimed, remembering a reference Bliss had made to a trip where her friends lived.

"I don't know Boston either," the guy said and shut the door. Which was fair.

Emory picked her way down the stairs to the street. Her head wasn't very clear, and she needed bandages for the blisters on her heels. Where was Bliss?

The flower shop. Maybe Bliss was at work. Something or other Park Slope, or Park Slope— She'd walk around the neighborhood until she figured it out.

No, she'd take the subway. Emory found the closest stop, but it wasn't running due to construction, and the instructions posted for the bus were confusing, and there were no cabs in sight. She limped along the edge of the park, counting on it to spit her out in Park Slope.

By the time she found the shop, Emory was completely sober. Or—was she? It seemed different. The sign outside called it SELMA'S PICKS, which wasn't what she remembered. The hours were newly lettered on the window, and the door with the old-fashioned glass was painted red. A mannequin stood in a display, holding a swirling bride's bouquet of flowers that looked almost identical to the one Bliss had texted her all those weeks ago. She had to be here.

Emory pushed the door handle down, but it was locked. She leaned forward to look in the window and banged her forehead against the glass.

Then she rested her cheek on the cool pane, probably leaving a smudge, and cried.

But not for long. She wiped her face in the reflection of the door, and when she did, she saw that across the street and behind her, there was a new craft store with a grand opening banner hanging across the front.

Come on, tiger.

twenty-two

BLISS DRAGGED HER SUITCASE BEHIND her. The left wheel of her carry-on had bit the dust when she caught it in the closing doors of the subway on the last leg of her journey. After a weekend spent with friends, she couldn't be mad about the wheel; it was a small sacrifice to the god of the good vibes. Her movers had finished dropping off her boxes before noon last Thursday, then she'd spent a little time talking to Selma, who'd covered Friday and then made her official departure for Vermont. Bliss had arrived in Boston in time for a fireworks cruise with the crew and had spent most of the weekend sprawled on Erika's floor, listening to her friends talk, sharing how hard she'd been working for the past weeks. Feeling like she was moving in the right direction for the first time in a very long while.

A vacation had been good for her. She had a spring in her step—one that scraped her suitcase along the sidewalk—as she rounded the corner for home. But she stopped in her tracks when Selma's Picks came into view.

Emory was kneeling there, on the sidewalk. Bliss's heartbeat quickened, and at first, she didn't believe her eyes. She blinked, twice, and Emory was still there.

And Emory was a disaster. Her long arms and legs were a lobster red that was going to sting and then peel. Her hair had been pulled into a ponytail, but tangled strands hung out on one side of her head. She was wearing an outfit unlike any Bliss had seen her wear before. And she was smudged from head to toe in rainbow colors. She was an absolute *mess*.

Surrounding Emory was an entire garden—a messy, scribbly one—etched in sidewalk chalk. Flowers and vines wrapped around her and radiated outward, broken by cracks and the imperfections of the concrete. "I came to get an apology gift, but you were closed, so—" Emory began, wiping away a stream of sweat and leaving a smear of blue across her forehead. She shifted back on her heels and clasped her hands together, suddenly interested in the colors that grimed her fingernails.

"Today's a holiday," Bliss pointed out, heartbeat quickening. She had wondered what it would be like to see Emory again, and this—this wasn't like anything she could have imagined.

It was *better.*

Emory nodded. "So I made you flowers."

286

She had. Bliss was in love with them. She could see where Emory had started drawing, shakily, swirling green for a vine and making a teardrop leaf. It meandered toward a childlike drawing of a cactus, each spine tipped with a tiny red heart.

Bliss stepped into the drawing, tiptoe. There were the dresses they'd picked out at Bellworthy's, pink and gold triangles on cockeyed hangers. A yellow square with blue dots, probably French toast. And at the end of it all, a rainbow wagon wheel with multicolored squares and a heart in the middle.

The Ferris wheel.

The ending to their perfect day.

"I don't have a contract. Only an ask, for you." Emory got to her feet without grace. She wiped her chalk-covered hands on her shorts with predictable results..

"I know how it feels to have someone—disrespect, I suppose, the relationship you thought you had. So I think I know a little bit about how it might have felt to walk in and see me with Mari." She took a deep breath in, like she was holding herself together on oxygen alone. "I hope it looked like goodbye, because it was."

Bliss stayed quiet as a lump grew in her throat. She'd jumped to conclusions, and then she'd avoided Emory because she was terrified of finding out that she'd been right all along. And Emory's appearance didn't mean that this wasn't an apology leading up to the confirmation of her worst fears, or to another rejection—

Emory shoved her hands in her pockets and kicked her toe into the ground. After a moment, she pulled a creased, ragged ball of paper from her pocket, and Bliss knew without looking that it was her copy of their questions sheet. "We didn't finish this. There's a lot about you I don't know, but I do know this: Of all the people in the world, you're the one I'd pick to spend a perfect day with, every time."

She was frozen in place. She couldn't move. Couldn't speak. Where was the refusal? The break? Surely something else terrible was coming, because Emory was green and sickly.

"I never meant to hurt you," Emory continued, voice shaking. "I never meant for things between us to get to a place where I *could* hurt you. I came here because I want you to know how truly sorry I am, and I will leave you alone if that's what you want."

She gathered herself and went on. "Mari surprised me at the reception, and she was drunk, and I wasn't managing the situation well, and you saw it—and you thought—I don't know what you thought, but what *I* thought then was that I wasn't in love with her at all. I was in love with *you*. That's why I—I want—I don't know what they call it these days, I don't think it's going steady, maybe it's talking? So I guess I have to be old school: will you be mine? I mean, will you go on a date with me? No obligations, no signatures, and no strings attached?"

Bliss put her hands on Emory's waist and pushed her, gently, up against the door of Selma's Picks and held her there. It was everything, this feeling. She wanted Emory to feel it too, to feel *her* too. "Be yours?" she asked in a whisper.

She'd never seen Emory so nervous. Emory nodded, once, almost reflexively. "If you want. Like I said, I'm not going to hold you to some stupid contract you don't want to be in—"

"I only want your word, and I'll give you mine." Bliss found her voice. "That we'll negotiate. That whatever we have to figure out, we'll talk it through and figure it out. And I'll always text you back."

"I promise you," Emory breathed.

Bliss stretched up on her toes, leaning fully into Emory, and kissed her, hard. "It's a start."

—————✺—————

Bliss took Emory's hand and led her up the staircase to the apartment that was hers as of Selma's departure last week. She couldn't get the door unlocked fast enough or her shoes kicked off quickly enough.

As soon as they were inside, she wrapped her arms around Emory, pulling her close again, ignoring the sweat and chalk and Emory's residual sniffles.

Emory put her chin on Bliss's head and threaded her fingers through Bliss's hair. "You're almost back to a bob again."

"Haven't had time to cut it," Bliss said. She shivered. The air conditioning was turned off, so it wasn't from the cold. Being around Emory again had all her senses on high alert. "I've been busy with everything, and then the move here—" She raised a tentative finger to Emory's chin. "You're going to need some aloe. I have some in—"

Then she gasped. "Oh no. My suitcase! Stay here."

Emory's voice followed her out. "Not going anywhere."

Her suitcase was still out on the sidewalk, thankfully, which wasn't a given in New York. Bliss lugged it up the stairs, rolling it on its one good wheel. When she got back to the apartment, Bliss dumped her bag next to one of the piles of boxes near the door.

Emory was looking at a framed photo hanging on the wall, the one thing that wasn't packed in a box or stacked into an unruly pile. "This is the woman from the shop, right?"

"And her wife, Rosie," Bliss answered. She stood hip to hip with Emory and wiped a ghostly fingerprint from the glass with the hem of her shirt. "Don't they look happy? I had Selma make me a copy so I'd have a little bit of their love and history here, even after they were gone."

She dug through her suitcase and pulled out a tube of aloe gel. "You need some of this right away. Um, but, maybe you should have a shower first?"

Emory took the tube from her and turned toward the door. "I'll hurry back."

"No!" Bliss hooked her hand around Emory's elbow. "I mean, you don't have to go. I have a shower here." She looked at Emory meaningfully. "I spent half the day on a train. We could both use a shower."

The hint landed. Emory shucked her shirt off. She cast about for somewhere to leave it and noticed the photo again. "I feel like we have an audience."

Bliss inclined her head toward the hall. In the tiled bathroom, they left the rest of their clothes on the floor and climbed into the shower, which Bliss set lukewarm to cool them both down. They huddled together under the rainfall spray.

"I love you too, you know," she said, her cheek pressed against Emory's arm.

"Please don't make me wait any longer for you," Emory murmured, molding their bodies together so tightly the shower water couldn't run between them..

Bliss felt her lips curl into a smile against wet skin. "Oh, but I'm going to."

The prediction came true almost immediately: Bliss's dream of wrapping them in fluffy towels came to a halt as she remembered she'd sprung for a new set at Bellworthy's, and they were in a shopping bag somewhere in the living room, tucked in with supplies of shampoo and mouthwash.

"We're going to have to make a run for it."

They did, dripping everywhere. Bliss handed Emory the bag with the towels, sending her back to the bathroom to dry off, and used her house key to slit open box after box, searching for one with sheets and her old air mattress.

When Emory came back, damp-dry and stark naked, Bliss was lounging on a pile of blankets and pillows in the makeshift bed. She'd found glasses to fill with water, and had also moved Selma and Rosie's picture to a place of honor on the kitchen island, where it faced away politely.

"Don't flop on this bed. It's temporary until I can get some furniture," she warned Emory. She held her hand out. "But I think it will do for now."

Emory lowered herself to the mattress, legs tucked to the side. "I'll have to be very careful."

"From here on, yes. I thought you never forgot sunscreen." Bliss opened the aloe and smoothed it over Emory's reddening skin while Emory rehydrated, covering all the places she knew would sting later.

There was no answer for a long moment, only the squishy smack of sunburn gel on skin and the rubbery squeak of the mattress against the parquet floor.

"I didn't exactly forget. But I also didn't exactly remember. And when I did remember, I wasn't stopping for anything." Emory combed fingers through her hair to release the tangles from their shower. "The plan when I left my apartment was find you and talk to you, and that was the extent of it," she admitted.

"You improvised pretty well otherwise." Bliss didn't bother trying to hide the grin that pushed her cheeks upward when she thought about the chalk garden. Planned or not, it was perfect.

By the time she was done spreading aloe over Emory's limbs and everywhere she'd been exposed to the late-summer sun, the streetlights had come on, giving the room a soft glow. "That feels nice," Emory said, leaning back on the mattress as Bliss rubbed a last, sticky dot of aloe gel onto her knee. "Thank you." Her eyes narrowed to slits, like a contented cat.

It was time. Bliss had been patient. "We're not done making you feel nice yet."

Bliss set the aloe aside and levered herself down next to Emory, which was a bit of a balancing act on the air mattress. She considered her options. Her preference was *everywhere*, but much of Emory was sunburned and off-limits. There was plenty for her to work with, though. She simply had to decide where to begin.

"Can I kiss you, or do your lips hurt?"

"Kiss me," Emory answered immediately.

She propped herself on an elbow and traced Emory's lips with the tip of her finger. They were pinker than Bliss remembered, and soft. She leaned forward to taste them and Emory surged up to meet her.

Bliss hovered an inch out of reach. "Hey, slow down."

Emory raised an eyebrow. "This, from you?"

She shrugged—roguishly, she hoped. "I like to take my time. Once in a while that time's fast. Tonight," she continued, pausing to run her palm up Emory's rib cage and drag her thumb along the curve above, "it's going to be slow."

"Could we compromise at a pacey medium?" Emory placed her hand over Bliss's, moving it higher so Bliss cradled her breast.

Bliss squeezed her fullness and Emory arched into the feeling. She rubbed her thumb back and forth over Emory's nipple, delighted to see it swell. "Medium like this?" Bliss asked. "Or like this?"

She bent her head to taste the hardening bud, rolling the pebbled skin under her tongue. Up and over, again, again. Bliss pressed Emory into the mattress, listening for how her breaths came quicker or not at all. When she had discovered the thrills of Emory's left side, she moved to the right, waiting until she writhed to suck her into a peak, then pinching her gently between thumb and forefinger while she captured Emory's mouth for a long kiss.

"Either," Emory breathed, squirming. The air mattress raised up on one side, threatening to tip them over. "Either of those. Bliss—"

She'd promised to strive for *medium*. That, to Bliss, meant another kiss.

It meant long, deep strokes along the borderlands of Emory's sunburn, careful not to stray to the tender places, and running her knuckles from Emory's throat to where her legs fell open. Bliss moved to the end of the bed and grasped Emory's ankles, moving her feet to where she thought Emory would be able to brace herself for what came next.

There were so many things Bliss wanted to do with Emory.

She wanted to learn every way to bring her pleasure, show Emory how to bring her pleasure in return. Find out how to match her, how to fit their bodies together.

But there would be so many nights when they'd have a real bed to stretch out in. Not to mention Bliss's other plan for a very squashy couch and a fine selection of armchairs, among the more mundane ideas she had.

For this night, though, they didn't need any surprises or ex-periments. They only needed each other.

Bliss traced her mouth over the ridge of Emory's hipbone, across the tops of her thighs, along the soft, silken skin where her leg met her body, into the dark golden curls above. Emory's ragged breaths came louder. She ran her finger down the slick line of Emory's center, lingering low, then she slid under to knead a fistful of Emory's glorious ass.

Emory lifted her hips, and Bliss used her free hand to spread her wide. It took everything Bliss had not to dive into her depths without permission. "This is what you want?"

Emory groaned her frustration. "I want you. Just you."

That was all Bliss needed. She took Emory with her mouth, laving every secret fold, every lush, smooth expanse while Emory gripped what she could of the sheets. Bliss found her way to where she knew Emory ached the most and circled her greedy tongue against the hot heart of her arousal.

One hand reached down between her own legs, and she closed her fervent lips around Emory's clit, sucking without cease while Emory's thighs quivered and she cried out. Her mouth worked as steadily as her hand between her own legs, and she raced after Emory to climax.

"Bliss," Emory rasped, and Bliss reluctantly stopped after one last, luscious lick.

She crawled toward the head of their bed and curled onto her side, careful not to brush the places where Emory's skin was particularly dire. With a little maneuvering, she was able to wrap an arm around Emory and pull her close, one hand over Emory's heart. She buried her face between Emory's shoulder blades.

They breathed together. In and out.

Drifting. Content.

Eventually, Emory shook off the stupor of wild abandon and reached for Bliss's hand. She kissed the tips of Bliss's fingers, one by one, and the creases in her palm, and the scratches she'd won in battle with a miniature Norfolk pine, special order, which she'd had to completely repot before it could be delivered. Delicious heat pooled low in her stomach as she thought about what else she'd like Emory to do with that mouth.

About what she could do with her own.

"We have a lot of catching up to do, I think," Emory said, voice thick and drowsy. She planted a quick kiss on Bliss's wrist, followed by a gentle suck that made Bliss's legs curl tight against Emory's backside.

"We do," Bliss agreed. *Catching up* was going to be her new favorite activity.

Her long day of travel was catching up to her, and Emory was clearly exhausted. In her past relationships, she wouldn't have dreamed of calling the game early, but—however much there was to be said between them, however much to be *done* between them—she knew, simply and surely, what to do next.

She reclaimed her hand and groped for enough blanket to pull over them both. "In the morning. Right now, I think you need to sleep."

Emory twined one ankle under Bliss's leg. "I don't deserve you. I don't deserve any of this."

"Maybe you don't," Bliss teased her, "but maybe I'll let you work for it."

april, again

twenty-three

IT WAS A CHILLY, BLUSTERY day for a walk in Prospect Park. Emory and Bliss were wrapped warmly in jackets and scarves. The sky was the soft milk-white of winter, but the cherry trees had blossomed during an early warm spell, and windy showers of petals fell on them, clinging to their clothes and hair. Bliss held a hand up as if it were snowing, and Emory tilted her head back and stuck out her tongue, earning her an indulgent chuckle.

Bliss sneaked her phone out of her pocket and raised it to check her messages. Even though it was her day off, she needed to know her plant children were okay.

Emory captured the phone and held it above their heads. "Selma's Picks will be fine. The flowers can live without you for an afternoon. And Brandon will be fine too. He's been working there for three months now. Surely he can handle a few hours alone on a Sunday!"

She gave Bliss's phone right back, because she'd never truly take it away—she'd just hold it for a few seconds, as they'd previously arranged, when Bliss was trying to disengage.

"Okay, miss 'I stayed late at the office every day last week,'" Bliss shot back with a wink. She did, however, put her phone away. Emory was right: Selma's Picks needed her attention, but not every second of every day.

"Speaking of staying late at the office, I could use your advice about something." Emory tucked her nose into her scarf and waited out a particularly strong gust. When it eased, she took a long time to speak again. "I've been thinking. About what I want. You know how you always say you want to make the world a beautiful place?"

"Yeah?" Bliss linked her arm under Emory's.

"And you do it. With the shop, but also with..." Emory trailed off. "What you do beyond that. The circle around your life."

Bliss nodded. She didn't exactly understand what Emory was getting at, but she thought she understood the sentiment.

"I worked hard, and I got lucky, and I was given perfect opportunities. I used that privilege and I made enough money that I can spend the rest of my life day drinking on the beach, if I want."

They came to a fork in the path and Emory halted. Most days, this was where they turned back. "That's not what I want."

Sometimes, you needed to see where the road took you. Bliss tightened her grip and they walked on.

"Tell me," she said. She didn't catalogue the details about Emory on a sheet of paper these days, but she wanted to know all of her answers.

Emory matched her pace. "I want to have my own private equity firm, and I want it to benefit people that private equity neglects. I don't want to spend my days propping up the same people who always get propped up. I want to microseed a business run by an immigrant family, or help a queer person who can't get a bank loan become a designer, or teach a woman how to manage her company's finances so their new cure for cancer can be offered affordably."

She scratched her nose. "I've been thinking about this for a long time. Weighing the possibilities. Worrying. I have all these ideas, but who's to say I won't make the exact same mistakes other people have? Who's to say that I haven't been put two and two together and come up with five?"

They stopped under a tree. Cherry blossoms piled up on Emory's head. "The plan could fail miserably. I might have to come scrub buckets at Selma's with you if that happens."

"Well, I let you move in with me, so I'm pretty sure that we could work something out." She tried a reassuring smile. Whatever Emory wanted to do, she'd succeed. Bliss was sure of it.

Emory heard her, yet there was more she wanted to say. "But I think—I think I could make something. A different way of investing in businesses, of helping people make the world beautiful for themselves and their families." Her voice crackled with excitement.

"I'd hire Beatriz, if she's interested, and I'm pretty sure Francis is ready to make the jump to entrepreneurship so she can spend more time with Sophie—"

Bliss said Emory's favorite phrase. "It's a start." She squeezed Emory's arm and offered some hard-earned wisdom. "Change is really, really scary. Sometimes you have to leap into the void and see what happens. Probably works best when you know what you're doing and when you can use the skills you're good at. I think you'll be amazing."

Emory swung her hip to bump Bliss's, an unspoken *thank you*. "And I stayed late because I was working on a very important presentation."

"Oh?"

Bliss usually took a pass through Emory's slides to spruce them up with her eye for design, and she was a willing listener while Emory paced the living room to practice her delivery. She always clapped at the end, no matter how boring and technical the business prospect.

The thought that Emory hadn't bothered to loop her in on this rehearsal made her uncertain. Or had she already heard the presentation and forgotten? "Which one?"

"A very important one," Emory answered.

They approached the boathouse, one of their favorite places to be quiet side by side and watch the swans, and her tone turned confessional when they changed course for the picturesque bridge that crossed a narrow point in the lake. "I'm pretty nervous about it. It could be life-changing. And when I started working, I was told to treat every presentation like it's a matter of life and death, so I like my presentations to be perfect."

No wonder Emory had been holding back, she supposed. "That's a lot of pressure to put on yourself. I can understand why you'd spend extra time rehearsing."

"Want to hear it?" Emory asked.

"Yep," she replied.

"Now?"

Bliss halted in the middle of the bridge. "I guess?"

Emory walked her feet apart so they were square under her shoulders and shook out her hands. She took a few deep breaths through her nose, her usual warmup before she ran through a presentation, and jumped up and down a few times.

Then she lowered herself to one knee and retrieved a small box from her pocket.

It was the same size as the one she'd handed to Bliss on their trip to Los Angeles almost a year ago, and printed in tiny daffodils, Bliss's favorite.

Emory struggled with the top. "See, this is why I needed to practice."

When Emory managed to open the box, there, on a pillow of deep blue velvet, was the ring she'd given Bliss to mark their status as fake fiancées—the vinelike one that had felt so right wrapping around her finger, the one that she'd been missing ever since she left it on a table in Malibu and escaped from the despair that Emory would never feel the same way she did.

Her engagement ring.

Falling to her knees on the cold stone, Bliss put her hands to Emory's cheeks, her collar, her chin. "Yes," she exclaimed, and pulled her in for a kiss, and another, and another. "Yes. Yes. *Yes.*"

Emory laughed against her mouth. "You haven't heard the presentation yet."

"I already know everything I need to know." Bliss pulled them to their feet. The bridge was both pretty and highly uncomfortable on the knees. "And I have one condition. In fact, it's non-negotiable. I want to get married on this day next month."

"That's not a lot of time to plan," Emory said, expression doubtful. "I'm up for an elopement, though."

Bliss put her foot down. "A thirty-day engagement. No more."

"A thirty-day engagement," Emory agreed. She slipped the sparkling ring onto Bliss's finger.

As they reached the exit of the park, warm golden rays broke through the dreary clouds. Cars passed, and people on bicycles, and parents pushing strollers. An elderly couple took turns rolling a cart of groceries. They waited for the walk signal at the crosswalk.

The world was full of beautiful, everyday things, Bliss thought. "Do you remember when I asked you about your perfect day when we were in California? And it ended on the Ferris wheel in Santa Monica?"

She'd loved Emory then, desperately, deeply. Bliss loved her even more now. They were going to have so many days to love each other.

Emory smiled. "I remember."

"Mine ends something like this," Bliss said. "Because I'm with you." She took Emory's hand, and they walked west, into the spring sunshine.

Together. For real.

author's note

I BEGAN WRITING THIS BOOK during a global pandemic, and I imagined a day when luck, time, precautions and personal protection, and vaccines let that pandemic be a thing of the past. That's when *The 30-Day Engagement* is set—a hopeful future that's meant to be contemporary, not speculative. When I was almost done drafting, the right to an abortion was rolled back in many places in the United States, and that court decision referenced *Obergefell*, indicating that the right to love and marry as we wish could be restricted soon as well. New laws were passed denying vital, gender-affirming healthcare. Authors faced new challenges to the content of their books, and other laws left educators scrambling to hide their relationships, to fight demands to out their students, and avoid acknowledging LGBTQ+ issues at all.

What do you do, then, when physical intimacy in your manuscript is a very real act between two women who are holding themselves out as engaged to be married? What do you do with another character, someone who has never wanted a child in the past, but *chooses* to give birth and raise one? What do you do when yet another character would face the prospect of arrest for sex with his boyfriend, and another be denied medical and legal support in her gender?

Reader, I wrote. Because I believe that we are facing a dark night and that with our voices and our votes, we can see the sun rise. And in the meantime, we deserve stories, both serious and lighthearted, both speculative and based in our own world, where we belong, matter, and are granted the right to live freely, privately, and happily.

Yours,

Waverly

about the author

WAVERLY DECKER IS A WRITER, editor, and (most importantly) reader of books of all kinds. *The 30-Day Engagement*, about two women who fake a relationship so that one can succeed in business—and also show her ex-fiancée that she has finally moved on after being unceremoniously dumped—is her debut novel. She is also the author of a novella: *Girl Gets Ghosted*. She lives in New York.

You can visit her online and sign up for her newsletter with book alerts and promotions at waverlydecker.com.

CPSIA information can be obtained
at www.ICGtesting.com
Printed in the USA
BVHW072304240123
657000BV00003B/43